Trouble in Rio:

A Family Business Novel

Trouble in Rio:

A Family Business Novel

Carl Weber

with

M. T. Pope

URBAN
BOOKS

www.urbanbooks.net

Urban Books, LLC
300 Farmingdale Road, NY-Route 109
Farmingdale, NY 11735

Trouble in Rio: A Family Business Novel

ISBN 13: 978-1-62286-586-4
ISBN 10: 1-62286-586-3

First Hardcover Printing March 2019
Printed in the United States of America

10 9 8 7 6 5 4 3 2 1

Distributed by Kensington Publishing Corp.
Submit orders to:
Customer Service
400 Hahn Road
Westminster, MD 21157-4627
Phone: 1-800-733-3000
Fax: 1-800-659-2436

Trouble in Rio:

A Family Business Novel

Carl Weber

with

M. T. Pope

Rio

1

"This can't be my fucking life," I muttered as I lay in the center of my canopy bed, wrapped in my duvet. It felt like the walls were closing in on me. I tried telling myself that what I was feeling wasn't depression; today was just one of those days, that's all. There was a house full of people, yet I felt alone. I was a Duncan. Royalty. I had all that money could buy plus some, but I was still unhappy. Unfulfilled. It seemed as if everyone in the family had a solid position in the family business except me. Not only that, but I felt like I was the outcast of the family, the loner, the gay one.

I know I was loved, but I didn't feel as if my family truly appreciated what I brought to the table. Granted, I wasn't a brilliant businessman like my father or my older brother Vegas, and I didn't have the book smarts like Orlando or London. I definitely didn't have the muscle power or physical strength of my oldest brother, Junior. And I didn't have the sensual prowess of my twin sister, Paris, or our cousin Sasha. No, I was more like our mother; I had not only inherited her amazing fashion sense, but her uncanny intuition and ability to detect when people were lying. Not only that, but my reputation in the gay community as being one of the best people to party with gave me an all access pass to the happenings in the club scene. I was valuable; it's just that my family couldn't see my true value, and sometimes I felt like they didn't even try. It didn't seem to matter if I was around or not. The only time they noticed my presence was when we were in the middle of a family crisis, which there'd been quite a lot of over the past few years. We'd endured everything from my niece being kidnapped, my father being shot, to my murderous uncle escaping a mental hospital and declaring war on us. We'd survived it all—as a family. But now that there was no drama to deal with, my presence wasn't needed.

My mother said she loved me often. My father was a different story. Our relationship had always been "different," and I had come to accept it for what it was. After all, he was LC Duncan, one of the most powerful black businessmen in America. Having a gay son, especially one as open as I was, wasn't an easy pill for him to swallow. He'd made his own sort of peace with it, especially after I put my life on the line during a recent family crisis, but I still felt like there was a distance between us that didn't exist between him and my brothers. It would've been nice to feel like their equal every now and then, even though I knew deep down Pop would never accept my lifestyle.

A lack of real friends only added to my sense of isolation. Other than my sister Paris, I wasn't really close to anyone. I had people I partied with, but there wasn't anyone I connected with beyond face value. No one I could really talk to about men, sex, fashion—about anything, really—from a man-to-man perspective. Not only that, but it had been a long time since I had someone special in my life. The last person I even thought about as a potential mate was brutally snatched from me before we even had a chance. His death contributed to the funk I'd been in the past few months.

Lately, I'd felt myself slipping deeper and deeper into a dense fog, and it was becoming harder to fight it. I needed to do something and do it quick. I made my way into the bathroom and took a long, steamy shower, hoping it would revive my spirits. It didn't. Even after I pampered my skin with the finest products and put on a fly Gucci outfit, I felt no different. My mood sucked, and it didn't look like there was anything I could do to change it.

It was about eleven on a Saturday morning, and I could hear the chatter coming from the dining room, so I went downstairs. London and her kids were seated at the table, along with Junior and his wife, Sonja, and Nevada, my sixteen-year-old nephew.

"Good morning, everyone." I greeted the room with the most cheerful voice I could muster. Their responses were all cordial, but as usual, I felt like I had interrupted their conversation.

I walked over to the breakfast food spread out on the buffet and made myself a plate, then sat in the empty seat beside Nevada. Like a typical teenager, he was too engrossed in whatever was happening on his phone to look up. The food didn't taste bad, but I still wasn't satisfied. It was the typical brunch we had every weekend: pancakes, eggs, bacon, sausage, fruit. It was good, but it was the same—just like everything else in my life lately. I realized that I wanted something different. I needed something different. I was tired of feeling this way.

"Where's the parentals?" I tried making small talk.

No one answered for a minute.

Just as I was about to have an attitude, Nevada looked up and said, "You say something, Uncle Rio?"

I turned and repeated my question. "I asked, where are the parentals?"

"Oh, my dad is down in the gym with Uncle Daryl and—"

I shook my head. "Uh, I wasn't talking about *your* parentals, nephew. I was talking about mine."

"Oh, my bad." Nevada shrugged.

"It's okay, Nevada. It's not like he specified whose parents he was referring to," London said.

I glanced up at my sister and asked, "Why the hell would I be asking about his parents?"

"Anyway, to answer your question, Momma and Daddy went out for a drive this morning," London said then went back to talking to Sonya.

As tempting as it was to respond with a snide comment, I decided to finish my breakfast without saying another word. Showing a serenity I really didn't feel, I walked out of the dining room and didn't stop until I was out the front door. When I hopped into my car, I knew exactly where I was headed.

Forty-five minutes later, I was at my spot. All the Duncan children had their own secret hideouts, including me. Mine was located in a country setting, surrounded by trees and a huge iron gate, all on a quarter acre of land. I pressed the password into the keypad, put my fingerprint on the sensor, and the gate to my small but adequate getaway opened and allowed me access. I drove up to the front of the small, two-story bachelor pad and bypassed the three-car garage, deciding to park in the driveway instead.

I entered the house and looked around at the décor I had meticulously selected. There were huge mirrors on all the living room walls, making it feel bigger than it really was. The color scheme of burnt orange, brown, and red gave the place a warm atmosphere. Mostly everything came from Pier One, my favorite go-to place for home décor because their pieces were unique, just like me. The focal point of the dining room was a huge glass table surrounded by cast iron chairs, with an elaborate olive-green dish setting at each seat. Everything matched perfectly: the rug, vases, and pictures throughout the room. Stepping into the black-and-white motif kitchen, I saw the sparkling clean stainless steel appliances—the same ones my parents had at their home. I figured if they were good enough for them, then surely they were good enough for me. I'd decorated the place with love and attention, and usually it relaxed me when I escaped to this space. My home away from home was a breath of fresh air. But, somehow, I didn't feel the usual peace this time.

I flopped down on the burnt orange sofa in the living room and checked my phone to see if I had any missed calls or texts. Not one. I started to scroll through my social media feeds to see if anything was popping in the city, but there wasn't anything I wanted to do on there. I loved New York, but shit was not lit for me right now.

Again, I was overcome by the urge to be somewhere else, somewhere carefree where I didn't have the pressure of being a Duncan, always worrying about my family's reputation. Everywhere I went, I had to think about how not to end up as a feature story on Page Six or TMZ. And God forbid my parents got a call from someone who had heard that I was somewhere doing something with someone that brought negative attention to the Duncans. Never mind the fact that the Duncan name brought its own set of drama because of the enemies who had it out for my family. We had more than our fair share of haters, that was for sure, and I didn't need or want anyone coming for me. Thinking about this shit all the time was getting so damn tiring.

"I need to get away. I just need a destination. Somewhere I can let loose and not care," I spoke out loud.

I asked Siri for gay hot spot cities. She came up with a few locations, Atlanta, Los Angeles, and Baltimore being the top three. Atlanta was the current gay mecca, but I knew that in my current mood, I wouldn't have patience for the drama queens down there. Los Angeles was too far to fly just to have fun and come back. Baltimore was a popping city, and even though it was ghetto as hell, it did have its hot spots, and the gay scene was on point for the most part. Plus, it was the closest. I decided to take a chance.

I went to the bedroom closet. My wardrobe selection here was pretty limited compared to my overstuffed walk-in closet at the family house, but I was able to grab a few pieces I knew would work until I got to Baltimore and did a little shopping. I didn't know how long I was going to be there. While tossing my things into my Louis Vuitton Weekender bag, I caught a glimpse of myself in the mirror. A couple of months ago, I had begun to grow my hair out. Once it was long enough to rock short twists, I dyed it into an array of blue and green ombre colors that I called my mermaid look. I loved it, and so did Paris; my parents, not so much.

When she saw it, my mother had simply asked, "And how long do you plan on wearing your hair like that?"

My father inhaled deeply, turned away, and shook his head, the same way he did pretty much every time he saw me. I believed the only way I would ever get his true approval would be to tell him I'd decided to be straight—and since that wasn't happening, we both had to deal with one another the best way we knew how.

As I stared at my reflection, I decided to make a change before I headed to B'More. I went into the bathroom to begin my transformation. It had to be something drastic, so I grabbed a can of shaving cream, smoothed it all over the top of my head, and started shaving. Before long, all my hair was sitting in the sink. I looked in the mirror and gasped. Because I had my mother's complexion, people always commented that I was her spitting image. But now, as I stared at myself, I looked exactly like a younger version of my father. Hell, I looked even better than he did. I decided to add one little touch, though. I popped in a pair of hazel contact lenses from the medicine cabinet, and then stepped back to admire my new look. Smiling at myself in one of the full-length mirrors, I was satisfied.

I sent Paris a quick text from my regular phone: Gonna vanish for a few days. Reach me on my bat phone if there's an emergency. She was probably the only one who would miss me, and I didn't want her to worry.

I went to the safe in my bedroom closet, removing a burner phone, some extra cash, and a box labeled *Magic Tricks*. Then I shut down my regular phone and locked it in the safe. I was ready to hit the road.

I walked out of the house into the garage, where I had two other cars—a BMW and a Honda Civic. Baltimore wasn't the safest place in the world, so I opted for the Honda. I pulled out of the driveway, and the gate closed behind me. I took one last look at my spot in the rearview mirror as I headed south, hoping to find the change I was looking for.

Corey

2

As my father walked into the visiting room, the first thing I noticed was that he was a little thicker than I remembered. It had been a few months since we'd seen each other, and he no longer looked muscular. If anything, he was a little flabby. His demeanor, however, was still the same. My father had always commanded attention in every room he entered. I was filled with all types of emotions as he made his way over to me. There was admiration for the way he carried himself even though he was going to be locked away for the rest of his life, pain because his presence reminded me that my mother was under six feet of dirt, and fear that clenched my chest because I was finally going to share a secret with my father that I'd been holding for as long as I could remember.

He passed by two armed guards, who were posted at the door even though there was almost no chance anyone in the room was carrying a weapon. Visitors were required to go through several security measures before they were allowed in. My father had been an inmate in the federal correctional facility in Cumberland, Maryland for over a year while waiting to be transported to another facility. Seeing him in this place was unsettling to me. He had warned me many times that this was a possibility because of his life in the streets, but I never thought it could happen to someone who was so good at his job. But he knew better than I did, and this was just the proof that made me a believer. Seeing him now made me wonder if this would be my home one day too. I had to live with the strong possibility of that happening because now that he was locked up, I was handling the day to day operations of his street business.

My father sat down with a serious look on his face. I wanted to smile, but I had to save face because, even though he was behind bars, he was still my blueprint in many ways.

"Good to see you, son," he said in an upbeat tone as he picked up the phone that was on his side of the thick barrier between us. The slight smile on his face let me know that he was happy to see me, and I hoped that would still be the case once I told him my news.

"Good to see you too, sir." I matched his tone.

"So, what's good?" he asked. I knew he was referring to the business. My father had been in the drug game a long time. Now the territory had expanded, and he had a hand in a little bit of everything in the city: clubs, liquor stores, payday loan stores, and, of course, drugs. They were all bringing in good money, even the clothing boutique I'd recently invested in. Life was busy and sometimes challenging, keeping all these things together and watching out for the backstabbers lurking everywhere. Thank God my business partner had my back. It made things a little easier for me.

"Everything is everything," I replied.

"Good. So why are you here?" he asked. It was a fair question. It wasn't like I'd been visiting regularly.

I paused, trying to get my heart rate under control. Over the last year or so, I had witnessed some downright dirty things: murders, torture, robberies, kidnappings—they all came along with the territory of the illegal empire I'd inherited—but to sit in front of my father on the opposite side of this glass to tell him what I needed to tell him brought me great fear. However, I had wrestled with this for a long time and had procrastinated long enough. It was time to tell him.

"I'm here because I need to tell you something that I should've told you a long time ago. I've been putting it off, but it's time for me to man up and just—"

He interrupted me. "Stop it. I already know. I've known for a while."

My heart began pounding so fast that I thought it was going to come out of my chest. He knew? How? When did he find out?

"Shit, at first I was cool with it," he continued.

"You were?" My voice cracked, and I cleared my throat to play it off.

"Yeah. I knew once I landed in here it was going to be a major transition for the business and you were going to need some additional support. You did what you had to do, right?" He nodded at me. "I am a little disappointed that you kept it from me."

I was both shocked and relieved at his explanation, so I simply nodded and said, "Uh, yeah, about that . . ."

"But things are getting out of hand. Which is why you're coming to me now, and that's what matters. Don't worry, son. I already got a plan in place. I got somebody on it already."

I was even more confused. This wasn't making any sense. Clearly what he was speaking about and what I was going to share with him were two different things. The anxiety I had when he first entered the visiting room returned full force.

"Pops, you don't—"

"I know I don't have to, Corey, but just because I'm on the inside don't mean I can't make shit happen. You took on a huge responsibility, but you still learning. Hiring faggots to sell dope wasn't something I'd ever do, but I can't be mad at you. From what I hear, those fruits are out there moving weight in the clubs. For what it's worth, it was a smart move. But now it's time to get rid of them, son. We can't have the reputation I built up be convoluted by having a bunch of candy asses—and now with Vinnie Dash being gone, it's prime time to make some major moves. We need real men working for us. So, now we gotta do what we gotta do."

I sat back and stared at him in silence. It was no secret that my father was homophobic. I'd heard him make disrespectful and disparaging comments about gay men my entire life. But the look in his eyes told me that what he was thinking about was beyond a phobia.

"And what is that?" I asked slowly.

"We gotta get rid of them. Kill them muthafuckas." A sinister smile spread across his face.

"What?" I glanced around. The guards nearby didn't seem to be paying attention to our conversation, thank God.

"Don't get me wrong. Like I said, they've done some good work, but at the end of the day, you know how they are. If we fire them, they will get all emotional, and there's no telling what they'd do. They could go crying to the feds and take all of us down. They're worse than women. Pansy-ass bastards," he growled. "They're all over the place in here, too, but they know not to fuck with me. I have shown and made it known that I will slice a sucker up without even having second thoughts if they even look in my direction." This time he spoke loud enough for the people near him to hear. One of the guards smirked, but he didn't look too concerned. He probably hated the gay inmates as much as my father did.

"You . . . we . . . can't do that. That's crazy. For a lot of reasons," I told him. "First of all, you sound like you're about to take out an entire demographic of people, which you can't."

"Maybe not. But don't worry. I got a plan I'm working on, and hopefully I can take out a good amount." He laughed casually. "What's Dre up to? He handling things like he's supposed to?"

I couldn't believe my father transitioned to asking about my business partner and second in charge like he hadn't been talking about his plan to murder folks only seconds before. I was too busy trying to process everything to respond.

"Corey, did you hear me ask you a question?"

"Huh? Oh, yeah. Dre is fine," I mumbled.

"What the hell is wrong with you, son? You're acting like something's bothering you." He became serious.

"I'm fine," I lied. "I just came through to make sure you were okay and check up on you. I gotta get up outta here. You need anything?"

"Nah, son. You know I'm holding my own in here. You know how I do. And don't worry about what we were talking about earlier. Like I said, I'm working on a plan to take care of it. You just keep doing what you're doing. I'm proud of you, because Lord knows what would happen if you had turned out to be one of those queer-ass dudes. Then I would have to be trying to figure out how to kill your ass too. Right?" He stared at me intensely, waiting for a response.

"Right." I nodded.

We said our goodbyes, and as he stood and hung up the phone, the little boy in me was crushed. The one who'd wanted his father's constant approval and hung on his entire word died in me at that moment. I realized that my father would never embrace his seed as a man should and love me unconditionally.

But it was all good. There was nothing I could do to change that, and although I was hurt, I told myself that I would be fine. I had no other choice.

I walked out of that facility a free man, but my father would be forever locked up, both mentally and physically, because of his thinking. Brushing away the tears that fell from my eyes, I decided that one day, I was going to embrace myself and live my life just the way I was. But that would have to wait, because I didn't know what kind of plan my father was working on, but I knew someone had to be ready to protect the gay men in our organization, including myself.

Diana

3

The amount of money I had spread across my bed was enough to make someone think that I was either a stripper or a lottery winner, but I was neither. I was simply a part-time college student who'd run into a lottery-like situation. When my boss, Corey, came to me with his proposition, I was a little bit hesitant, but the money he offered and the opportunities that came with it were too good to turn down.

We'd met one Saturday in the mall. Ironically, we were both looking at shoes—me, as a birthday gift for my father, and him, just because. The saleswoman had really convinced him that the ugly three hundred–dollar pair he was trying on were a must-have. Feeling sorry for him and not wanting him to go out looking like a sucker, I shook my head and told him the truth. Luckily, he listened to me, and after I helped him select not only the perfect pair but a matching ensemble to go along with them, we went to lunch, and a beautiful friendship was born. He was good looking, fun to be around, and he had money. I was shocked when I found out he was in the dope game, because he definitely didn't seem like the type. Corey was far from a thug, but he was about his business at the same time. He had power but didn't flaunt it, and I liked that about him. He was also easy to talk to. When I shared my dreams of one day having my own clothing line, he was very supportive.

"I can see you doing that," he told me.

"Really?"

"Hell yeah. You definitely have an eye for fashion, and you stay helping a brother look fresh in the latest gear."

"Yeah, you do have a point. If it wasn't for me, there's no telling what you'd have on. Probably some whack-ass overpriced moccasins," I teased.

A couple of weeks later, he said he had something to talk to me about. He asked me to meet him at one of the buildings they were renovating downtown.

"What's this?" I asked when I walked inside.

"You like it?"

"It's a nice space, but for what?"

"I was thinking about putting a boutique in here. Well, if I had someone to run it for me. You know anyone?"

My mouth gaped open. "Are you serious? Stop playing, Corey."

"I'm dead ass. I'll pay you fifteen hundred a week to manage it. But if I do this for you, I'm gonna need you to do something for me."

I paused, preparing myself to cuss him out in response to whatever sexual invitation he was about to extend. I knew the fact that he'd never pushed up on me was kinda strange, but now I figured all of that was about to change. "What the hell do you think I'm about to do for you? Because you know I don't get down like that."

"Shut up, Di. It ain't like that. But there are some other job requirements that you'll be responsible for."

"Like what?" I folded my arms.

"Like I'm gonna need for you to hang out with me a couple of nights a week at Wet Dreams."

"The gay bar?" I was familiar with the hottest gay club in town. Most of my gay classmates hung out there on the regular, and I'd been a few times with them. It was a great place to party, even for straight people.

"Yeah, I own it now, so I gotta make my presence known."

"And you don't wanna be caught up in there by yourself because people might think you're gay. I get it. But why me? I'm sure you got plenty of bad bitches you can take," I said.

"This is true, but you know how it is: if you take a chick somewhere more than once, she naturally assumes shit. I don't need that type of pressure in my life. And you're a bad bitch that I don't mind being seen with," he said with a cute laugh.

"Well, I am that." I struck a supermodel pose.

"And, if things go the way I'm thinking they are, this boutique, along with the club, are gonna be a match made in heaven. They'll profit from one another. Same clientele."

"Damn, you're right." I nodded.

"So, we got a deal?" He held his hand out.

Fifteen hundred dollars to do what I love to do—play in clothes and party? There was no way I was turning it down. I quickly pushed his hand away and jumped into his arms, hugging him tightly. "Hell yeah, we got a deal!"

So far, things had been going perfect. Business at the boutique was booming, and I was having a blast hanging out at the club with Corey a couple of nights a week. As the owner, he had a permanent spot in VIP, where we spent most of our time. I couldn't have asked for a better job. I was stacking my loot—hence the pile of money on my bed at the moment. After purchasing a new car, my next move would be to move out of my parents' house. I had been there long enough, and it was time.

Knock. Knock. Knock.

"Hold on." I quickly grabbed the money and shoved it underneath the bed before I opened the door.

"Wassup, Pop?" I greeted my father with my "innocent daughter" smile.

"It's kind of late for you to be getting in the house. Were you at work?"

"Yes and no." I turned and walked back toward my bed, flopping down on it like I was a big kid.

"That's not an answer." He looked at me seriously. He was such a protective parent, which was why I was in such a rush to leave the nest. Even though I was over twenty-one, he still treated me like a teenager. It was like I would never be grown in his eyes.

"Dad, I'm sorry. I went out with the girls after work to chill for a little bit. I should have called. I was just releasing a little bit of stress from work and school." I batted my eyes and pursed my lips to soften him up.

"Next time, think of others and not just yourself," he said, then he came over and kissed me on the forehead. "I love you, and I am proud of you."

He left the room, and I felt my stomach twisting into knots. His last statement hit me kind of hard. Was I really a daughter to be proud of? Yeah, I was in school completing my degree and working at one of the hottest boutiques in the city, but I was also doing something I never thought I'd be doing. It wasn't just clothing I was selling at the store. I was also selling drugs and working for Corey Parks, one of the largest street dealers in Baltimore.

Rio

4

I zoomed past the WELCOME TO BALTIMORE sign in the median strip as I entered the city. "Wrecking Ball" by Miley Cyrus blasted from the radio, and I was filled with anticipation of all the things I might get into down here in B-more. I didn't have a plan other than to arrive in the city. Now I was beginning to wonder if this was a good idea.

"What the fuck!" I yelled out in anger as a crazy driver swerved in front of me with no blinker. Being a native New Yorker, I was used to erratic driving, but that shit still irked my soul. As I tried to calm my nerves, I realized that I wanted, no, what I needed was a drink.

I pulled over into a random parking lot, googled "Baltimore hot spots" and then scrolled through the choices. One name stood out: Wet Dreams. The title alone was intriguing. I popped the directions into Maps on my phone and headed toward the club.

The streets of Baltimore reminded me of New York on a smaller, poorer scale. I saw tons of abandoned buildings and boarded up houses, but I also passed by the Inner Harbor, with all its museums, shopping, and restaurants. That was the section of town that had been cleaned up for tourists.

When I got to Wet Dreams, I was surprised by the number of people lined up outside. It looked promising. If the décor inside looked as good as the façade, then this place might be just what I was looking for. Something about it reminded me of the nightclubs I frequented in Paris a while back.

There were only a few parking spots left about as far away from the door as I could get, and that pissed me off a little. Why wouldn't a place this jumping have valet service?

"Stop being so bourgie, Rio. Just go have a good time," I told myself as I climbed out of the car and hit the lock. The neighborhood didn't look too bad, but this wasn't my city, and I didn't want to take any chances. Last thing I needed was to end up in B-More with no ride.

I walked toward the front of the club and checked out the people in the line. It was a mixed crowd, with people of all colors and nationalities—a clear indication that this was a well-established club that brought people from all over who wanted to have a good time. I was impressed. If I had any doubt about finding some gay men in the crowd, that disappeared as soon as I started listening to some of the conversations happening around me in the line. The word *bitch* was used between dudes, like, more times than I could count. A true sign.

The line moved quickly, even though every person who entered was given a pat-down and scanned with a metal detector. A few people in line complained about it, but after that mass shooting in Orlando, you couldn't be too safe these days, especially in a gay club. I was glad they were taking extra measures.

As I stepped up for my turn to be searched, I could hear the music pumping. The guard patted me down, taking a little longer and pressing a little harder than he needed to.

"Damn, was it good for you too?" I asked when he finished.

He looked at me like I was crazy, but I gave him a slight smile, letting him know that I wasn't offended. Real talk, it had been a minute since I'd been dicked down, so I didn't mind being felt up in the name of safety.

"Next time, ask for my number first. You just might get more than a few cheap feels."

He smiled back at me, and although he was noticeably cute, the night was still young. I wanted to get inside and prowl a bit before I chose my entertainment. If anything, he would still be there when I left, in the event that I didn't meet anyone else.

Inside the club, the room was packed to damn near capacity, with beautiful people on the dance floor, doing their thing. Several bars and lounge-type booths spanned the entire perimeter, with a few tall tables scattered here and there. It was plush, but not stuffy. Up above was a balcony, where the high-money clients were getting bottle service and surveying the scenery beneath them.

I was enjoying the vibe—and definitely the sights—as I strolled over to the bar. The men were gorgeous, even the straight ones. Some of the gay brothers looked a little flamboyant, but others were more reserved about it. There were even a few thuggish queers in the mix. I was loving the variety I had to choose from!

"What can I do for you?" the bartender asked with a quick glance down at my package.

"That's a loaded question." I smiled flirtatiously.

"Did you want a drink?" he asked, suddenly all business.

"Oh, sorry. Didn't mean to offend you," I apologized. *Shit, did I read him wrong?*

"No need to apologize. It was funny. Thing is, I just don't shit where I eat. Feel me?"

I shrugged. "I totally understand. Give me a margarita on the rocks."

He walked off, and I turned to scan the room for someone who wasn't on the clock and would be more open to whatever. When the bartender returned with my drink, I left him a semi decent tip, then walked over to one of the booths. I wanted to sit down and observe from a comfortable spot.

People watching was one of my favorite pastimes, especially in the club. Some of the couples were grinding so good that they were damn near having sex, and that shit was starting to turn me on. One guy in particular was giving the people a show and getting it in with a few of the females in the room. He was well built and knew how to work his body. As I watched him from across the room, I began to feel a slight pulsation in my crotch, and I moved around in my seat to readjust.

I enjoyed his little show for about ten minutes, watching him work that ass with a whole group of women. At one point, he turned around, and I took my eyes off his ass long enough to get a glimpse of his face. It was pretty dark in the club, but something about him was instantly familiar. He had a swag that let me know he had to be from New York. I leaned forward to try to get a better look at him, but he left the dance floor and disappeared into the crowd. I spent the next hour hoping to see someone else interesting on the dance floor, but no one even came close.

Three drinks later, I knew it was time to leave or I'd be too drunk to drive. "Fuck it. Let me get out of here and get me a good night's sleep," I muttered to myself. I headed for the exit.

Standing just outside the entrance, I started looking around for the bouncer who'd caught my eye, when suddenly I spotted the sexy-ass guy from the dance floor walking out. This time, I got a perfect view of his face. My heart dropped in awe and surprise. I couldn't believe my eyes as I stared at him, standing near the front door, talking to a couple of people. My buzz was gone; seeing his face had instantly sobered me.

"You a'ight? Hey, you good?"

I realized the bouncer was talking to me. "Yeah, I'm good."

"You sure you good to drive?" he asked.

I continued to stare, unable to tear my eyes away as the guy from the dance floor put his arms around some woman and kissed her neck.

"I'm good," I muttered to the bouncer.

It wasn't until the two of them walked off in the opposite direction that I finally left. Inside my car, I sat for a few minutes, still in a state of disbelief.

"It can't be," I said aloud to no one. "He's dead. He's supposed to be dead. I know he's dead. I had his blood all over me." I could feel myself trembling as I sat there, trying to make sense of this.

The honking of a car horn somewhere in the parking lot brought me out of my trance. I needed to get out of there, but I realized I didn't know where I was staying for the night. I grabbed my phone and searched the internet for five-star hotels and was happy to see the Four Seasons in the city. I booked my reservation online and finally pulled myself together enough to turn the car on and leave.

My mind was still all over the place as I drove to the hotel, but as I pulled up in front of the enormous glass structure, it put a smile on my face. I loved hotels, especially lavish ones.

"May I park your car?" a cute Asian guy with a thick accent offered.

Normally I would have responded with something like "At your house?" but I was still in a state of shock after seeing a man come back from the dead. I needed to get inside and check into my room so I could sort this all out in my mind. So without even a hint of flirting, I took the parking ticket from him and watched the valet take my luggage from the trunk.

At the front desk, I paid for a week-long stay, even though I had no idea how long I would be in the city. I got my key card and headed up to my suite on the eleventh floor. There were breathtaking balcony views of the skyline, a luxurious king-sized bedroom, plus a living room with a kitchenette. This was a suite meant for entertaining, but here I was, alone and much too shell-shocked to think about partying. I flopped down on the bed and stared up at the ceiling, still in a daze.

That could not have been him. I watched him die on the floor. I shook my head in confusion. *At least I thought he died. I left him there to die. Could he be alive?*

I went out onto the balcony. As I leaned on the railing and stared out into the darkness, the same questions played over and over in my mind: *Is Kennedy alive? Was that really him in the club? Did he fake his death to get away from me? Did my father have anything to do with this?*

Memories of that night were so vivid that it could have happened yesterday. Normally, when they came to my head, I would force myself not to remember; but tonight, I allowed them to replay. It was my father who sent Kennedy, who worked as a part of the Duncan security detail, with me on a mission during the height of our family's feud with Brother X and the Muslim brothers. We got caught up in an ambush type of situation, and Kennedy took two hot ones for me. His last words still made me tear up every time I remembered them: "I would have come out for you, Rio. Please go. Please."

I mourned a lost love that never got to happen, one that I didn't even realize was possible until it was too late. His death had affected me in a way that I'd never imagined. Now, it seemed as if he was very much alive and well. Or at least, I thought he was. Either way, I was going to find out.

Corey

5

I couldn't remember the last time I'd slept in, and this day was no different. I woke up to the sound of my phone ringing, same as it did each and every morning. Seemed like I was always handling business. One thing about being a kingpin, it was demanding as hell. I knew it was hard work even before I took over, because I'd had a front row seat to my father's action, but damn! Shit was getting to the point that at times, I wanted to walk away from it all. I had a lot of perks and power, but I never had time or energy. I wasn't even thirty years old and I felt like an old man. Something had to give. This wasn't the life I'd planned for myself.

I checked the caller ID on my cell phone and declined the call. It was Ant, one of my street lieutenants, a guy who always had something to complain about. I wasn't in the mood to hear his whiny ass first thing in the morning. I climbed out of bed and headed into the bathroom to take a quick shower. As soon as I stepped out and put on a pair of pants, my phone rang again. It was the same annoying-ass dude.

"What the fuck is going on?" I snapped, letting him know I didn't appreciate the multiple calls.

"Boss, these faggots are getting out of hand. I can't work with them dick chasers. They fucking up my mood."

I wanted to go off on him, because technically he was insulting me even if he didn't know it. But I had to be smart about it. I couldn't sound like I was favoring my gay workers, because the second I looked soft to him or anyone else, someone would step up to challenge my reign. Besides, this wasn't even really about them being gay. Ant was just mad because truth was, the gay corner boys were outperforming the straight dudes lately.

"Is money gay?" I asked.

"What?" he asked, sounding confused.

"Is money gay?" I asked again.

"I ain't following you."

"Money is green. Money is paying your bills. And money don't give no fucks, so neither do I. Call my shit again with some petty shit, and I promise your bitch ass will be replaced with another faggot. Now, get my fucking money and grow some balls instead of worrying about who chasing them!" I hung up on him before his simple ass wanted to say something else.

I was pissed, but it didn't take me long to come up with a solution. I dialed another number.

"Yo, Marcus. You wanna move up the ladder?"

"Hell yeah!" he answered.

"Then kill Ant and you can have his spot."

"Word?" he asked for reassurance.

"Word! Handle that." Problem solved. I looked forward to not having to deal with Ant's homophobic ass anymore.

I moved on with my day, making calls and giving orders as I left the house. Once all of my soldiers had their marching orders, I checked in with Dre.

Dre and I had been friends ever since he moved from New York to Baltimore. He was working for my old man, and truth be told, I was pretty jealous in the beginning. Pops took an instant liking to him, and it was always, "That Dre is so damn smart. That Dre handles his business like a real boss." It wasn't long before Dre became his right-hand man. When my father got locked up, I thought for sure he was going to turn everything over to Dre, but to my surprise, he gave it all to me. He told Dre that he expected him to treat me with respect and to look out for me at the same time. Ever since then, Dre had done what most disloyal muthafuckas on the streets won't do: he'd proved that he truly did have my back. We didn't always agree on everything, but we made it work.

"Dre, what's going on today?" I asked when he answered the phone.

"I'm gonna make my rounds on a couple of spots, and then we can meet back up later to go over some things."

"A'ight. I got a couple runs to make myself, and then I'll be heading over to the club for a drink or two. We can meet there."

"Cool. I'm doing a pickup at the boutique, so let ya girl know to have her ass there. I ain't got time to be wasting like she does," Dre said. "And she better have made some decent money this week."

I laughed. "Man, come on. You know Diana is gonna be there. Don't do that." One of the things Dre didn't agree with me on was opening the boutique. He didn't see the point. I tried to explain that the boutique was a money maker, especially with Diana running shit. That chick could sell ice to an Eskimo if she needed to. She was smart, funny, and fine as hell—the kind of woman that men wanted and other women aspired to be like, so they listened to her. Dre still thought the store was pointless until he realized that it could also be used for other purposes. Not only were we able to filter money through it, but we could store contraband in the back. We bought a truck for deliveries that could also transport narcotics throughout the city all under the cover of a legitimate business.

"Listen, I know that's your girl and all, but I don't like her, and I don't trust her either," Dre said.

"You're tripping, Dre. But I'll give Diana the heads up that you'll be stopping through, so she'll be prepared."

"Yeah, you do that. I'll see you later." Dre hung up the phone.

I immediately called Diana. She seemed just as thrilled for the stop as Dre was. They were like oil and water, those two.

"Can't you just come and do the pickup?" she whined.

"You know that ain't what I do," I told her. "Just have shit ready when he gets there, please."

"I will. But it won't matter, because he *stay* having shit to say about me. I swear one of these days I'm gonna cuss his ass out, Corey. I mean it. I bust my ass in this place, and—"

"I know, Di. You're a hard worker. We all know that. Dre is just Dre."

"Whatever. Oh, and we're running low on X. Pierre came in to place an order, and we're down to the last."

"Man, I knew shit was gonna get tight sooner or later. I thought what we had would last longer than this," I replied. We had plenty of weed and heroin, but X had become harder for us to come by, especially without Vinnie Dash, who had been my father's supplier for years.

"He wanted way more than what I gave him, but I held onto some. You know they sell out of that shit like crazy at the club. That's the drug of choice for the sugars," Diana said with a laugh.

"Yeah, you're right." I pretended to be amused by her statement. Unlike Dre, I trusted Diana. I knew she didn't have a problem with gay people. She probably thought calling them "sugars" was cute. But still, she had no clue about my sexuality, and I wasn't ready to share that information with her. If she slipped and anyone else found out, I could be putting myself in danger, especially now that my father was talking reckless.

"I gave Pierre a partial order, but what are we gonna do about the rest?" she asked.

"I'll get with Dre, and we'll figure something out. Just tell him to give me a couple of days and I got him," I told her.

"You're the boss," she said. "I got some real customers who just walked in. I'll text you when Dre gets here."

"You coming to the club tonight when you close up shop, right?"

"Did you really have to ask, Corey? I'll be right there beside you in VIP, drinking up all your liquor and backing that ass up on you like the good girlfriend that I am." She laughed.

I ended the call, put my silver Range Rover into gear, and backed out of the driveway. In a perfect world, I'd be heading to a spa for the day to relax, but that wouldn't be happening anytime soon. Instead, I set out to locate a new supplier of ecstasy and make sure the other business operations were running smooth. Just another day in the life of a drug dealer.

Diana

6

Although Corey owned Chic World Boutique, it was my baby, and I put my heart and soul into making it the most popping spot for fashion in the city. It was one of my favorite places in the world to be other than Maryland Institute of the Arts, the school I attended. Running the boutique not only gave me retail experience, but it gave me the opportunity to make some serious connections with buyers and suppliers that I would be able to work with once I started my own fashion line. Not only that, but I was also able to gain some clients that I designed original pieces for. But, as much as I loved it, working for Corey also meant I had to deal with Dre's mean ass. He would come by twice a week to make drop-offs and pickups, which should've only taken ten minutes tops, and didn't require much conversation. But, it never failed; he always had something to say.

I had been giving myself a pep talk ever since Corey called and gave me the heads up, and I was determined to remain polite.

"Hey, Dre," I sang out when he walked in the door. I was in the middle of ringing up two guys who had come in moments before. Both of them turned to stare at Dre—rightfully so, because Lord knows he was fine as hell. Tall, with a nice build, strong-looking shoulders and a chiseled face, he was a man's man who just oozed testosterone. Had he not been such an asshole, I probably would have fucked him by now.

"'Sup." He gave me a nonchalant shrug as he walked to the back of the store.

I quickly completed the customers' transaction and bagged up their items.

"Hope to see you again soon," I said as they left the shop.

I heard my name being called. I took a deep breath and hurried to the back, still determined to keep things civil with Dre. I was not in the mood for drama with him today.

"What's up?" I asked.

Dre was looking in one of the cabinets we kept under lock and key with a frown on his face. "Where the hell is the rest of the X?"

"Pierre came and made a buy. That's all that's left," I explained.

"Pierre? Really?"

"Yes, Pierre," I said and folded my arms.

"Why didn't you tell him we ain't have it? Better yet, why you ain't call nobody?"

"I—"

He cut me off before I could finish. "So you let Pierre's fruity ass make a buy instead of telling his ass no? You do realize Pierre's bar is our competition, right? So now his customers are gonna have product while ours don't. Or did that thought not cross your mind?" Dre snapped.

"First of all, that thought did cross my mind, which is why there's still product left for us to have at the club. If I hadn't thought, I woulda sold his ass all of it like he wanted. Second, I already told Corey what the fucking deal was when it happened, and he said he'd take care of it. So don't come at me like I'm one of your little flunkies you got running around here, because I'm not."

It was no secret that Dre didn't like me, nor did he trust me. I'd never done anything other than be nice to him, so I didn't know what that was about, and really, I didn't care. He was from New York, and they were known for being the utmost assholes, so it was kind of expected. He was also used to having women faun over him. Being a nice-looking guy with swagger and money who could also dance made him the center of attention at the club. He had his choice of females and left with a different one each night. Not only was he an asshole, but he was also a man-whore.

"You got that right." Dre took a step closer to me and stared with such intensity that I damn near felt naked. I was determined not to be intimidated by him. We were so close to one another that I could feel the heat from his body. Neither one of us moved, and the tension was thick.

The chime of the front door alerted us that someone had come in, and although I hated to, I was the first one to move. Just as I was about to walk out, I felt his hand on my arm, and again, our eyes met.

"What?" I asked him.

His eyes traveled from my face down to my breasts, where they stopped. My body betrayed my mind, and against my will, my nipples hardened under his gaze. I snatched away and crossed my arms in front of me, hoping he hadn't noticed.

"Next time, you call me if there's going to be a problem." He raised an eyebrow at me.

I didn't say anything as I walked away. For the remainder of the day, all I could think about was sex. I was already horny before Dre had come in, and after our little "heated moment," I was even more so.

I had no choice but to call Ashton, a preppy white boy I met at school who I'd been seeing for a few weeks. He was well spoken and kind of a nerd, but he was nice. Normally, I didn't go for white boys, but there was something different about Ashton that interested me, and one day when he "accidentally" sent me some *dick-ture* mail, I realized exactly what it was. His manhood was impressive, and I immediately wanted a chance to see if he knew what to do with it. He did not disappoint; my first ride on it almost took me out. I came within minutes and quickly learned that Ashton was a closet freak. He twisted my little body up into positions that I never knew existed.

Ashton was always ready, and it didn't take him any time to show up at the store. As soon as I saw his car pull up, I closed the blinds and put the WILL BE BACK SOON sign in the door. I wasted no time pulling him into the back of the store.

"Damn, baby, you must've missed me," he said.

We stood in the exact same spot that Dre had been in earlier. Thinking about what almost happened between us made me even hornier. I put my arms around Ashton's neck. His hands immediately went under the little black dress I was wearing—without any underwear—and he began to massage my sweet spot with his very capable hands. We shared a sensual kiss as my dress slipped to the floor. Ashton's hands cupped my ass, and I stood on my tiptoes to give his mouth easier access to my breasts.

He began sucking slowly, and I moaned with anticipation as he lifted me off the floor.

I wrapped my legs around him. "I have been waiting for this all day," I whispered into his ear.

He carried me over to a nearby desk. My hands quickly began fumbling with the belt holding up his khakis. I couldn't wait to get my fingers on his massive dick that I could see was already growing to its full girth in his pants. My heart began racing in anticipation of having his hardness in my hands—and in other places.

While I moved to unfasten his pants, Ashton meticulously unbuttoned his shirt and removed it. I ran my fingers along his muscular chest and torso with a big smile on my face. He might have been a white boy, but he could definitely give the brothers a run for their money. He was sexy as hell. By the time he was finally naked, my wetness was oozing down my inner thigh. I was ready. But Ashton wasn't going to let me have it that easy.

"You ready for me?" He waved his hard piece at me with no hands.

"Damn straight, I'm ready."

I watched as he strapped on a condom, and then I leaned back on the desk and spread my legs wide. He pressed it up against my wet lips, and I shuddered as he slid just the swollen tip in then took it out, teasing me.

"You want it?" he asked, slipping the tip in again, this time holding it there for a few seconds before taking it out again.

"Mmmmm," I moaned through pursed lips.

He pushed inside of me with one quick thrust, causing me to yelp. My body tensed up at his girth, but I took it like a big girl. He took a slow pace at first, and then his stroke quickened until he worked me to a fevered frenzy. He grabbed the back of my thighs and pushed my legs back farther until they were damn near touching my head, but I didn't care. I was too busy enjoying the thrust of his thickness as he entered me.

Just as I thought I couldn't take anymore, he slowed down once again and started caressed my clit.

"You like that?" he asked.

I nodded my head, too focused on the sensations to give him a verbal response. Then, he stopped abruptly. My eyes flew open.

"Tell me." He stood there smiling, his dick still pulsating inside of me.

"Ashton, please," I begged him.

"Please what?" he teased. He loved to talk during sex. I didn't, but I knew if I wanted him to finish the job he'd already started, I had to oblige.

"Please fuck me," I moaned, reaching behind him and pushing on his hips to make him start moving again.

He started pumping again, still talking with each thrust. "You like this, don't you?" Push. "You love this dick." Push. "I can feel you getting wetter." And so on, until he let out a roar and we both climaxed at the same time. As his sweat-covered body collapsed on top of mine, I found myself thinking about the last person in the world I should have been thinking about: Dre.

Rio

7

I slept until damn near three in the afternoon. It was a restless sleep, and Kennedy was still on my mind when I woke up, so he was probably all I'd dreamed about.

I considered texting Paris to tell her what I saw the night before, but I decided I needed to figure shit out on my own. I made my way into the bathroom that was just as lavish as the rest of the suite, and instead of taking a shower, I indulged myself with a bath in the massive porcelain tub. I filled it with hot water and scented oil, then turned on the jets and slipped in. The tension and anxiety I'd been feeling since the night before finally began to melt away. Soon, my head felt clear enough to formulate a plan of action for the night. Going back to Wet Dreams to find Kennedy was a must. I needed answers, and I wasn't leaving Baltimore until I got them. With hours to waste before I could go back to the club, I decided to pamper myself a little more—with some retail therapy.

"Good afternoon, sir." The attendant who took my ticket at the valet station was pretty cute, a little bit of eye candy for me to admire while I waited for my car. "It's a beautiful day, isn't it?" he asked, and I wondered if he was flirting with me.

"It sure is," I replied. "Guess I should have brought my sunglasses."

"Well, there's plenty of good shopping around for you to go get a new pair," he suggested.

I laughed. "I like that idea. It's not like I ever need an excuse to go shopping."

"Yeah," he said, letting his eyes wander up and down my body. "I can see you have good fashion sense."

Now I had no doubt this guy was flirting. I didn't mind the attention, but with Kennedy still on my mind, I wasn't in the right frame of mind to pursue this.

"Thanks," I said a little coldly, so he'd understand this wasn't going anywhere.

The driver pulled up with my car, so I gave the attendant a little wave as I went to get in the Honda. I rolled down the passenger-side window and leaned over to ask him, "So, where would you go shopping in Baltimore? I need something to wear to the club tonight."

He stepped up to the window and leaned in. "Well, I go to a couple of spots, but there's this nice little shop that just opened up. It's called Chic World. Nice clothes that I think will suit your taste: high quality and unique."

"Hmm. I like that. High quality and unique, just like me," I said. "How do I get there?"

He smirked. "How about you give me your phone number and I'll text you the address?"

Apparently, he hadn't gotten the hint earlier. I shook my head. "Not happening. I'm only in town for work," I lied.

He shrugged. "Can't blame me for trying, can you?"

"Nah, I guess not, but I mean, you guys down here probably wouldn't know what to do with all this New York swag," I joked, and he laughed along with me. At least he wasn't going to get all pissy now that I'd shut him down.

He told me the address. "You have a nice day, sir. And I'll be here till seven if you change your mind about your availability," he said.

I flashed him a mysterious smile and pulled away from the hotel. Poor guy would probably be waiting around all day, hoping I'd come back for him. Chances of that happening were slim to none, but hey, at least it felt good to know I still had it.

I let the GPS take me to the address he'd given me, and twenty minutes later, I was in what looked like a newly renovated business district. I was happy to see that the streets were clean, and there didn't seem to be any unsavory types lurking around on the corners. Maybe that sounds funny, considering the business my family is in, but just because we sold drugs to them didn't mean I wanted to spend my free time in their presence.

The shop was the size of two row homes made into one shop, with an all-glass front. The *Chic World* logo on the sign was simple, maybe even a little disappointing. It didn't really give me the feel of a luxury boutique. Maybe that valet attendant had a different idea of high-end than us New Yorkers. Even though I was doubtful, I parked my car and went to check it out.

My opinion of the place changed as soon as I stepped inside. The décor was fresh and modern, and the clothes looked a whole lot more stylish than the sign outside had led me to expect. Right away I spotted a few things that I could wear out to the club.

"How are you today?" a pretty black chick behind the counter spoke. I was glad to see that she was already helping someone and wouldn't be able to hound me as I looked around. I liked to shop freely.

"If you need any help just let me know," she said.

"Okay," I answered, with no intention of actually doing so.

I started looking through the racks, pulling out a few pieces I liked. None of the labels were well-known designers, but the designs were unique, and the quality was impressive. This was definitely my type of shop.

"You like what you see?" The cashier had finished with the other customer and walked over to me.

"It's okay." I shrugged in an effort to downplay my enthusiasm for the place. If she thought I was too into it, she'd become way too pushy, and I hated that.

"Just okay?" She looked offended.

"It's okay, I guess, for Baltimore."

She just walked away without responding, but I could see she was irritated. If you ask me, she was too damn sensitive to be working in sales. I went back to looking through the rack of shirts in front of me.

Minutes later, she returned with a pair of pants in hand. "I think these would look very nice on you."

I stared at the eggplant-colored trousers with a look of horror. "A bitch just gonna try me, huh?" I looked at her like she was crazy. "Who the hell do you think I am, Prince?"

"Yes, *this* bitch has coins to make, and clearly you have some to spend. You don't like the pants, cool. It takes a special kind of man to rock them anyway. My apologies. Now, is a bitch going to buy some shit or what?" she said with a saucy attitude just loud enough for me to hear.

"I think I'd rather give these coins to the polite chick who greeted me when I first walked in," I shot back. "Do you think you could pull her out again, Miss Multiple Personalities?"

As much as this chick annoyed me, I had to admit when I looked back down at the pants that they would indeed look good on me. I reached over and took them from her.

"On second thought," I said, "you can have these coins. These pants, I like."

"Oh, so now my multiple personalities aren't a problem, huh?" she said with a smirk.

I laughed. She was sassy, but her attitude kinda reminded me of my sister Paris, so she got points for that. "Yeah, I love a chick that can transform and work from every angle to get money."

She side-eyed me. I guess she didn't understand it was a compliment. "I do what I have to do. Keep looking around and pick out what else you want. I'll be over near the cash register when you're ready."

"Cool. I got you."

By the time I walked over to pay, I had my arms full with items, including the purple pants and a pair of fabulous sunglasses, my reason for going there in the first place.

"So, where are you wearing these fabulous clothes? Church?"

"I'm going to spare your life and ignore the shade you just threw my way." I gave her a quick once over. "But, since you asked, I'm thinking about hitting up this club called Wet Dreams. I went the other night, and it was a lot of fun."

She perked up a little. "I know that spot very well."

"Is that so? You going tonight?" I asked.

"Actually, I am." She didn't offer any more info. "Your total is four hundred sixty-seven dollars and twelve cents."

"Damn." I reached into my crossbody bag and handed her my Black Card.

She took the card with a smile. "Yep, you ain't do as much damage as you thought, huh?"

"Shit, I did more," I told her. "I was hoping Baltimore was gonna be a bargain basement for me."

"But it's worth it. Trust me. You got some pieces here that no one else will be wearing, and you're gonna look fabulous in them. Make sure you tag the boutique on social media, too, because I know you gonna be flossing," she said, going full salesgirl on me. The thing is, she was right. I was going to look so damn hot, and I wasn't going to run into anyone else who had my style in the club.

"Damn right. As a matter of fact . . ." I took out my phone and posed for a selfie. She immediately leaned in to the shot. We were both laughing as she completed my transaction and bagged up my items.

"Thank you for shopping at Chic World, and please come back again," she said cheerily.

"You ain't gonna be taking all of my coins, Miss . . . what's your name anyway?"

"I'm Diana. Di for short. And you are?" She extended her hand, and I shook it.

"I'm Rio. Nice to meet you, Di."

"The pleasure is mine. As a matter of fact, take my number and text me when you get to Wet Dreams tonight. I'll buy you a drink."

"It's the least you could do after taking all of my damn money today." I laughed as I handed her my phone. She took it and programmed her number in.

The door chimed, and a couple of customers walked into the store. She went to help them, and I gathered my bags off the counter, waving at her on my way out.

Back in my car, my mood was much lighter than when I had arrived. Once again, retail therapy did the trick. Not only did I get some fly new gear, but I had also made a new friend. If I didn't find Kennedy to get some much-needed answers, at least this sassy chick would be at the club to cheer me up with a drink or two.

Corey

8

I was placing stacks of money in the office safe when I heard someone walk in. Dre was the only other person who had a key, so I turned around to make sure it was him.

"What's good?" he asked after he closed and locked the door behind him. The bass from the music downstairs was so powerful that it made the floor shake underneath us.

"What's up?" I said. "You got anything to put in here?"

"Nah, not right now. I made a bank deposit for the boutique for nine grand earlier, and the rest I reinvested."

"Sounds like Chic World had a damn good week." I slammed the safe door and laughed, knowing that of the nine grand he deposited into the boutique account, most of it wasn't from selling clothes.

"Yeah, a decent week for sure." He gave a nonchalant shrug.

"I told you it was a good investment. Admit it. I was right."

"I ain't say it was a bad one . . . but we got some shit to discuss." Dre sounded irritated, which gave me cause for concern. Based on the amount he just said we brought in, he should've been satisfied.

"A'ight, let me grab a drink first. Sounds like I'm gonna need one." I went to the fully stocked mini bar in the corner of my office and poured us both a glass of Hennessy XO. I handed him his glass then took a seat behind the desk. Dre sat on the leather couch along the wall.

He took a long sip and then said, "You know Di let Pierre get half our X inventory, huh?"

"You say that like she gave it to him. But, yeah, she told me earlier. I'm working on finding a new connect so we can re-up as soon as possible. You know Vinnie Dash was my pops' go-to guy, and now that he's gone, I still haven't been able to find anyone that can keep up with our demand," I reminded him. This problem wasn't something new, so I was still confused by his irritation.

"Which is why I don't understand why she let Pierre's sissy ass get half the fucking inventory. That was a call she wasn't supposed to make without clearing it first."

Hearing him use the word *sissy* caused a slight sting, but I knew better than to react. "You're trippin', Dre. Di wasn't about to turn down that money he had, and neither would you. Cash money in hand? The decision she made was a good one. Now, if she gave him all we had, that woulda been a dumb-ass move and out of line."

"He's the fucking competition, Corey. He runs a bar not too far from here." Dre frowned. "We helping him take our customers now?"

"He ain't the competition. He's a fucking customer and one of our best ones," I pointed out. Pierre came to us for all of his narcotic needs: X, Molly, Percs, weed. If we had it, he got it. Dre just had a problem with him, and I knew why.

Dre's phone started vibrating, and he picked it up to answer. "Yo. . . . What? When? What the fuck happened? . . . Shit, I'm on my way." He stood up and downed the last of his drink.

"What's up?" I asked.

"Fuck. Someone just killed Ant," he snapped.

"Oh yeah, bet," I said calmly.

"What the fuck you mean, bet? You knew some shit went down and you ain't tell me?"

"I made a call this morning and had it handled. He was becoming a cancer and causing all kinda issues. It was time for him—"

"Damn it, Corey! You can't be making these kinds of decisions and not tell me. That ain't how you handle shit. You putting out hits and shit on our own soldiers? He was one of our best men. Now what the fuck? I gotta find somebody to—"

"I already took care of that too. I put Marcus in his position. Everything's good," I said calmly.

Dre stared at me for a few moments. "Marcus, huh? You think that was a smart move?"

"Yeah, I do." I nodded. "Dre, I may not have been in the game as long as you have, but I'm still my father's son. He raised me well and taught me shit the same way he taught you. He believed in both of us. You've made moves and decisions without discussing everything with me first."

"And that was for the good of the business!" he yelled.

"So, you can but I can't? You think I'm supposed to report what I do to you?"

"That's not what I'm saying at all."

"That's what it sounds like to me!" I stood up. Both of us were yelling at this point, and I was grateful for the loud music so no one would hear us. Dre was used to intimidating people, but I wasn't about to let him think he had any kind of power over me. He may have been my Dad's right-hand man, but I was his seed and the one he left in command.

Dre's phone buzzed again, and he looked at it without answering. He said to me, "I gotta go. All I'm asking is that from this point, if you're gonna decide some shit that's gonna affect the entire operation, we need to have a conversation. It's respect."

"I don't have a problem with that. And I expect the same thing of you," I told him.

When he opened the door to leave, Diana was standing there about to knock.

"Oh, damn. Hey, Dre," she said.

"Yeah." He looked her up and down, then brushed past her on his way out the door.

I got up and poured myself another double shot.

"Uh, is this a bad time?" She walked in.

"Nah, you're good." I sighed. "You want a drink?"

"Of course," she said with a laugh. "You sure everything's okay? Y'all both looked angry as fuck, and I thought I heard yelling."

"We were just having a business discussion that got a little loud, that's all. Everything's good." I handed her a drink. "What's the crowd looking like downstairs?" I asked, trying to change the subject.

"Packed as usual," she answered, then brought our conversation right back to Dre. "You know, he came to the boutique earlier and had the nerve to tell me some bullshit that I was supposed to call him first before I make decisions."

"What did you tell him?" I frowned, wondering why all of a sudden Dre seemed to think everyone had to run everything by his ass like he was the damn boss.

"I told him I don't work for him, I work for you. Fuck him." She laughed.

I liked her answer. It showed me that Diana was loyal and I could trust her. Hiring her was a good move to keep my business safe, and also my secrets.

"Besides, I wouldn't call his ass anyway. He hates me for no reason."

"He doesn't hate you," I said, not really sure if that was true.

"He does, but I don't give a shit. As long as he doesn't fuck with my money or disrespect me, I'm good." She turned to one of the mirrors that hung on the wall and adjusted her full breasts in the tight dress she wore. "I think he hates me because deep down, he wants to fuck me, and he knows that ain't happening."

There was no doubt she was a beautiful woman with a banging-ass body. Any man in his right mind would want to sleep with her. Hell, I found her attractive, and I ain't even swing that way. But was she right about Dre? Did he want to fuck her?

I raised an eyebrow and said, "I find that hard to believe."

"What? That he wants to fuck me? What are you tryna say?" She laughed.

"Nah, that you wouldn't let him if he tried."

"I wouldn't. Dre is an arrogant asshole who thinks everybody wants his ass. He loves being the center of attention. To me, that's a turn-off. I could never be with a man who loves being in the spotlight more than I do. No, sir. I'm selfish like that," she stated proudly.

"Okay, selfish. You ready to head down and enjoy being the center of attention?" I asked.

"I stay ready."

I grabbed her by the hand, and we ventured downstairs to the club and went straight to VIP. Diana was right; the crowd was thick. Folks were having a good time already, and it wasn't even eleven o'clock. I checked in with the bartenders and security, who were working double duty, so they would be on alert that our supply of "party favors" was limited. I instructed them to only sell to select customers. Now that Dre was on edge, the last thing I needed for him to hear was that we had run out completely. One thing was certain: I had to find a new supplier and find one quick.

Diana

9

Twenty minutes after I went to the VIP room with Corey, I got a text from Rio, the guy from New York who came into the boutique that day. He was outside, so I sent him a message to bypass the line and go to the front door, where I would meet him.

"I'll be right back," I told Corey.

"Where you going?" he asked. One thing I'd learned, he hated being left alone in the club. It was like he was paranoid and having me by his side was some kind of personal security. It got annoying at times, but because of the amount of money he paid me, I didn't complain.

"I gotta get somebody in. It'll only take a minute," I reassured him. He relaxed a little, and I made my way down to the main floor of the club, squeezed through the crowd, and to the front entrance. Rio was looking fabulous in the outfit I'd styled for him earlier.

"Why you are looking at me like you want to fuck me or something?" he asked with a big-ass smile on his face.

"I was admiring my creation on you, smart-ass." I pushed his shoulder as he got close to me.

"I do look good in this shit. You got some skills."

"Sure do," I agreed. "Let's get this party started. You ready?"

"You have no idea."

"He's good." I nodded at the large security guy at the door. He gave us the go-ahead, and I grabbed Rio's hand and led him inside.

"This shit is on fire in here!" I yelled over the music as I pulled him through the throng of people. We made our way to the elevator that led to the premium areas and hopped on.

"Where are we going?" he asked.

"Don't worry; I got you. You are about to get your life. Bet."
I pushed the button for the second floor. Moments later, we
were standing in front of the area that led to Corey's personal
VIP section. The security guards looked at me and then at Rio,
then back to me, as if I didn't have permanent access—which, of
course, I did.

"He's with me." I gave one of them a look.

"I know you, but he's new. The boss doesn't know him. He gets
the treatment."

"What the fuck is the treatment?" Rio looked at them and then
at me.

"They have to search you and scan you for weapons."

"Okay. This isn't the first time I got searched before." Rio
waved his hand nonchalantly. "That ain't no problem."

Rio assumed the position against the wall without being told. I
waited and watched as they searched and scanned him and then
waved us in.

"That shit felt good. I think I'm in love with this muthafucka
over here," he said as he looked at Tay, the larger of the two
guards, who had olive skin and a body to die for. It was amusing,
because as fine as he was, he was also gay, but very few people
knew it. He didn't respond to Rio's comment.

Rio followed me into the well-protected area reserved for
Corey and his guests. There was a perfect view of the dance floor
and bar areas, and anything you couldn't see from that vantage
point was perfectly displayed on the large TV screens which
hung overhead. Nothing went on in the club without being seen.

"Hey, boo, you missed me?" I walked over and sat on Corey's
lap and kissed him playfully.

"Damn right, I did." Corey smiled and slapped me on the ass,
then turned and looked at Rio. "Who's this?"

"How are you doing? I'm Rio." He held his hand out confi-
dently to Corey, who hesitated a bit before shaking it.

"Rio, this is Corey, the owner," I said.

"Really? Nice spot you got here," Rio told him, looking around.
"I'm feeling it."

"Yeah, cool." Corey's tone was emotionless and dismissive, and
I was not feeling his attitude at all. I figured it had something to

do with the loud exchange he'd had with Dre earlier. Still, that didn't give him a reason to be rude to Rio.

"You want something to drink, like some red wine?" I asked Rio.

"Sure, give me something light," he answered, moving closer to the balcony to look down at the dance floor.

The VIP area had its own bar, and it didn't take long for me to get Rio's drink. Corey had a few other guests he began talking to, making it a little easier for me to slip away and hang with Rio. The music was pumping, and he was bouncing to the beat of the Lady Gaga song that was playing.

"I see you're having fun," I told him.

He took a sip of his wine then said, "I am. So, how'd you meet Corey?"

"Shoe shopping in the mall. We've been dating for over a year," I said.

"Oh, you two are love birds?" He raised an eyebrow.

"You can say that." I smiled. "Why do you ask?"

"He just doesn't seem like your type, that's all. You're all footloose and fancy free, and he's all uptight and serious. I don't know about that."

Having him question my relationship with Corey made me nervous, especially since it was the first time he'd ever met him, or me, for that matter. We'd been in our "arranged relationship," and no one had ever questioned it. Everyone just thought I was Corey's woman and he was my man.

I quickly explained, "Because to you and me, being here is fun. For him, it's business, that's all."

"Okay. If you like it, I love it." Rio shrugged and went back to bouncing to the music, and his attention went from the dance floor to the bar area, then up to the screens.

"Are you looking for someone?" I asked.

"No. Well, yeah. Kinda." He sighed.

"Who is it?"

"A guy I saw last night while I was here. Tall, muscular, cocoa brown with a close cut," Rio said.

"Boy, that's half the brothers that come in this place." I laughed.

"I know. I don't see him, but it's some fine-ass guys here, that's for sure," he said, still scanning the dance floor with his eyes.

"How about we hit the dance floor so you can get a better look?" I pulled him by the hand, and we slid past Corey, who was so deep in conversation that he didn't notice.

Dancing with Rio was so much fun. He made me laugh with his skillful, yet exaggerated dance moves. The two of us entertained the crowd until finally, we were both hot and tired.

"Who the fuck is that?" Rio stopped dead in his tracks, damn near causing me to bump into him.

I turned to see who he was asking about, then laughed. "That's Pierre."

"Dirty Diana! Come give me a hug wit' yo' sexy ass." Pierre waved as he and his entourage headed in my direction.

"Hey, Pierre, what the hell are you doing on this side of town?" I gave him a hug and a kiss on the cheek, glancing up at the balcony to see who might have been watching. No one was looking down, but who knows what was on the screens up there.

"I actually came to talk to your man," Pierre said.

"I don't know if I want that to happen," I teased.

"No worries. I promise not to take him from you. Besides, everyone knows you got that dick on lock, Di," Pierre replied jovially. "I need to ask you for some pointers. Lord knows I don't have a problem getting a man, but I damn sure can't keep one."

Laughter erupted, and I glanced over at Rio, who seemed to be enchanted.

"Pierre, this is my friend, Rio. Rio, this is Pierre."

"Nice to meet you, Rio." Pierre not only shook Rio's hand but air-kissed both of his cheeks. "I am loving those pants you're wearing."

"Thanks. My stylist told me they were one of a kind." Rio winked at me.

Pierre shook his head and said, "Funny, that heifer told me the same thing when she sold me that exact same pair last week."

"What?" Rio's mouth dropped open.

I slapped Pierre in the chest and said, "Stop lying, Pierre. You couldn't fit your fat ass in those pants if you wanted to."

"Okay, she's right. But I must say, you wear them well, Rio," Pierre said. "Now, Di, where is that fine-ass man of yours? We need to talk business."

Rio

10

I didn't see Kennedy at the club that night, but it wasn't a total bust. I had a blast hanging out with Diana for the short time Corey let her off her leash. That girl was entertaining as hell, although her man was a whole damn different story. Once we returned with fine-ass Pierre and his crew, Corey agreed to meet with him in his office, but he insisted that Diana come with him. I didn't know why he had her ass on such a short leash, but she didn't seem bothered about following his orders. She asked me to wait for her, saying that it wouldn't take long. I didn't mind, because I hoped to holler at Pierre anyway to see what was up with him. Unfortunately, that wasn't meant to happen. After waiting about an hour for them to come out of the office, I got bored and decided it was time to leave. I sent Diana a quick text to thank her and then headed back to the hotel.

I didn't realize I was hungry until I was in my suite, and I definitely wasn't going back out to get anything, so my meal would consist of whatever was on the late-night room service menu. I was scanning my choices when my phone rang.

"Where the fuck are you?" Paris screamed so loud I had to pull the phone away from my ear. Still, the sound of her voice brought a smile to my face. My twin always had that effect on me.

"I'm in one of the most luxurious hotel suites I've ever stayed in," I told her.

"What the fuck ever, Rio. Who are you there with?"

"I'm all alone, believe it or not. I did hang out at the club tonight, and it was fun as shit."

"Which is why you're probably not alone. You know how you stay picking up a fuck buddy from the club."

"This is true, but I'm sitting here about to order some hot wings and spinach dip and call it a night," I said with a sigh.

"What the hell is wrong with you?"

"I'm hungry," I replied.

"So, take your ass down to the hotel bar and get some dick to go along with your midnight snack, Rio. I thought you got away to relax and regroup. You're acting like an old fucking man," she whined.

"I'm not. I told you I'm good, and I am relaxing. Today I went shopping and met a cool chick who I hung out with tonight."

"Chick? Oh my God, it's worse than I thought. You're not trying to become straight, are you? Is this about Daddy? Are you trying to change for him?" Paris asked.

I sucked my teeth in disgust. "No, bitch, ain't nobody switching sides. I'm still strictly dickly, the same as you. And this has nothing to do with LC and his hangups about my sexuality," I told her forcefully.

I heard a car horn beeping in the distance, then Paris was yelling, "What the hell is wrong with you? Use a damn turn signal!"

"And where the hell are you?" I asked her.

"Unlike you, my night is young, and I'm heading out to have some fun."

"With who? Sasha?"

Paris and my cousin Sasha were like oil and water; they didn't mix well. The competition between them to be queen diva of the family was fierce at all times, but they still went out to the clubs together most nights. The two of them were so fucking hot they could pull any guy they wanted. Unfortunately, most nights they wanted the same guy, and that didn't always end peacefully.

"Nope, I don't know what that bitch is up to tonight. I met a guy at the gym last week, and I decided I needed a late-night workout. He's the right one to help me stretch my muscles."

"You're such a whore," I teased.

"And you are too," she shot back affectionately. "Well, you used to be. But seriously, Rio, I do miss you, and I hope wherever you are, you are enjoying yourself."

The sincerity in my sister's voice almost made me want to pack my suitcase and go back home. I knew she was concerned and missed me. Still, that wasn't reason enough for me to leave, not yet. A flashback of Kennedy walking out of the club came across my mind, and I instantly lost any feelings of homesickness I felt. I couldn't go back home until I figured out what the hell had happened with him.

"I'm fine, Paris. How's everyone else doing?" I asked about the rest of my family, even though I knew they weren't concerned about me.

"Same shit. Mom asked if I'd talked to you, and Orlando asked if I'd checked on you too," she said.

At least a couple of folks were worried about my well-being, so all wasn't lost. "Tell Mom I'll give her a call soon. And tell Orlando I'm cool."

"Well, keep me posted on your happenings—or not happenings, I guess. I love you."

"I love you too, P." I ended the call. Looking down at the menu sitting beside me on the bed, I decided I wasn't hungry anymore. I climbed under the covers and went to sleep in my fabulous new pants that Pierre said made my ass look perfect.

The next morning, I woke up to a text from Diana inviting me to brunch, which I accepted. I was glad because not only did it give me something to do, but because I hadn't eaten, I was starving now. I jumped up, showered, and changed.

We met at a low-key spot not far from where I was staying.

"You look cute." I greeted Diana, who was already seated when I arrived. The black jeans and fitted top she wore were simple, but she had tied an African print scarf around her like a halter top that set the outfit off just right. It showed off her cute figure, and the gold jewelry she wore accented her gorgeous face.

"You do too," she said as she stood up and gave me a hug.

"If we're here enjoying brunch, who's running the boutique?" I asked, taking the seat across from her.

"It doesn't get much traffic before noon, so I'm good. Folks know if they really need me, they can hit me on my cell."

A waitress came over with two cups of coffee and took our order. Diana ordered a pineapple mimosa and French toast.

"That sounds good. I'll have the same," I said.

"I'm mad you left last night," she said after the waitress left.

"I waited for-damn-ever. Y'all were taking too long, and I was ready to go."

"Well, I wasn't the only one disappointed that you left." She smirked.

"You weren't?" I whispered. "Do tell. Was Corey asking about me?"

"Bitch, you tried it!" She laughed. "Hell no, he ain't ask about you."

"Who, then?"

"Someone I think you'll be glad to hear."

"They bodyguard? The one who felt me up? What was his name, Trey?"

"Tay, and no, it wasn't him either. Pierre noticed you were gone. *And* he asked me for the inside info."

Despite my delight, I acted unimpressed. The last thing I wanted to do was seem pressed. Diana would have run right back and told Pierre, and I couldn't have that. I reminded myself that I was the prize, not him.

"And what info did you give him?" I asked.

"None, because that's all I had. I told him that the only thing I knew about you was that you had great taste in clothes and knew how to shop. Whatever he wanted to know, he was gonna to have to ask you directly."

I poured some cream into my coffee and took a sip, then tried to seem nonchalant as I asked, "So, what's the deal with Mr. Pierre?"

"He's mad cool. He shops in the boutique all the time. One of my best and most favorite customers."

"And where does his coins come from? And don't lie," I warned her.

"Here you go. Two pineapple mimosas." The waitress set our drinks on the table.

Diana took a sip then set down her glass. "He's an entrepreneur."

I tilted my head. "Isn't everyone these days?"

"No, seriously, he is. He owns this really nice bar called Oz."

"Oz?" I recalled seeing it listed when I was looking for happening gay spots in the city.

"Yeah, next to Wet Dreams, it's the place to be for the gay population."

"I'll have to check it out." I leaned back in my seat and took a sip of my mimosa. "You know, I gotta say, I'm kind of surprised someone as uptight as Corey would own a place like Wet Dreams," I told her.

"It didn't start out that way, trust me. When Corey bought it, it was a traditional crowd at first. It was kinda dry, but then y'all sugars kinda infiltrated the place and took over." Diana laughed.

Just as I was about to respond, our food arrived. I was kind of grateful for the interruption. No need to cuss out a new friend—the first one I'd met in this city. I would address the "sugars" comment some other time. We dug into the French toast and bacon like we hadn't eaten in weeks.

"Damn, this is good," I said between bites.

"It's one of my favorite spots. Pierre turned me on to it."

I glanced up from my plate. "Was that supposed to be a hint?"

"Not at all, but you were asking about him, and he was asking about you, so maybe y'all should ask each other. You did say you wanted to meet a fine-ass man. This may be the love connection you're looking for."

"Hold the fuck up, friend. Ain't nobody say nothing about love," I corrected her.

"Well, whatever it is, it's a damn connection." She shrugged as she picked up her phone that had started ringing.

"Hello? Oh, hey. . . . At brunch. . . . Uh-huh. Yep. He's right here. Hold on."

My eyes widened as she passed the phone to me. "What the hell?"

"Here. Someone wants to talk to you."

I hesitated for a second, but the smile on her face made me curious. I took the phone. "Hello?"

"Well, hello to you. How are you on this fine morning?" a voice sang into my ear, and I instantly recognized it.

"I'm doing well, and yourself?" I gave Diana a threatening look, albeit jokingly.

"I would be doing better if I would've gotten a brunch invite from you," Pierre said.

I laughed. "Unfortunately, I didn't host this event this morning, and I wasn't told I could bring a plus one."

"Point taken. Then how about I invite you out tonight? And no, you can't bring a plus one."

There was a slight pause while I tried to remember the last time I'd been asked out on a date. I didn't really know this guy, and I wasn't the type to trust someone too quickly—that was part of how we Duncans were trained because of the business our family was in. But, hey, I had come to Baltimore looking for some attention and appreciation, right?

What the hell. If Diana likes this guy, he's probably okay.

"I think I can make that happen," I finally said.

"Wonderful. I'll text you the address. I'll see you at nine tonight."

"Nine it is," I said.

Before I even passed the phone back to Diana, my phone buzzed with a text from an unfamiliar number. When I opened it, I saw an address and a heart-eye emoji. I was slightly disappointed to see that it wasn't directions to his home or a restaurant, but to Oz, the club Pierre owned. I hoped he wasn't going to be doing business all night the way it had been at Wet Dreams the night before. Either way, I was going to make the best of it.

"How the hell did he get my number?" I asked Diana.

"I don't know." Diana couldn't hide the guilt on her face even as she tried to deny it.

"Liar."

"Prove it. Anyway, come on, let's go. We need to hit the shop and make sure you look fabulous tonight." She sounded excited.

"How do you know I don't already have something fabulous to wear?" I asked.

"Whatever it is, it can't compare to what I have for you. Now, come on." She reached for the check sitting in the middle of the table, but I stopped her.

"This one is on me," I said.

"But I invited you out."

"Honey, if tonight goes as well as I hope it will, I'll be owing you. Let's call this a down payment."

Diana

11

Between school, working at the boutique, being Corey's arm candy at the club, and seeing Ashton, my free time was limited. The only time I was home was to sleep, bathe, and change clothes, although I did try to make time to have dinner with my family once or twice a week so I wouldn't have to hear my parents' mouths. They weren't the only ones who complained about my busy schedule, though.

My younger sister, Mona, walked into my room without knocking.

"Di, can I borrow—"

I turned away from the mirror. "Damn, Mo, what have I told you about knocking first?"

"Are you going out again?" she whined, looking me up and down. I had just changed out of the leggings and oversized shirt I wore to dinner into a pair of jeans, a colorful top, and tall leather boots that reached the tops of my thighs.

"I don't know about *again*, but I am going out."

"You're never home to spend time with us."

"What are you talking about? I just had dinner with the entire damn family the other night."

"You know what I mean. You and I never hang out." She flopped down on my bed.

"I'm sorry, Mo. I just have a lot going on right now. You know that. Things are going to slow down soon, I promise." I walked over and touched her shoulder. She looked up at me, and I could see she didn't believe me. "What did you come in here for anyway?"

"I wanted to borrow your black MK crossbody purse," she said.

Even though I had planned to carry the bag that night, I reached into my closet and handed it to her. "Here it is."

"Thanks," she said unenthusiastically. "Where are you off to now anyway?"

"Just going to a study session with some friends," I lied. Truth was, I was going to meet Ashton at the Inner Harbor. We would grab a bite to eat and then fuck the rest of the night away at one of the nearby hotels. It was our weekly routine.

"So, let me come with," Mona suggested.

"What? No, not tonight. You wouldn't have fun." I shook my head.

"Fine, then let me hang out with you another night. I'm twenty-one now, and I want to be out here living my best life the same way you are."

Mona and I were like night and day. Even though she was only a couple of years younger than I was, she was still what I considered "green." By the time I was her age, I'd had way more life experiences. I began dating at fourteen, behind my parents' backs, of course. At sixteen, I'd already had sex, drank, smoked weed, and perfected stealing my parents' car. Even though I was a wild child, I still made good grades and graduated with honors. Despite several scholarship offers, my father had refused to allow me to go away to school, which was why I stayed at home. Mona didn't even think about leaving and decided to postpone attending college at all. As far as I could tell, the only dates she'd been on were junior and senior prom, and both guys went to our church. She pretty much lived her life through the stories I shared with her. I couldn't see having her tagging along with me when I went out.

"Mo, don't you have friends you can hang out with?" I asked. "What about your coworkers?"

"They aren't really fun. You know most of them are kinda older women." Mo was referring to the teachers at the daycare center she worked at, and she was right. Most of them were mid-dle-aged ladies. "I need some excitement in my life. Speaking of which, are you hiring at the boutique yet?"

"Girl, I wish. You know we're not making that much money yet, but as soon as my boss gives me the okay to add staff, I got you," I told her, even though I had no intention of letting my sister work there. I couldn't have her around to see the other ways I made money these days. Focusing my attention back on the mirror, I pulled my long braids into a bun on top of my head. I kinda didn't know why I was bothering when they would be down before the end of the night from Ashton pulling them.

"Fine. Well, thanks for letting me borrow the purse. Have fun at your little study session. I guess I'll go in my room and Netflix and chill till I fall asleep." Mona stood up from my bed.

"How about we plan a girls' night in a couple of weeks?" I said, feeling a little guilty. "We can go get manis and pedis, catch a movie, and then do dinner?"

She smiled. "I would really like that, Di."

"It's a date." I gave her a quick hug. "Now, I gotta get out of here before my study buddies start blowing my phone up."

"Damn, you look sexy as fuck." Ashton's face spread into a huge grin when I walked up to where he stood in front of the entrance to Bistro 3000, a restaurant in the Inner Harbor. He looked like the typical preppy white boy dressed in a pair of khakis, button-down shirt, and casual leather shoes. At first glance, no one would suspect he was hung like a damn horse and had the stamina of a stallion, and that was fine with me. It meant I could have my boy toy all to myself.

"Why, thank you." I put my arms around his neck and kissed him. He cupped my ass and gave it a quick squeeze, making me even more excited about what we'd be doing later.

"You ready?" I asked as I reached for his hand.

"I am. But we're not going inside," he told me.

"What do you mean? You're not hungry?" I paused, then gave him a seductive look. "Oh, you want to start with dessert, huh?"

Ashton laughed. "That's not a bad idea, but no, tonight I thought we'd do something different."

"Like what?" I asked cautiously. "I'm not down for no weird shit, Ashton. I told you I don't get down like that. I ain't doing no threesomes or orgies—"

"No, Di, calm down. It's nothing like that."

"What is it then? I'm not dressed to go anywhere fancy either. You should've given me a heads-up first if that's where you're trying to go." I looked down at my chic yet casual outfit.

"You look amazing and absolutely perfect for where I'm taking you."

"But I need to know where first."

"I wanna take you out dancing at a club. We're going to Wet Dreams."

"What?" I stared at him blankly.

"I wanna go somewhere fun, and I know you hang out there, because I heard a couple of people from school say they've seen you there. From what I've been told, you are a natural on the dance floor. I wanna see you in action." He smiled and pulled me close.

I felt myself panicking. What had the people from school told him? Hopefully they hadn't seen me with Corey. I mean, being with him was all an act, but I was a damn good actress, and most people who saw us together at Wet Dreams believed we were a couple. From Ashton's demeanor, I didn't think he'd heard anything like that, but that didn't bring me much comfort.

There was no way in hell I could show up at Wet Dreams with Ashton. Now way, no how. I could imagine it all unfolding now: folks blowing Corey's phone up to tell him that I had shown up with a white boy. Corey never said I couldn't have a man, but one of the stipulations of our agreement was that if I did have one, I'd better keep it on the low. Bringing Ashton to Corey's spot would be anything but low-key.

"Wet Dreams? I don't wanna go there, Ashton. It's mad crowded, and tonight's not a good night for us to go. There are plenty of places we can dance and have fun. We can find another club to go to," I told him.

Ashton's face became serious. "Diana, what's the deal? Is there a problem?"

I glanced around and saw a few people looking at us. Not wanting to make a scene, I plastered a fake smile on my face and in the brightest voice I could muster, I said, "How about we talk about this in the car?"

"Fine."

I followed him to his silver Durango, and he opened the door for me to climb in.

Once he was in, he turned to me. "So, what gives?"

I almost giggled because the way he said it was so "white," but luckily, I had enough self-control to maintain my composure and simply say, "Nothing."

"Oh, there's something." He stared at me.

"Ashton, you're the one tripping, not me. I got all dolled up and cute, excited to have a great night, and now you got an attitude for no fucking reason." I felt a little bad flipping it on him like that, but he'd left me no choice. I could not let him guilt me into going to Corey's club. Damn, my life was becoming complicated with all the secrets I had to keep.

"No reason? Is that what you think?" He frowned.

"Yeah, it is."

"Diana, for the past three months, all we do is eat and fuck. That's it."

"Okay." I shrugged, knowing where this conversation was headed but trying to delay it as long as possible.

"Are you ashamed of me? You don't want to be seen with a white boy, is that what it is?"

"Here we go again." I blew out a frustrated breath. "Ashton, if I didn't want to be seen with a white boy, I wouldn't go out with you in public. That makes no sense."

"We go to hotels and tourist attractions, Diana. There's no sign of me on your social media anywhere. I haven't met any of your friends outside of the ones at school. Hell, I haven't met your family. I need to know what's up with us."

Ashton's whining was turning me off. In my mind, he sounded like a bitch. True, we hung out and had a good time, and God knows he was a beast in bed, but I didn't really consider him my man, and we damn sure weren't what I considered in a relationship.

I sighed. "We're good, Ashton. And for the record, I haven't met your parents either, or your friends. And as far as social media, you know I don't even get on there like that other than to promote the boutique."

"You've never even asked to meet my family or friends," he said. "And I see you had no problem posting this pic!" He took out his phone and went to my IG page where the selfie that I'd taken with Rio the day before was posted. "Who the hell is he?"

"First of all, Ashton, this dude is gay. Anybody can see that. Look at his fucking perfectly arched eyebrows and the hazel contacts he's wearing, not to mention that pose he's making is even more feminine than mine. He came in the store yesterday and spent five hundred dollars, thus the hashtags #anothersatis-fiedcustomer, #tookallhiscoins, #newfaveshopper. Did you pay attention to any of that?" My attitude was in full force now, and it wasn't an act anymore. He was really starting to annoy me. "And what, are you stalking my IG page now? You don't trust me? Listen, I told you when we started doing this that I had a lot going on in my life and I wanted to just let shit happen, and now you're demanding to meet the parents and have me changing my relationship status on social media? You know what kind of pressure that is for me?" I raised my voice an octave and tossed his phone into his lap.

"No . . . I . . . " he began to stutter.

"Pressure I don't need and don't want. I got class, the store, I'm trying to design custom items for people and get my name out there. You know I wanna have my own label one day. I don't need this shit. Goodbye, Ashton." I reached for the door handle.

"Diana, wait. Don't leave." He grabbed my arm. "I don't want you to go. I'm not trying to put any more pressure on you. I'm sorry. You're right; I was tripping. Come on."

I let my hand fall from the door handle, relieved that my angry black woman moment had worked once again. The tables had turned, and I was in control. I remained silent, giving him some time to become even more nervous.

"Diana, say something."

Finally, I turned around and faced him. He looked like he was about to cry, and I felt a little sorry. "What do you want me to say, Ashton?"

"That we're good."

Shaking my head, I smirked and said, "We're good."

The worry on his face changed to relief. "Can I get a kiss?"

"You're asking for a lot now," I said.

"Please." He leaned over, and I kissed him softly.

His hands cupped my face, and his tongue pressed against my mouth until I relented and opened it, welcoming the feel of it inside. The heat between us began to rise. My hands made their way to his crotch, where I felt his manhood, enormous and still growing. I was tempted to take it out of his pants and deep-throat it, but I resisted because we were parked in a well-lit spot.

"I see you're happy now," I said.

He grinned. "I am. You wanna go have dinner now?"

"Nah, I'm not really hungry," I told him. His face dropped until I added, "Well, not for food anyway."

He smiled and said, "Well, I think I have something that will fill you up. Only if you let me eat first."

He wasted no time taking me to the nearest hotel. For the rest of the night, I kept him well occupied, and he didn't mention going to the club or anywhere else.

Rio

12

I took one final glance at myself in the mirror in my hotel room. The ensemble Diana had put together for me was impeccable. The red mesh shirt I wore under my denim blazer was a perfect fit and showed off my broad shoulders. Although I wasn't chiseled like Orlando or Vegas, who both worked out regularly, I still had a damn fine body. After a last-minute spritz of eau de parfum, I grabbed my keys and wallet and headed out.

Even though I would never admit it to him, I was a little apprehensive about meeting up with Pierre. As I drove through the streets of Baltimore like I had been there for years instead of a couple of days, I replayed the pep talk Paris had given me the night before: Pierre was the lucky one, not me. Besides, I told myself, I had nothing to be nervous about. This was just a meetup at a bar, nothing special.

Oz was nestled in the heart of Baltimore, not far from Wet Dreams. As I walked to the front door, I checked out the other patrons standing around outside. Had I not known, I wouldn't have guessed it was a gay bar. No one was dressed in anything too outrageous—it was mostly tasteful and casual outfits.

I smiled at a transgender woman who really stood out. She was wearing an eye-popping, form-fitting black dress and four-inch heels.

"Bitch, you are wearing the hell out of that outfit," I said.

"Thank you, love." She wiggled around a bit and gave me a sexy shake. "I see you ain't here to play either, are you?"

"Not at all."

There was a bouncer at the door, but he didn't give me an in-depth body search like they did at Wet Dreams. After a quick wave of his wand, I got the okay to enter. The vibe inside was laid back and chill, with people filling the booths along the wall, and the deejay playing music that kept the dance floor full. I looked around but didn't see Pierre anywhere, even though I was fifteen minutes late, just as I'd planned.

I sent Pierre a quick text: I'm here. Where R U? Then I walked over to the bar and ordered a drink, enjoying the atmosphere while I waited.

"Whet can ah get yah?" a sexy-ass bartender asked me with his Jamaican accent.

I was tempted to say "A fuck and a smile" but instead ordered a blackberry martini. When he brought my drink, I gave him a ten-dollar tip, which earned me a wink. I was just about to ask his name when a well-dressed guy walked over to me.

"Rio, welcome to Oz."

How the hell did this guy know my name? "Uh, thanks," I said, frowning at him.

"You can follow me. Pierre is waiting for you," he said without introducing himself. I guess Pierre was into drama, sending some dude over to deliver me to him. I gulped the remainder of my martini then followed him to a secluded booth in the corner.

Pierre stood up and greeted me. "Rio!" He air-kissed each of my cheeks. "You arrived."

"Pierre, I have." I did the same to him, kind of enjoying the theatrics.

"And not only do you look amazing, but you smell just as fabulous." He smiled and then added, "Silver Mountain Water. Impressive."

The fact that he recognized my four-hundred-dollar cologne let me know that he enjoyed the finer things in life as much as I did. He motioned for me to take a seat.

"This place is nice." I nodded, looking around.

"Thank you. It's decent, and it gives members of our community a safe place to hang out. It's not as lively as Wet Dreams, but people seem to enjoy it," Pierre said with understated pride.

"I see. The vibe in here is cool as hell. The music is chill, and if the drinks are as good as the one I had over at the bar . . ."

"Trust me, they are. I make sure all the bartenders are as talented as Fred over there with his sexy ass. I love a foreign man, don't you?" Pierre winked.

I couldn't help staring at his handsome face. His smooth, naturally tan skin and thick wavy hair, which was slicked back, made me suspect that he was of Latino descent—maybe Puerto Rican, Mexican, or even Spanish. "They are quite intriguing. Tell me, exactly where are you from?"

"Me? I'm from Florida," he said.

"Miami, huh?" I sat back and relaxed a little.

"Miami? No, not Miami. Why would you think that?" Pierre laughed. A waiter walked over and placed another blackberry martini in front of me and a regular one in front of him. He raised his glass to me and said. "To new friends and a great night."

"Cheers." I lifted my glass, clinking it against his then took a sip. "Let's be real," I said. "You are what some might consider a 'pretty boy,' and I knew you were Hispanic, so when you said you were from Florida . . ."

"Pretty boy? That's hilarious." He laughed so hard that his eyes began to water.

"What? You are."

He finally stopped laughing long enough to say, "I am far from being a pretty boy. I'm not Hispanic, and I damn sure ain't from Miami."

"What the hell ever." I took a long sip of my drink. "Pretty boy ass."

"So, because I'm a little on the light side and originally from Florida, that makes me a pretty boy? I should be offended, but I'm not. I am from Pensacola, and I'm very much black. Now, I've been told that my people are of creole descent, but I'm as African American as you are."

"Let's not forget your name is Pierre," I teased.

His eyes widened, and he drank the last of his drink. "And yours is Rio. So, what is your ethnicity?"

"Trust me, you already know I'm as black as they come. I'm from New York, born and raised," I told him.

"I already knew that."

"Really? And how's that?" I wondered if he'd tried to run a background check on me. I hadn't told anyone my last name, and all my social media accounts were private or unsearchable. If anyone did try to find me, it was damn near impossible.

Pierre smiled. "Your walk, your sense of style, all that swag. It's very obvious you're a New Yorker."

It was hard not to blush at the compliment. I started a dialogue in my head to try to calm myself down. *It's just a casual meetup and nothing more. We are sitting in the back of a bar. This isn't a real date.*

"Are you hungry?" Pierre asked but then didn't wait for an answer. He made a motion with his hand, and a waiter arrived at our table with a rolling cart full of food. He placed a basket of bread and a large bowl of salad in the center of the table. In front of each of us, he placed a set of linen-wrapped silverware, then reached onto the cart and took out two covered plates and set them in front of us.

"Will there be anything else?" the waiter asked like we were at some fancy French restaurant and not a nightclub.

Pierre looked around the table, then at me. "Would you like another martini, maybe some wine instead? Your glass is empty."

"Wine would be nice," I said, pleasantly surprised by the whole presentation.

"Bring us a bottle of Chardonnay, please, Deon. Oh, and some Perrier."

"Yes, sir," Deon said as he rolled the cart away.

"I hope you like surf and turf. I took the liberty of having my chef prepare it for us," Pierre said.

I lifted the cover off my plate, and my mouth instantly watered at the sight of the most beautiful NY strip I'd ever seen, along with a broiled lobster tail and a side of asparagus. I didn't even realize I was hungry, but as the aroma of the food entered my nostrils, my stomach began grumbling. "Wow, I wasn't expecting this."

"I invited you out. Surely you must've known that I was going to feed you. Normally, I would've taken you to one of my favorite restaurants, but there are some things going on, and I needed to be here tonight," Pierre explained. "So, I figured I would make the best of it."

"Well, I appreciate all of this," I said, unwrapping my silverware. "It looks amazing."

"I promise it will taste as good as it looks."

I looked up from my plate. Something about the way he said it told me that he wasn't just talking about the food. He was flirting with me, and I didn't mind one bit.

While we ate, the conversation flowed naturally, with topics ranging from politics to pop culture. I found that we had traveled to a lot of the same places, both in the U.S. and abroad. It felt almost like talking to an old friend, instead of someone I'd met only twenty-four hours earlier.

"I'm surprised we've never run into each other before," I said as we sipped on after-dinner cognac. "How long have you lived in Baltimore? And what brought you here?"

He sighed. "A very rich, much older Caucasian gentleman that I met over ten years ago."

I frowned slightly, hoping this wasn't about to be some kind of secret-lover-type situation. I was too smart, too fine, and too fabulous to be anyone's sidepiece. I didn't care how gorgeous and easygoing Pierre's sexy ass was. A guy had to have standards.

"Oh, so you have a partner?"

"Had. He moved me here from Pensacola. He was the one who bought Oz for me. A birthday gift a year before he died of cancer." Pierre's eyes became sad, and I could hear the grief in his voice. I immediately thought about Kennedy and felt my own heartache. The memory of his bleeding body lying on the floor flashed in my mind.

"I'm sorry for your loss. I've been there." I had to blink away my tears.

Pierre straightened his back like he was trying to pull himself together. "He wanted to make sure I had something to call my own, although the half million dollars he left me in life insurance would've been sufficient."

"Damn." I gave a low whistle. "He must've really loved you."

"Right?" Pierre laughed.

Suddenly, Deon came rushing over to the table and said something in Pierre's ear. Pierre frowned and turned toward the bar area; then he stood up and apologized. "Rio, excuse me for a few, will you? I won't be very long."

"Take your time. It's cool."

He walked over to the bar and got into an intense conversation with Fred and another guy. I tried not to stare, instead turning my attention to the other tables and nodding my head to the beat of the old school Usher song that was playing.

"Is everything okay?" I asked a worried-looking Pierre when he returned to the table.

"Yeah, it's fine," he said, his eyes darting around the room.

"Are you sure? You look a little stressed."

Pierre inhaled deeply and said, "Can I be honest?"

"Of course."

"We've run out of party favors, and they're worried because the crowd is getting thin," he said. "Normally, we're packed by now."

Now that he said it, I realized that the crowd was little lighter than when I'd first arrived. At one point, while Pierre and I were eating, a few couples had started dancing in the open area near the deejay, but they were all gone now. And even though the music was still decent, the vibe had lulled a little. I looked down at my watch and saw that it was only eleven thirty, still early.

"Party favors?" I asked.

"Some of our customers like a little something extra with their drinks to help them unwind, if you know what I mean. So, we oblige." Pierre took out his phone and sent a text, then placed it back down on the table.

"I get it." Hell, if anyone understood what he meant, it was me. I had indulged in more than my fair share of party favors, and I didn't even have to be at a party to enjoy. "What kind of goodies do you offer? And how did you manage to run out?"

"Nothing major. Just X and Molly, nothing harder than that. I don't fuck with that hardcore shit. Like Whitney said, 'Crack is whack!'" Pierre joked.

"You do know she smoked crack though, right?"

"I refuse to believe that, and I shall not allow you to sit here and slander her name. She is my guardian angel and could do no wrong."

I tossed my head back and laughed loudly. It was a laugh that came from deep within, from my belly. A laugh that I hadn't had in a long time.

I stood up and said, "Hold tight. I'll be right back."

"Are you okay?" Pierre asked.

I touched his shoulder and smiled at him. "Yep. This will only take a few minutes."

I slipped out the front door of the club and went to my car. Opening the trunk, I fumbled around until I found the black box I was looking for. I popped the top off, took out what I needed, put the top back on, and closed the trunk. Looking up, I whispered, "I sure hope I'm doing the right thing."

"You good?" Pierre asked when I slipped back in my seat across from him.

"Yeah. I had to run to my car and get something. You sound like you missed me."

"You sound like you wanted me to miss you," he said.

"You flatter yourself. But I do have something for you." I reached into my jacket pocket and pulled out four small pills. I held my hand out to him, palm up, so he could see what I was offering. "You can take one and give the other three away."

Pierre stared at the tiny tablets that looked similar to pink Tic Tacs. "What the hell are these?"

"I call them Pixie Dust."

"They look like damn ice cream sprinkles," Pierre joked. "What do they do?"

"They're kinda like a cross between Molly and X. They give you a quick buzz, then you feel euphoric and mellow out. Just try it." I popped one into my mouth and chased it with wine. Pierre watched me for a second, then took a pill from me and did the same.

"YOLO. Isn't that what the kids say these days?"

I shook my head. "They don't say that anymore. That was, like, two years ago."

He shrugged and gave me a cute smirk.

It wasn't long before the pill took effect. I felt like I was floating. "Let's dance," I said to Pierre.

"Dance?" His voice sounded like he was at the other end of a tunnel.

I grabbed him by the hand and pulled him up. We laughed and swayed to the music right there next to our table. He pulled me close, and I realized we were almost the exact same height. I closed my eyes and enjoyed the synchronicity of our bodies.

He gave me a big grin. I could tell that his pill had kicked in too.

"Hey, play some Whitney!" he yelled to the deejay. The music changed quickly, and "I'm Every Woman" began blasting from the speakers. We had our own personal dance party until we were both sweating.

"Oh my God, that was fun!" I said when we finally returned to our seats.

"I feel fucking amazing," Pierre moaned. "Those Sprinkles are the shit."

I corrected him. "Pixie Dust."

"But it's not dust. Sprinkles sound better. Where the hell did you get them?"

Pixie Dust—or Sprinkles, as Pierre referred to it—was the brainchild of my brother Orlando and me. We'd started developing the party drug a couple years earlier, but then he became engrossed in the creation of a much stronger, more profitable street drug he called HEAT. It was successful in the test market, and we thought it was destined to be the next best thing. We started selling it in clubs, and I swear we were on the way to becoming billionaires until Orlando discovered that HEAT could cause cancer. It wasn't easy to give up all that profit, but my family decided that HEAT was not worth risking the lives of millions of people. You know, criminals with a conscience and all that. So, the drug was destroyed, along with the formula. I had hoped that one day Orlando and I would resume the development of Pixie Dust, but it never seemed to be the right time. I kept my own personal supply for entertainment purposes, but that was it.

Of course, Pierre didn't need to know all that. "Uh, I know a guy," I said vaguely.

"I need to meet him," he shot back. "Sprinkles is just what we need in here. You got any more?"

"I have a few."

"I tell you what. How about you let me buy what you have left and do a test run tomorrow night? I'll pay you double what you paid for them."

I thought about it for a little while. I had promised Orlando that I would only use my stash for personal consumption, but as I sat across from Pierre, whose hand now covered mine as he stared into my eyes, I realized that I liked him, and I wanted to help him. And I wanted to spend more time with him.

So, with the sound of Whitney singing about million-dollar bills in the background, I nodded and said, "I got you."

Corey

13

"What the hell is going on?" Dre asked when he entered the VIP area.

"What's good, Dre?" I nodded toward him.

"Not the intake for this week, that's for sure." Dre sat in the chair closest to me.

"Yeah, Marcus told me sales were kind of low, but we've had off weeks before. We'll recover," I said. When I'd gotten the call giving me the update about the numbers for the week, I knew Dre was going to be in some kind of mood about it. "It's because we're out of X. And I'm working on it."

"Nah, that's just part of the problem." Dre shook his head. Looking around, he said, "I need a damn drink."

I waved my hand for the bartender to bring us a round of drinks. "Dre, we're good. I got this."

"Got what? It ain't just about the X, Corey."

I prepared myself for what I knew was coming next: Dre placing the blame for the low sales on the gay dealers we had out in the streets. They were always the easiest scapegoats, but I knew they had nothing to do with it, and I was ready to come to their defense. "Look, I already know what you're about to say, and—"

A waitress brought our drinks over. Dre immediately picked up a glass and swallowed it down in one gulp. I couldn't help but notice his eyes on her ass when she walked away.

"Like I was saying," I said to get his attention. "I am—"

"Sales are off for Molly, too, and weed." He leaned over closer so only I could hear what he was about to say. "I think somebody's tryna make a move on us."

"What?" I frowned. "You're tripping for real. Ain't nobody that crazy. We lost a couple grand this week, that's all. You're overreacting."

"I'm not. You ain't been in the game long enough to realize—"

"Here we go with that bullshit again." I sat back in my seat and glared at him.

"Hey, y'all!" Diana popped up out of nowhere and threw her arms around my neck. I gave her a quick hug then moved over so she could take a seat.

"'Sup, Di," I said.

Dre looked her up and down without speaking. "Corey, I'm telling you, I'm right about this."

"Right about what?" Diana asked.

Dre cut his eyes at her. "None of your business, that's what. Your parents ain't teach you that's its rude to interrupt grown people when they're talking?"

"They did, but since I'm a grown-ass woman, I decided to join the convo," Diana snapped back at him.

Dre slid to the edge of his seat, and I touched his arm.

"Dre, chill," I warned him.

"I need a drink." Diana stood and walked over to the bar.

Dre stood up too, looking thoroughly pissed off. "I'm outta here."

"Man, sit down and let's finish this."

"Naw, this ain't the time or the place; and you don't wanna hear what I gotta say anyway. But I'm telling you right now, whether you like it or not, we got a problem."

There was no reasoning with Dre when he was like this. So, I just said, "You see what you can find out, Dre. I'm gonna work on getting us a new supplier for the X."

"You leaving already?" Diana walked back over with a drink in hand. "Come on, Dre. Don't leave. I'm sorry I interrupted your conversation."

I appreciated her making an attempt to smooth things over.

"Nah, I got some shit to handle," Dre said.

"Looks like ain't nobody here tonight anyway," Diana said, looking over the balcony.

"What?" I asked, standing up to look.

"Look, people are here, but something's off." She pointed to the crowd below. "Ain't no sugars here."

"Sugars?" Dre gave her a strange look. I knew exactly who she was referring to, but I didn't respond.

"Yeah, the sugars. The fun boys. That's what they do; they bring the fun," Diana explained.

"Oh," Dre said. "Where the hell are they?"

"I don't know." Diana shrugged and sipped her drink. "Why do you care anyway? Normally you're complaining about them being here, and now you wanna know where they are."

"You need to find out," Dre told her.

Diana looked over at me, then back to Dre. "I don't need to do—"

I touched her arm and smiled at her. "Di, just see what you can find out. For me. Please."

She inhaled deeply then said, "Fine, for *you*, because *you* are my boss."

"Thank you," I said. Dre looked beyond pissed off, but he kept his mouth shut. She put her glass down and headed downstairs. It only took her a few minutes to return with the answer to our question.

"Well, just as I suspected, they're at Oz. No big deal."

"Oz?" Dre and I said simultaneously.

"Yeah, Pierre's spot. It's where all the sugars hang out anyway." Diana laughed.

"Pansy-ass Pierre," Dre growled.

The smile left Diana's face. "That's so disrespectful."

"So, does he have some kind of special guest there tonight or something?" I asked, ignoring the little feud going on between them. Pierre was well known and well liked, and celebrities would stop by from time to time, drawing a crowd. That could explain what was going on.

"I don't know. I haven't really talked to Pierre for a couple of days," Diana answered.

"He ain't make a buy this week?" I asked.

"Nope."

I glanced over at Dre, who was giving me a look that said, *I told you so*. Pierre was usually one of our best customers for party drugs. Now it appeared that our low supply really was affecting us more than I'd wanted to admit.

"Why didn't you say anything? You didn't think that was a little odd?" I asked Diana.

"Not really. He's been a little preoccupied," she said with a smirk.

"Preoccupied how?" Dre pressed.

"He met a new boo," she said. "But lemme check his social media and see if anything is up there." She pulled out her phone and scrolled through some pages. "Nope, nothing but selfies. It does look packed in there, though." She held up her phone for us to see.

There was a long pause. I felt myself starting to panic as the reality of the situation set in. Our business could be in serious trouble.

Dre was fuming. He barked an order at Diana. "Call Pierre and see what the fuck is going on."

She looked at him like he was crazy, then turned and looked at me with her eyebrows raised, like, *Didn't I just tell this fool he's not my boss?*

I sighed. "Di, we just need you to holla at him and see what the deal is, please."

Dre's attitude was making this way harder than it needed to be, but he wasn't wrong about the level of problem we had.

"Fine." Diana pouted. "I'll text him. It's too loud in here for a conversation."

"True," I said.

She got a reply from Pierre almost instantly. "He says it's all good. The bar is packed, and he's gonna come through the boutique tomorrow around two to holla at me and fill me in on what's been up."

"Bet," I said.

"Can everyone relax now and enjoy the rest of the night? We'll know what the deal is tomorrow. As soon as I know, then y'all will know."

I wanted to relax, but I would have felt better if he'd said he was coming through to buy some shit, not just to fill her in on whatever he had going on. If our biggest buyer was no longer a customer, it would just give my father one more reason to blame everything on the gays. And judging from the way Dre screwed up his face every time he heard Pierre's name, I was beginning to understand that he had a big problem with gay men too.

Diana

14

I was hanging up a new shipment of shirts in the boutique, blasting Mary J. Blige and singing along, when the door chimed and Pierre floated in, wearing a smile from ear to ear. Now, Pierre already had flawless skin thanks to good genes and his bi-monthly appointments with his aesthetician for facials and dermabrasion. But there was something different about the way he looked—almost like he was glowing.

"Well, damn. Either you got some good dick or won the damn lottery. Which one is it?" I asked.

"Neither." He gave me a quick hug and air-kissed each cheek.

"Liar."

"I'm not lying." He giggled.

"There's only one other reason you would be around here looking like that, and I know your ass ain't pregnant, bitch." I folded my arms and faced him. "Now, dish."

Pierre put his hands on his stomach and said, "You never know. I could be with child, you envious hussy."

"That's fat, not a baby," I teased.

"You're so fucking mean to me, Diana. I don't know why I torture myself by bringing my ass in here. I'm so glad I have high self-esteem, because if I didn't, you would have me doubting how amazing I am. And yes, I am amazing, bitch."

I couldn't help but laugh. "Fine. Since you ain't gonna come out and tell me why you're on cloud nine, then tell me where the hell you've been. I ain't seen your ass all week, and you haven't called me. Is it safe to assume your little disappearing act has something to do with my new customer? Whom, I might add, I also haven't seen or heard from in a few days."

I knew Pierre and Rio had been hanging out. I hadn't talked to either one since the day after their first date, when each one called me to gush about the other. Rio had gone on and on about how classy and attentive Pierre had been. Pierre couldn't stop talking about how funny and engaging Rio was. It was safe to say that they were both feeling each other—which was why I hadn't really thought anything about Pierre not making a buy like he usually did.

"It's possible a certain someone has contributed to the smile on my face," he said coyly.

"Possible? In the famous words of TLC, I believe that's actual and factual. So, you did get some good dick?"

"No, we haven't even gone there. No sex at all. Just great conversation, laughs, and enjoying each other's company. That's it. Now, I'm hoping some good dick accompanies all of that soon, but for right now, I'm just letting shit happen as it happens." Pierre leaned against the counter and picked up one of the shirts. "This is cute."

"Thanks. You can be the first to buy one," I told him. "So, I heard Oz was the place to be last night. Who the hell was there that had all the people coming through?"

"First of all," he started, "Oz is always the place to be. We ain't have nobody special other than the usual headliner: *moi*."

"Stop lying, Pierre. Who else was there?" I was now just as curious as Corey and Dre about what Pierre had going on at the club, especially since he was being so evasive.

He shrugged. "I swear, no one. Just the usual and a couple new faces that stopped by. We've just been having a good week. The deejay has been fire, the crowd has been lit, and we just been having a good time."

"And where is all this fun coming from? Because you ain't come by to pick up nothing from me." I got straight to the point, surprising myself, because I sounded like I really was a drug dealer—which I damn sure wasn't. Or was I?

"Hey, you ain't have nothing for me to pick up." Pierre walked toward a nearby rack of jackets and took one out. "Or did you? Heffa, when did you get these?"

I took the jacket from him and said, "Yesterday, and you know what I'm talking about."

He continued to casually look through the jackets, "Di, sweetie, you're acting a little perturbed, and I'm starting to get worried."

"What the fuck ever, Pierre."

"Hey, you need a little something to help mellow you out?" He grabbed my hand and turned it up, then dropped something in my palm.

"What the hell is this?" I asked, looking at the tiny piece of candy. "Are you tryna tell me my breath stinks, jerk?"

Pierre laughed. "That's not candy, although you could use a little freshening up."

"Go to hell and tell me what the fuck this is." My eyes went from staring at my hand to staring at his face while I waited for his answer.

"It's a little piece of happiness. Or what I call a Sprinkle."

"A Sprinkle? What the hell is a Sprinkle?"

"It's kinda like a cross between a Molly, ecstasy, some good weed, with a hint of Vyvanse. Try it."

"Nah, I'm good." I shook my head and went to hand the pill back to him. Although I did smoke weed every once in a while, I really wasn't a pill popper.

"Di, I'm telling you, this is the new shit. The effect isn't long lasting, but you don't crash, have mood swings, or get the munchies. It's like a jump starter for a good night. And best of all, you won't test positive."

"How do you know all this?"

"I tested it, and I passed out a couple of samples."

"So, where did this magical jumping bean come from, Jack?"

"I'm not going to reveal my sources." The smile now spreading across his face gave me a hint.

I took a wild guess. "I'm thinking you got this from the same person that's got you ignoring my phone calls and floating on air."

He smirked. "I plead the fifth. But lemme just say folks are loving it, and it's selling like top shelf vodka at the bar," he gushed.

I shook my head. "Pierre, you can't be serious. You getting party favors from somebody you barely know? What the hell is wrong with you? Do you know how fucking dangerous that is?"

"First of all, like I said, I tried it first to make sure it was legit. Second, I know him as much as I knew you when we first started doing business, remember? And lastly, I'm a businessman who had a need to fill, and you had nothing to fill it with."

Pierre made some valid points, but I was still a little irked. "We're working on getting some product in here soon, Pierre. And we still have other shit—"

And then he said exactly what I didn't want to hear. "But with this new favor I got, I don't really need that other shit right now. I'm making money hand over fist. I'm telling you, just try it and see for yourself, Di. Here. Take one more for later." He held his hand out toward me with another pill. I hesitated, but took it, placing both pills in my bra for safekeeping. I had no intention of taking them, but I needed them to show Corey.

"I hope you're sure about this," I said.

"About as sure as I am about this fly-ass jacket I'm about to buy." He walked back over to the counter and held up the four hundred–dollar leather jacket. I rang up the sale and placed the jacket into a plastic bag with the boutique logo on it.

"Thank you for shopping at Chic World for your *fashion* needs. Please come back again," I said sarcastically.

"You're being really childish right now." Pierre gave me the hardest side-eye in the world. "You know that, right?"

"I don't know nothing," I told him.

His cell phone rang, and he smiled as he looked down at the caller ID.

"Hey, Rio. . . . Yeah. I'm here with her now, but she's got a major attitude. . . . Uh-huh. Yep. Hold on."

I didn't move when he held the phone out. "If he wants to talk to me, he knows how to reach me."

Pierre put the phone back to his ear. "See, I told you she had an attitude. I'll call you back in a little while."

No sooner had he ended his call than my cell phone began ringing. I looked down and saw that it was Rio. I waited until my voice mail was about to pick up before I finally answered.

"Yes?"

"Bitch, you better had answered the phone. What's your problem?" he asked, sounding like we were besties or something instead of a customer I just met.

"I don't have a problem. But I do have a customer I'm with right now," I told him.

Pierre shook his head at me. "You are doing the absolute most right now."

"I'm not," I told him.

"Okay, so we doing brunch tomorrow? Just the two of us so we can catch up," Rio said.

"Are you asking or telling me?" I asked.

"I'm telling you, heffa," he responded.

"I'll think about it."

"Think about what?" Pierre asked.

The door chimed. I nearly dropped the phone when I saw Mona walking in. I was worried that something might be wrong, because she should've been at work.

"Rio, I have to call you back." I ended the call before he said anything else.

"What's wrong?" Pierre frowned, then turned to see what I was staring at. "Who is that?"

"Trouble. Listen, I gotta go handle this. You good?" I asked, handing him his bag.

"Yeah, are you good? Do I need to stick around?"

"Naw, I'm fine. It's just my sister, that's all. I'll text you later," I told him.

He picked up his bag and headed toward the door, giving Mona a once-over as he passed her. I felt bad, because although my sister was harmless, my reaction to seeing her made him think otherwise.

"Who was that?" Mona asked when she stepped up to the counter.

I didn't answer her question. "Hey, what are you doing here? Shouldn't you be at work?"

"I called out," she said nonchalantly.

"Why? Clearly you aren't sick, so what's wrong?"

"I don't know. I was headed to work, and then I just didn't feel like going. I think I'm burnt out, seriously. I don't like it anymore." She sighed.

The door chimed again, and a couple of customers I'd never seen before came in. "Welcome to Chic World. Feel free to look around. I'm Diana, and if you need anything, let me know." I whispered to Mona, "We all have those days, Mona. You just need a break. Take today and chill out. Go get a mani/pedi, treat yourself to lunch."

"Can you go to lunch with me? We can go together," Mona suggested.

"Excuse me." One of the ladies who'd just entered called out to me as the door chimed and more people entered.

"I gotta go help these customers," I told her. Then I asked, "Is that my shirt?"

She looked down at the cute shirt she was wearing and gave me a guilty smile. "Uh, yeah. Can I borrow it?"

I just shook my head as I walked away to go help the customers. I felt bad about not being able to go to lunch with Mona, but making sales was my priority, especially if my sales of "other items" to Pierre was going to slow down to nothing. Besides, she was the one who popped up unexpectedly.

I glanced up and saw her walking toward the door. *I'll call her later*, I thought as I went back to helping my customers. A few minutes later, I was shocked when she came walking back into the store. This time, she was not by herself.

"Di, you ain't tell me you had a sister, especially one as fine as this," Dre announced loudly.

I excused myself and hurried to where the two of them stood. "Uh, I thought you were leaving, Mona," I whispered.

Mona shrugged. "I was about to. Then he walked up as I walked out, and we started talking."

"I couldn't let this beautiful creature walk by and not tell her how good she looked today. Besides, she looked like something was bothering her, and I felt the need to put a smile on that pretty face." Dre was looking at my younger sister like she was a perfectly cooked ribeye and he was a hungry lion who hadn't eaten in days. I didn't like it one bit.

"Well, I'm sure she appreciated the compliment. I'll call you when I get off, Mona, and we can go grab something to eat."

She stood her ground, even though I was trying to nudge her toward the exit. "Actually, Dre mentioned that he was one of the owners here, and I told him I'd been asking you about possibly getting a job," Mona said.

"What? He's not—"

"Di, I think Corey and I wouldn't have a problem with Mona working by your side," Dre interjected with a smirk. He knew this was making me uncomfortable, and clearly he was enjoying it.

I glared at him. "Well, like I've told Mona, once business picks up, we might be able to get her in here, but right now, there's no need. You were just complaining last week about how low the numbers are, remember? Certainly adding another person on the payroll wouldn't make sense."

"Maybe she can work part-time while you're in class or on the days you open late," Dre replied, then he turned to Mona and said, "We'll figure something out."

"Seriously?" Mona gushed, "You don't know how much I would appreciate that."

"Mona has a job at a daycare center that she works during the mornings," I told him, still trying to put a stop to the whole thing.

"I can change my schedule and just do the after-school program," Mona said.

"Like I said, Mona, we'll definitely figure something out," Dre said.

"I think we're ready." The customers I'd been helping walked over with the items they wanted to purchase.

"Sure, you can come on over here and I'll take care of you," I said, leading them toward the cash register.

As I rung up their purchases, I could barely focus, because I kept looking over at Dre. He was whispering something into Mona's ear, which caused her to giggle and blush. I made the fastest customer transaction in history and then practically pushed them out the door.

As soon as they were gone, I called out, "Hey, Dre, can I see you in the back right quick?"

"Wait right here," he told Mona.

As soon as we were in the back, I snapped at him, "What the hell are you doing?"

"What are you talking about?" He had the nerve to act like he really didn't know.

"Oh, for starters, stop looking at and talking to my sister like you have a chance in hell to screw her. You don't!" I snapped.

"Whatever. Your sister is fine as hell, and I'm just making myself known. Are you jealous?" He smiled and looked me up and down, making me even more pissed than I already was.

"No, I ain't jealous!"

"I can't tell."

"Second, why the fuck did you offer her a job? She can't work here."

"Why not? It's just part time, and she's your sister. Why wouldn't you want to give her a job?" he asked.

"Because despite what's displayed on the racks out there, high-end clothing ain't the only thing we sell here, Negro!" I reminded him as I pointed to the unlabeled boxes sitting on a couple of shelves. "Those ain't shoes in there. Did you forget?"

Dre blinked for a second, then slowly exhaled. "Shit."

"Exactly, and if you think for one second I'm letting my little sister get caught up in this shit that I ain't even supposed to be involved in, you're crazy. What the fuck is wrong with you?" I shook my head.

"Okay, point taken. But honestly, I felt bad. She was looking like she lost her best friend when she walked out the door, and I was just tryna help."

"You were trying to holler," I corrected him.

"That too," he admitted.

"Why the hell are you here, anyway?" I asked. "Your pickup day is tomorrow."

"I came to see if Pierre talked to you."

Ugh. Just what I didn't want to talk about. I already knew Dre wasn't going to like what I had to say.

"He was here earlier," I said vaguely.

"And? What did he say?"

Something about the way Dre was peering at me made me uneasy, like he wanted to blame me for the drop in sales. So, I lied.

"Nothing. Like I told you, he's got a new boo that's been hanging with him at the bar. A really fun dude that's been hyping the crowd up. That's about it," I said with a casual shrug.

"What about making an order?" Dre pressed.

"We ain't get into all that. I told you; he's in love. I don't think his mind is really on business right now," I said. "But if he says anything else, I'll let you know."

Dre looked disgusted. "Typical gay dude. He's worse than a woman. Fall in love and stop handling your business."

"Wow. Listen to you being homophobic and misogynistic all in one sentence," I said.

"Oh, listen to the college student using big words," he shot back. "Besides, you know it's the truth," he said.

I rolled my eyes and started walking back to the front, relieved that I hadn't told him shit about what was really happening at Oz.

Mona was still waiting for us, and seeing her erased the scowl from Dre's face. "So, Mona, where do you hang out?" he asked.

"I don't," Mona told him.

"You're twenty-one and you don't hang out?"

She shook her head. "No, not really."

Dre grabbed her hand and said, "Well, that's about to change. You gotta come and hang with us tomorrow night."

"Where?" Mona asked, looking into his eyes like she was mesmerized.

"Wet Dreams. Your sister practically runs VIP."

Mona turned to look at me with her eyebrows raised. "Oh, she does? You got it like that, Di?"

"Don't worry. You 'bout to have it like that too. Just wait." Dre's voice deepened, and he grinned mischievously.

"Mona isn't the club type," I said, interrupting his game. "Besides, I don't even know if I'm gonna hang out tomorrow night. I have study group," I said.

"Don't even try it. You'll be there, and Mona will be too. Right, Mona?"

Mona nodded. "Definitely."

"Well, I gotta get outta here. I'll holla at you later, Di. Mona, I'll see you tomorrow night."

I watched in horror as he reached to give her a hug, and she wasted no time pressing her body against his.

"I'm leaving too," she said.

Dre smiled at me and told her, "Then I'll walk you to your car."

"Mona, I thought you wanted to talk to me," I said, making one last attempt to put a stop to this.

"Nah, we can just talk later when you get home. And you can help me figure out what to wear tomorrow night." She waved as she and Dre walked out.

I couldn't believe Dre was pressing up on my sister. One thing was for damn sure: I wouldn't let her fall for him or his bullshit. I was going to stop it before it even got started.

Rio

15

Diana having a semi-attitude because I went MIA for a few days made me feel a little guilty, because I knew I hated it when my sister Paris did the same shit. The couple of times she texted me, I hadn't ignored her, but my answers were super brief. I could see why that might have come across as rude, and I didn't want her to feel that way. Even though we'd just met, she was cool; I liked her, and she deserved better than that.

She was also the one who'd introduced me to Pierre, who was the reason I'd been too busy to talk. We had gone shopping, spent a day at a spa, and swapped stories over some great meals—breakfast, lunch, and dinner. Pierre was like a breath of fresh air, helping me shed that looming darkness I'd felt when I left New York. When I was with him, I almost forgot this was just a vacation and I would be leaving soon. I could see myself falling for someone like him, and I had to remind myself that there was no point in getting caught up.

It wasn't all pleasure, though. We'd also talked business. Sprinkles was an instant hit at Oz. He'd sold out of the few pills I gave him so fast, and he kept pressuring me to get him some more. I was supplying him from my own stash, which was running really low. Pierre didn't know the truth about where the pills came from, so he kept asking who my supplier was, and asking if I would hook them up. He had all these big business ideas, like making Oz the exclusive spot to sell Sprinkles in Baltimore and making me his partner. At this point, I was interested in being his partner—in business and even more so in life—so I got up the nerve to call Orlando to see if we could work something out.

"Yeah," Orlando barked into the phone.

"Is that how you answer the phone for everyone or just me?" I asked.

"Pretty much," he said.

"That's not an answer," I told him.

"What's good, Rio? You back?"

He was using his I'm-too-busy-to-be-bothered tone, but I needed something from him, so I decided not to be petty and call him out again on his rudeness.

"Everything is cool, and no, I'm not back yet. I'm still out of town. What are you up to?"

"I'm working. In the lab right now, as a matter of fact." Orlando had been trained as a pharmacist, which had once seemed like a weird choice considering he was always going to be a part of the family business; but in the end, it worked out perfectly, because he could develop the drugs that we would eventually sell. There's no better way to keep control of your product than to design it yourself. And although he was Pop's right-hand man, being in the lab was his passion, and it was still where he spent a lot of his time.

"Oh, that's cool," I said, still trying to find the right way to explain my call.

"A'ight, Rio, what's wrong? What happened?"

"Why does something have to be wrong, Orlando? Can't I just call to see how my big brother is doing?" I asked, trying my best to sound sincere.

Orlando laughed. "Your ass don't even believe that yourself, so you know I don't. Now, what's up?"

Hearing the lightheartedness in his voice lessened my anxiety. I took a deep breath and went for it. "A'ight, I am calling to holla at you about something."

"What is it?"

"I need you to hook me up with some more Sprinkles."

"What? What the hell are you talking about, Rio? Are you drunk?"

"No, I'm not drunk. And I meant Pixie Dust."

"Oh, hell no! Rio, what the hell do you have going on? Hold on. Let me close my damn door." I heard him clicking the locks. "Where the hell is the Pixie Dust you had? I let you have the entire batch I created last year, Rio, and that was at least three hundred pills."

"I—"

"Wait. Did you take all those pills? Do you have a substance abuse problem? Is that why you've been acting so fucking weird lately and went on this little trip?"

My brother was talking so fast. I could picture him pacing around his lab with an angry scowl on his face as he grilled me. You know what was weird, though? I should have been offended that he thought I had a drug problem, but instead, I was grateful that he seemed so concerned about me.

"No, Orlando, I don't have a substance abuse problem. Do you really think I'd take all of those damn pills?" I asked.

"I don't know what you'd do, Rio. You know how you're in your own little world lately and don't wanna talk to nobody."

I tensed up, feeling misunderstood. I knew my brothers loved me in their own way, because we were taught that family sticks together, but sometimes I wondered: if we weren't family, would they want to know me at all? We didn't exactly have anything in common. I liked shopping and fashion; they liked fast cars, big guns, and beautiful women. I mean, was there really any question why I didn't spend much time with them? But now was not the time to have that conversation with Orlando.

"Well, I didn't take the pills. I sold them," I said matter-of-factly.

"You what? Sold them to who?" Orlando yelled so loud that I had to hold the phone away from my ear.

"O, calm down," I said. "Stop yelling at me like I'm your fucking kid."

"I knew I should've just put those pills in the fucking incinerator. You promised you would just hold them for yourself. You promised, Rio." He sounded distressed. Ever since we had that problem with HEAT, Orlando was extra cautious about the formulations he created. He wanted to invent drugs that made the family rich, but he also wanted to make sure they were safe, and we hadn't really gotten to the testing phase with Pixie Dust.

"This is my fault," he continued. "It was my product, and I should've disposed of it. I can't believe this. I'm not going down for this shit."

Translation: he didn't want to piss Mom off. She had really gone off the deep end when she found out HEAT could cause cancer. Who knows what she would do if she found out about this.

"You're acting like Pixie Dust wasn't just as much mine as it was yours. We developed it together, remember? And you were just as excited about it as I was. Now you're tripping." I got up from the side of the bed and began pacing back and forth in the hotel suite. Even I was kind of surprised myself by how intensely I wanted this product. I still wanted to do this for Pierre, even though I knew it went against my family's wishes—something that Orlando reminded me of loudly.

"That's not what I'm saying, Rio. You're right, it was a collaborative effort, but you know what Dad said after what happened with HEAT. We're not supposed to be putting nothing new out on the street. It's too risky for us; us meaning you, me, and the entire fucking family," he yelled. "And you're out here selling them, Rio? What if something goes wrong or you get caught? Rule number one: you never touch the product. We got people in place to do that shit for us."

"Orlando, listen. Nothing is gonna go wrong. I got this. I'm not out standing on a street corner. I only sold to one person. He owns a bar, and that's the only place you can get Sprink—I mean, Pixie Dust," I explained.

Orlando was not convinced. "How do you even know you can trust this guy? Wait, let's start with this: where the fuck are you?"

I stopped pacing. "I'm in Baltimore. I got a room at the Four Seasons, and that's where I'm staying."

"And the guy you sold to?"

"His name is Pierre. He owns a spot called Oz."

"Oz?"

"Yeah, Oz. It's a gay bar, and it's really nice, and so is Pierre."

"Rio, don't tell me you and this dude . . ."

"No, we're just friends, O. Damn." I sighed. "Man, I get it. I know that when it comes to Duncan family business, everyone believes I don't have shit to contribute—"

"Rio, that's not how anyone feels."

"No, O, let me finish. You know I'm speaking facts right now. This is my chance to prove to you and everyone else that I have a spot in the Duncan family too."

"You already proved that when you allowed Dad to use you as collateral with Alejandro," he said.

"Okay," I said, "but that was a one-time thing. Pop only sent me because he didn't want to send one of his more valuable sons."

Orlando was silent for a minute, meaning he didn't want to acknowledge there was some truth to that statement. When Pop sent me out to California, the Duncans were holding Alejandro's son at the same time. Things could have gone very badly for me if Paris hadn't come out and rescued my ass.

"I want to prove that I can do more than plan parties," I said. "You remember when I came to you with the idea for Pixie Dust?"

"Yeah, I do."

"At first you thought I was joking, until you took the time to listen to me. The gay club scene is an opportunity for us. We can do this on a lower scale and limit the risks. If we set it up right, this will work." I closed my eyes and said a quick prayer that my brother would be reasonable.

Orlando was quiet for a few extended moments, then finally said, "What you tryna do, Rio?"

I wasn't a religious man, but at that moment, I wanted to praise God like I was a church mother. "I need you to make more product. I have some left, but I'm gonna need more. A lot more."

He let out an exasperated breath like he couldn't believe I'd talked him into this. "This is how we're gonna do this. First, I need to know everything you know about this Pierre cat so I can make sure he's legit. He may be telling you one thing, and we find out something different. If he's a bar owner who's dealing on the side, then he had to have a supplier before your ass got there. Who does he normally cop shit from?"

I hadn't thought about that. All I knew was Pierre said he couldn't get his hands on any X. "I have to find out."

"Yeah, find out soon and let me know."

"So, you're gonna help me do this once I get that info to you, O?" I asked.

"I'll get a hundred pills over to you, Rio. It's gonna take a couple of days."

"A hundred? Come on, Orlando. I need five hundred to start."

"Nah, I ain't sending that much. It's too risky, Rio. Either we do this my way, or don't do it at all."

"Man, you know a hundred ain't shit," I told him. "You gotta give me a little more to at least show Pierre I'm legit."

"Rio . . ."

"Come on, O."

"I'll get you three hundred," he relented.

I wanted to squeal with excitement, but I didn't. I pumped my fist into the air and said, "Thanks, O. I appreciate you."

"Rio, you got twenty-four hours to get me that information or I'm not doing this."

"I'll get it to you."

"And another thing. This shit is to be kept between me and you, nobody else. Not Paris, not Sasha, no fucking body else, Rio. And if Dad gets wind of this before we have a chance to tell him, or if anything goes wrong . . ."

"He won't find out, and nothing is going to go wrong. I won't say anything to anyone, I swear."

"You strapped?"

I thought about the condoms that I'd placed in the nightstand that I had yet to touch. "I don't need—"

"You out in the streets of Baltimore and don't have a piece with you, Rio?" Orlando raised his voice, and I realized what he was talking about.

"Ohhhhhh, a gun?" I laughed. "Yeah, I got one with me."

"Yes, a gun! What the fuck did you think I was talking about? You know what? Never mind. Get me the info on this dude Pierre. I'll take to you later." Orlando ended the call.

I tossed my phone onto the bed and did the victory scream and dance I'd been holding onto. Things were truly looking up for me. Coming to Baltimore was turning out to be one of the best decisions I'd made. First, I met Diana, my new friend, then there was Pierre, who was potentially more than a friend, and now I was making major business moves with the support of Orlando. I looked over at the clock on the nightstand and saw that I needed to start getting dressed. Pierre and I had plans to meet for an early dinner before heading over to Oz. I was already looking forward to our date, but after speaking to Orlando, my anticipation increased, and I was ready to learn everything I could about Pierre.

Corey

16

I was sitting in the office, talking to Marcus, one of my foot soldiers, when Diana called.

"Hey, we need to chat," she said.

"I'm kinda in the middle of something right now. Is something wrong?" I asked.

"No, nothing's wrong. Have you talked to Dre?"

"Not since earlier." I hoped the two of them hadn't gotten into it again. I had enough on my plate without having to deal with them going back and forth like little kids. "What happened now?"

"He came by and wanted to know what Pierre had to say."

I glanced over at Marcus, who was engrossed in his phone. "Did you talk to Pierre?"

"Why the hell are you whispering?" Diana asked.

"No reason. Did you?" Maybe I was being paranoid, but I didn't want Marcus to hear me mentioning Pierre's name, even if this call was about business. Everyone knew Pierre was gay, so the less I was associated with him, the better.

"Yeah, Pierre came by earlier, and we talked. I got the info, but I didn't tell Dre shit. You know I don't like him like that," Diana said.

"Cool. Listen, I'll come by the boutique a little later, and we'll discuss it. Around nine, okay?" I asked.

"That's fine. You know the store will be empty then because I'll be closing up shop."

"I'll see you then, Di." I ended the call.

Marcus looked up from his phone. "Everything a'ight?"

"Yeah, it's cool." I nodded. "Women. You know how it is."

"True dat. You still wit' Diana?" Marcus asked. "Y'all been rocking for a minute, huh?"

"We have." I smiled.

"Interesting."

"Why do you say that?" I gave him a strange look.

"I don't know. I mean, she's cool and all. I just never thought she was your type." Marcus shrugged and looked back down at his phone.

"My type? Diana is one of the baddest bitches in the city. Why wouldn't she be my type?"

Marcus had just started working for my father right before he got locked up. He'd continued to be loyal and one of my best dealers, which was why I'd asked him to handle Ant for me. That job instantly moved him up the ranks, but we weren't cool enough for him to be saying some shit like that.

He put his hand up defensively. "Yo, I ain't mean to upset you, man. You're right; she's bad. And hey, like I said, y'all been rocking for a minute, so it's all good, right?" Marcus shrugged. "Let's get back to business."

"Yeah, let's," I said, sitting up.

"So, our numbers are still looking decent right now. We know there's a slight shortage of X, but we're making up the difference with Molly. You know Molly costs a bit more, so folks know they gotta pay if they wanna party until we get more ecstasy," Marcus said.

"I'm working on that now," I told him.

"Yeah, I heard Dre is working on it too. He's supposed to be meeting with a couple of dudes later to see what they can do."

"Yeah, we'll see what happens." I acted like I already knew this information, even though Dre hadn't mentioned anything to me about meeting with anyone. Seemed like my business partner was holding out on me, and I wondered why.

"So, here's the deposits from the south side." Marcus reached into the duffel bag sitting on the floor in front of me and gave me a handful of stacks. I took it from him and put it into the safe behind me without counting it.

"Good deal," I said. "Everything else cool? No issues or concerns from anyone?"

"Nah, nothing my boys can't handle," Marcus answered. "You know Dre ain't the easiest muthafucka to deal with sometimes wit' his rude ass, but they know it comes with the territory."

I wanted to agree, because I found Dre disrespectful at times, but gay or not, if you were going to be a part of the drug scene, you damn sure needed thick skin. As much as Dre and his anti-gay comments irritated me, we were business partners, and I had to show loyalty.

"Hey, if they don't like it, they asses can leave," I explained.

"Nah, boss, they ain't going nowhere. Real talk, I was kinda worried when you took over for your pops. I ain't think you were going to be able to run shit. But you proved to me and everyone else you could do it. You run a tight ship, but you're fair, and that's why folks respect you." Marcus looked me in the eye. "No doubt they respected your pops and Dre because they had to. It was out of fear. They respect because you earn it and deserve it."

"Good." Hearing that the corner boys and lower level employees respected me made me proud, and more than a little relieved. "I appreciate that."

Marcus's phone rang. "Yo, I gotta take this."

"Go ahead," I told him, and he exited the office.

When he was gone, I sat back and thought about calling Dre to ask what the hell Marcus was talking about. Then, a memory of my mother came to me. When she was alive, there was talk about my father sleeping with one of our neighbors, who was one of her best friends. I was furious and told her, expecting her to be just as upset as I was.

"Yeah, I heard they was messing around." She was actually smiling when she said it.

"What are you going to do about it? Are you gonna ask him? Are you gonna ask her?" I questioned.

"No," she said, still calm. "Trust me, there will come a time when you'll learn you don't have to share all of the information you know."

I was confused, especially when she was still loving and kind to my father, who was staying out all night. And she was nice to her friend. Then, one night, her friend called, screaming in pain because she was suffering a miscarriage and needed a ride to the hospital.

"Sorry, but it's late, and I'm too sleepy to drive," my mom told her. "Why don't you call the muthafucka who knocked you up?" she said and hung up.

A couple hours later, my father came in, and she told him about the phone call. He didn't say anything; just turned around and walked back out the door. The next day, he returned home with a new diamond watch for my mother, and his late nights now ended earlier.

I never forgot that lesson. There was power in holding onto information, so I would do just that. I would know if and when the time was right to reveal what I'd just learned about Dre. I'd never doubted Dre's loyalty before, but maybe it was time for me to start paying closer attention to him.

"What's the deal?" I asked Diana later that night when I walked into Chic World a few minutes after nine.

She walked past me, locking the doors and flipping the OPEN sign over. "Long day, busy day."

"Money-making day, I hope."

"Yes, boo. I earned some coins today too. I earn coins every day. Don't trip." She winked at me.

I followed her into the back of the store, and we sat in the makeshift office. I could see that she was tired, but she still looked amazing in a white crop top, jeans that seemed to be created just for her curves, and black stiletto pumps. Her outfit was simple, but somehow, she still looked like she'd just stepped off the cover of a fashion magazine. Like I'd told Marcus, she was definitely one of the baddest bitches in the city. I had been with women before, and though the relationships weren't quite satisfying, looking at Diana made me wonder if she could be different. My life would be so much easier if I liked chicks for real.

"Why are you staring at me like that?" She frowned.

"Huh?" I shook my head. "I didn't realize I was staring."

"Liar." She laughed.

"So, what's up with Pierre? What does he have going on over at Oz?" I changed the subject.

"At first, he tried to act like there's nothing new going on, but I eventually got him to tell me," she said.

"What is it? He got a new supplier, doesn't he?"

"He does." She nodded.

"Son of a bitch." I hit my fist on the desk, and she jumped.

"Wait, wait, let me finish." Diana gasped and put her hand on her chest. "Damn, son."

I relaxed a little and said, "I knew he took his business elsewhere. Where the fuck did he get it? Philly? Because it ain't no ecstasy to be found nowhere in Maryland or D.C. right now."

"See, that's the thing, Corey. He ain't selling X at his club, I don't think."

"What the hell is he selling then?"

She reached into her cleavage and took out a neatly folded Kleenex. "These."

I took it from her and unfolded it to see the contents. "Candy?"

"It's not candy. They're called Sprinkles, and he says they're selling like hotcakes."

"What the hell are Sprinkles? Did you take one?" I asked. "What do they do?"

"Now, you know I ain't take one. He told me to try it, though. Apparently, it's new," Diana said. "And whatever it does, people are loving it."

"Where is he getting it from?"

"He didn't say, but I got a feeling I know where." She sat back in the chair.

"Where?"

"His new boo."

I stared at her blankly. "And who the hell is that? You act like I know who that is."

"Remember that guy Rio who I was with the other night?" she asked.

"Which guy?"

"He was wearing the flyest gear in the club that night."

"That was probably me," I joked.

"Nah, that would've been you if you would wear some of the shit I sell in here." Diana smirked.

"Nah, I'm good with my wardrobe selections," I told her. Diana was an amazing stylist and had great taste in clothes, but most of the stuff she sold at the boutique was not my style. Unless I wanted to announce my sexuality loud and clear, I had to steer away from the colorful, flamboyant clothes she sold. Some of that shit just screamed "homosexual." I had to dress the part: jeans, T-shirts, and a fresh pair of Nikes on most days. My wardrobe would raise no questions about my sexuality, and I needed to keep it that way.

"What's the point of owning a boutique if you can't take advantage of the clothing?" Diana asked.

"Focus, Di," I said. "Now, who the hell is this Mario cat? How do you know him?"

"It's not Mario; it's Rio. And I just met him. He came in the boutique and bought some stuff, and we hit it off. He was at the club that night, and I kinda set them up on a date. And they hit it off."

"So, Rio is a dealer?" I asked.

"I don't know what he is. Now, I will say this: he does have some coins and doesn't mind spending them. I'm meeting Rio for brunch tomorrow, so I'll see what I can find out."

"I'ma need you to confirm if he's the one supplying Pierre with these." I nodded at the Sprinkles in my hand. "And I need to know what else he's got going on."

Diana looked at me. "You sure got me doing a lot of extra shit these days, Corey."

I stood up and put the Sprinkles in my pocket. "And don't I compensate you nicely? Where else are you gonna get paid for going to brunch and coming to work late all the damn time?"

"You do have a point." Diana laughed and grabbed her purse out of the desk drawer. I waited as she made sure everything was locked up, then turned on the security system. We headed out the back door and into the back parking lot.

"I'll see you tomorrow night at the club," I told her as I walked her to her car.

"Yeah, speaking of tomorrow night, can you tell Dre to stay the fuck away from my little sister? I don't need his ass pushing up on her," Diana said.

"Dre pushed up on your little sister? Wow, when did all this happen?" I asked.

"Today when she popped up here at the store and so did he," Diana answered.

Now I realized why she'd had such an attitude when she called earlier. "You know how Dre is. When he sees something he likes, he goes for it. Didn't you say the other day that he wanted to fuck you?"

"I'm not kidding, Corey. I can see through his bullshit, but my sister isn't used to his kind of attention. I will fuck him up. And that's not a threat, that's facts."

"Di, chill. I'll tell Dre to fall back if he speaks on it or I see it," I said. I'd never seen Diana so worked up over anything. She looked like she was about to cry. I took a step closer and gave her a hug.

"Thanks, Corey."

"You good?" I asked.

She stood on her toes and kissed me on the cheek, then nodded. "I am."

I opened the door of her car, and she climbed in.

"I'll talk to you tomorrow."

"Okay," she said and headed out of the parking lot.

As I walked to my BMW X5, I reached into my pocket and took out the crumpled tissue holding the Sprinkles. I got in and turned on the ignition, waiting for my phone to connect to the Bluetooth speakers before I dialed a number.

"Yo."

"Marcus, where you at?" I asked. "I need you to meet me. I got something new for you to try out."

Diana

17

As I was pulling out of the parking lot, Ashton called. I wasn't in the mood to talk to anyone, so I sent him to voicemail. He immediately called back, and I ignored the call again. He called a third time, making me even more irritated than I already was.

"Yes?" I snapped.

"Where are you, Di?" He sounded annoyed too.

"Why?" I asked.

"Because I wanna ask, that's why. Now, answer the question."

"Is this really Ashton? 'Cause I sure feel like I'm talking to my daddy."

"Look, I only asked because—"

"You know what? I don't care." I hit the END button. I didn't know what the hell was wrong with him, but whatever it was, he didn't have the right to speak to me in that manner, and I damn sure wasn't about to let him. He called twice more, but I didn't answer.

I waited for a few minutes to teach him a lesson, and then I called him back.

"Have you calmed down?" I asked when he answered.

"What the hell is wrong with you, Diana? Why you hang up on me?" he asked, sounding angry and a little hurt.

"Because you were talking to me like you lost your damn mind."

"Why? Because I asked where you were?"

Suddenly, a car pulled up behind me and began flashing its lights. I moved into the right lane to get out of the way, but when I glanced in the rearview mirror, I saw that the car had also moved over and was still behind me. The lights flashed again. Now I was nervous. I put my foot on the gas and sped up, but the car remained right on my tail. My heart began pounding.

"What the fuck? Hold on, Ashton. Some asshole is behind me flashing their lights. And now it looks like they're following me," I said.

"That asshole is me, Diana."

I looked in the rearview mirror again. Sure enough, the vehicle behind me was a silver Audi. "What the fuck are you doing, Ashton?"

"I'm trying to get you to pull over so I can talk to you," he said.

I hung up the phone and turned into the first parking lot I saw, which happened to be a strip mall with my favorite Chinese restaurant. I pulled into one of the parking spaces near the back of the lot, and Ashton parked beside me.

I sat for a few moments, just staring at him in anger and disgust. When he figured out I wasn't moving, he got out of his car and walked over to mine.

"Are you crazy?" I said when I rolled down the window.

"No, I'm not."

"Yeah, I'm thinking you are. First, you call me with an attitude asking where I am; then you start following me like some maniac, nearly scaring me to death."

"I wouldn't have to be driving behind you like a maniac if you would've answered your phone the first time and not had a damn attitude when you finally did answer." His tone surprised me. We'd had disagreements in the past, but he'd never been so aggressive toward me.

"How did you know where I was anyway? That's pretty creepy, Ashton."

He rolled his eyes. "Stop being so dramatic. I know what time you close the boutique, and I know which roads you take to go home."

It made sense, but it was still a little weird. "Well, you know where I am now, so what's up?" I tried to remain calm.

He folded his arms and said, "That's a great question. I've been trying to figure out what's up for the past couple of weeks."

I leaned my head back against the seat and groaned. "Ashton, please don't start with that again. I've had a long day, and I just wanna go home and take a shower."

"I'm not starting with anything," he responded. "You know what? I'm lying. I do want to start with a question."

"What question?"

He grabbed his phone and held it out to me. "Who the fuck is this?"

My eyes went wide. I was totally taken aback by what I saw. There, on the screen, was a picture of me and Corey in an embrace, taken moments earlier in the parking lot. I opened the door and jumped out of the car.

"Oh my God, are you fucking kidding me?" I said through clenched teeth.

"No, I'm not kidding at all. Who the fuck is he?"

I reached out to snatch the phone from him. "He's my fucking boss, you asshole!"

"Your boss, huh? This is what you do to your boss?" Ashton took a step back and ran his finger along the screen. It changed to another picture of Corey kissing my cheek. I was smiling in the picture. I could see how that would look bad to someone who didn't know the deal, but I wasn't about to admit that to Ashton, because I was fuming at this invasion of privacy.

"So, you're stalking me now? That's what we're doing?"

"No, I called myself surprising you with roses that I was going to have waiting on your car when you came out of work. But I was the one who got a fucking surprise." His face was flush, and beads of sweat were forming on his forehead, soaking his hair and making it stringy.

"You're crazy. You know that? I can't believe you." I shook my head. I couldn't believe he'd actually been taking pictures of me like some damn super spy. "If your psychotic ass would've come over to us, he could've just told you who he was."

He smirked. "I didn't want to interrupt the beautiful moment y'all were having. And I find it hard to believe that he's just your boss. Bosses don't look at their employees like that, and they damn sure don't kiss them. Not with all this 'Me Too' stuff that's going on these days. . . . Unless their employees *want* to be groped and kissed."

I rolled my eyes. "I can't even believe I'm going to justify your bullshit with an answer, but here it is: First of all, he's not grop-ing me. That's a fucking hug. And he kissed my cheek goodbye, the same way a lot of my customers and friends do."

"Oh, so that must be a black thing, huh?" Ashton said bitterly.

"What the fuck did you just say? A black thing? I'll show you a fucking black thing!" I lunged at Ashton, and he held his arm out to block me.

"Diana!" A voice came from across the parking lot. Ashton and I both turned to see my sister running toward me.

"Mona?" She was holding a bag of what I knew was beef and broccoli, shrimp fried rice, and an order of wontons—her favorite meal from China King.

"What is going on? Who the hell are you, and why are you grabbing on her like that?" She stood between me and Ashton, screaming in his face.

"I'm not grabbing her! She tried to hit me!" Ashton said. "Who the hell are you?"

"That's my fucking sister, and don't you talk to her like that!" I snapped.

"Are you okay, Di?" Mona asked me.

"I'm fine," I told her. "He's the one you should be worried about."

"Listen, your sister and I are just having a conversation, that's all. You can leave," Ashton told her, struggling to keep his voice calm.

"I ain't going no fucking where. *You* can leave," Mona said.

I couldn't believe what I was witnessing. First Ashton flipped out on me, and now my sister was showing a side of herself I didn't even know existed. She was the mild-mannered one of the family, the bookworm who jumped whenever someone said "boo." Now she was ready to go toe to toe with Ashton, even though he was a foot taller and almost a hundred pounds heavier than her. I was proud.

"It's cool, Mona. I got this. You can go." I touched her shoulder.

She turned around and huffed. "I ain't leaving until you leave. Fuck that."

Hearing her curse, something she rarely did, and seeing the concern in her face let me know that she meant what she said. I nodded at her and said, "You can wait in the car. I won't be but a few minutes."

"Your car or my car?" she asked, and for a brief moment, the innocent little sister I was used to returned.

"Your car."

She looked Ashton up and down once more, then slowly walked back across the parking lot, turning around to look at us every few steps. Once she got into her own car, I focused my attention back on Ashton.

"I guess you don't think that's my fucking sister either, huh?"

"I didn't say that," he answered.

"I don't appreciate you creeping up on me or taking those little snapshots. I also don't like the fact that you act like you don't trust me. I'm done," I told him.

"What do you mean, *done*?" He looked confused.

"I mean what I just said. I'm done. This shit was supposed to be fun and enjoyable. Now, I'm stressed and quite frankly, unhappy. So, don't call me, don't text me, damn sure don't follow me, Ashton. We are done."

He looked like he wanted to cry. I didn't mean to hurt him, but I felt violated and creeped out. No doubt the white-boy dick was good, but it wasn't worth the drama that now came with it.

"Diana, please. I'm sorry. Don't do this. Let's talk about this." He reached for me, and I stepped back. "Baby, come on. Listen, I really am sorry."

"Ashton, you're a nice guy. I've enjoyed you, I really have. But I can't do this anymore." I left him standing there, looking like he was about to cry.

I got into my car and flashed my lights at Mona to let her know I was leaving, and she pulled out of the space she was parked in. As I drove out of the lot, I looked over at Ashton. He was still standing in the same spot.

"Wait, so that white guy is your boyfriend?" Mona asked. We'd driven straight home, changed into our pajamas, and were now eating the Chinese food that she'd picked up.

I shook my head, hoping it would be enough to end her questioning. It wasn't.

"No, he's something." She gave me a knowing look. "I doubt that he was just some random white guy grabbing on you in the middle of the hood."

"Okay," I relented. "Not a boyfriend, but we were friends. . . . Well, a little more than friends. But not—look, it's complicated, okay?"

"So, y'all were fucking?"

I almost choked. Granted, that's what Ashton and I were doing, in a sense, but having my sister confirm it was a bit much for me. I swallowed hard, ready to tell her to mind her business until I remembered how she had stood up for me. I owed her at least a little honesty about who Ashton was. Besides, as far as I was concerned, he and I were over anyway, so there was no harm in admitting it now.

"Yeah, we were."

She gave me a strange look. "Wow, Di. You were with a white guy?"

I laughed. "What? Trust me, Ashton was *not* your typical white boy."

"Was? So, it's over? You're not going to sleep with him anymore?"

"Nope. He got to be a little too much, and he wanted more than I was willing to give right now. And tonight, he crossed the line, and that was it," I explained.

"What did he do? Did he put his hands on you?" Mona sat up straight.

"Hell no! He was still standing when we left, right? If he had put his hands on me, he woulda been lying on the fucking ground," I said.

"Well, what was it then?" she asked.

"It doesn't matter. It was just time." I reached out and touched her hand. "I appreciate you having my back, though. You came through like Wonder Woman ready to save the damn day, Mona."

"What was I supposed to do? I came out the restaurant and heard this yelling, and then realized it was you. I almost dropped my food, and you know how much I love my beef and broccoli. But, if I woulda had to let it go, I was going to."

"Thanks, girl." I gave her hand a squeeze. "I'm sorry I wasn't very attentive when you came by the store earlier. I had a lot going on, though, and I just wasn't expecting you. And I'm sorry you had a bad day."

"It's cool. I understand. I shouldn't've just popped up on your job like that. But, Di, I am frustrated at my job, and I'm ready to do something different. I really wanna work at the boutique with you," she said.

"I know. And I'll talk to my boss and see what he says. That's all I can do."

"But Dre said—"

"Yeah, about that. Dre isn't my boss, Mona. I know he was fronting like he runs the place, but he doesn't. And another thing, he's a fuck boy of the worst kind." I said.

"What do you mean?"

I made sure her eyes met mine so that she would fully grasp what I was telling her. "He will say whatever he has to say and do whatever he has to do in order to get whatever it is he wants from whomever he wants it from."

"So, in other words, he's a man," Mona said.

"Of the worst kind."

"Diana, listen, I get it. You think I'm young and gullible. But I'm also twenty-one, and I know more than you think I do. And what I don't know, I want to learn. I can't do that if you keep treating me like a five-year-old that's begging to go with you to the park up the street."

I couldn't help smiling at the memory. Mona used to constantly beg to go to the neighborhood park with me and my friends. I thought she was just the most annoying little sister back then. One day, she stopped asking, and when I got to the park, she was already there on the swing, having a ball.

"I get it. You've grown up," I told her.

"Let me hang out with you. Come on," she pleaded.

"Fine. Under one condition."

"What is it?" she asked.

"You stay the hell away from Dre."

She nodded.

"I mean it," I warned.

"Deal." She jumped up and gave me a hug, then headed out of the den.

"Where are you going?" I called after her.

"To raid your closet and find something fierce to wear. I know if I'm gonna be hanging with you, I gotta look amazing!"

Rio

18

"So, what did you find out?" Orlando asked when I answered the phone.

"Shit, what time is it?" I groaned, rolling over onto my back and rubbing my eyes and trying to get my head together enough to have a conversation.

"It's ten minutes till ten," Orlando said. "Now, wake your ass up and talk to me."

"All right. Hold on." I pulled the phone away from my ear and sent Diana a quick text, letting her know that I wouldn't be making it to brunch. Then I asked Orlando, "Did you send the package?"

"It's ready to go once you give me the information I need. Did you go back and talk to that Pierre dude?"

Did I? I thought with a satisfied smile. My night with Pierre was the reason I'd overslept and was now hungover.

Instead of dinner and drinks at the bar, Pierre had invited me over to his house, which wasn't far from the hotel. I was damn near blown away by his sky-level condo on the twenty-seventh floor of a building that not only had security, but a concierge as well.

"This is nice," I told him as he gave me a tour. I had no doubt that Pierre was living fabulous, but I hadn't expected this. Everything was pristine and crisp: from the light gray Italian leather furniture to the mirrored artwork and decor. But the most impressive thing about the magnificent residence was the floor-to-ceiling windows, which gave a panoramic view of the entire city.

"Thank you. It's okay for now." Pierre shrugged as we sipped wine in front of those fabulous windows.

"For now?" I smirked.

"Yes. I plan to either sell this place or rent it out and buy a home. A real house, like maybe in Arlington or somewhere like that. I want to get married and start a family one day."

"Oh," was all I could say. I'd never dated anyone who had those types of goals, and it wasn't anything I'd ever really considered. I liked the nightlife too much. Could I really see myself slowing down to become a stay-at-home dad kind of guy?

"Yep, and this building isn't really kid-friendly. There's no yard to put a swing set for my daughter or a basketball hoop for my son to practice his jump shots." He laughed.

"Got it all planned out, huh?" I said, taking a sip of my wine.

"A guy can dream, can't he? What's the point of working hard if you don't have dreams and goals?" Pierre said.

The private chef that Pierre hired to cook for us came in and announced, "Mr. Pierre, dinner is ready."

Pierre took me by the hand and led me into the dining room. The table was set with fine china and tapered candles. Soft jazz was playing from the overhead speakers.

"Should I sit here?" I pointed to the end of the table.

Pierre stared at the beautifully set table with a place setting at each end and then looked at me. "Sure." He walked to the other end of the table, then moved his own place setting to be right next to mine.

"Better?" he asked.

"Definitely better." I smiled.

The chef served us a scrumptious meal of shrimp, grits, and the largest crab cakes I'd ever seen.

"Shall I bring out the dessert?" he asked when we were done.

Pierre shook his head. "Hold off on that. Why don't you go clear out the kitchen, and then you can go."

"Thank you, sir," the chef said and then left us alone again.

"Shall we go and hang out on the balcony?" Pierre asked.

"I'd love to."

Pierre refilled our wine glasses, and then we headed outside, where he fired up two cigars for us to enjoy.

"So, have you thought about my business offer?" he asked after a while.

I was glad that the conversation had turned to business, because Orlando was still waiting for some answers. "I have."

"And have you made a decision?"

"No, I'm actually still considering," I told him. "Let me ask you a question."

"Ask away. You know I'm an open book," Pierre said.

"Where were you getting your party favors before?" I asked him.

Pierre looked over at me eagerly. "You said *before*. Does that mean you're leaning toward a yes and I'll be buying from you from now on?"

"Nice try. I'm still working on a couple of details," I said.

"Such as?"

I took a sip of my wine. "Business with pleasure."

Pierre cocked his head to the side, looking confused. "What about it?"

"You know what they say."

Pierre laughed. "Rio, you don't seem like the type to care about what 'they' say. And who the fuck is 'they' anyway?"

My mind went to the lecture Orlando had given me earlier. "Trust me, there are a lot of 'theys' out there, and we both know it."

He locked his eyes on mine. "Listen, you know you can trust me, right? Real talk, we can trust one another. I damn sure would not have invited you to my house if I didn't trust you, in case you didn't realize it. And honestly, your swag and the way you carry yourself, letting the world know that you don't give a fuck what anyone has to say, is one of the things that attracted me to you." Pierre slid his chair closer to mine.

I set down my wine glass and turned my body toward his. "Oh, so you're attracted to me, huh?"

"Damn right. As if you didn't know." Pierre smiled and leaned his face close to mine.

Our lips met, and I closed my eyes and opened my mouth to taste his. It was the most enjoyable kiss I'd ever experienced, and I wanted it to last forever.

When we finally pulled away, Pierre said, "Spend the night."

The throbbing desire between my legs told me to quickly accept his invitation, but I couldn't—partly because there was a possibility that we would become business partners, but mostly from fear. I was scared. The more time I spent with Pierre, the more I liked him. Now he'd made it very clear that he liked me too, which made me even more anxious. I'd hung out with men and slept with men, but this was different. This wasn't turning into the casual fling I was expecting. Pierre was pursuing me, something I wasn't used to. But, I wondered, was it because he had some type of agenda? Was he doing all of this just to get more Pixie Dust?

"I wish I could, but I can't." I sighed, caressing his neck with my fingers. "I'm meeting Di in the morning."

"I understand. And I hope you're not offended that I asked," Pierre said.

"Not at all. I'm flattered."

"Well," he said, "to answer your original question, that's where I buy my shit."

I frowned, confused by what he was saying. "What? Who?"

"Diana, Chic World. That's where I buy my party favors. Her boss, Corey, he's the plug," Pierre said matter-of-factly.

"Wait, so do you know this dude Corey who owns the boutique?" Orlando asked when I told him everything that I'd discovered last night at Pierre's decked-out condo.

"Not really. I know Diana, the girl who works for him at the boutique. I've met him. He owns Wet Dreams. It's one of the hottest clubs here," I told him.

"You don't know Corey's last name or where he's from?"

"Nope, but I'm hanging out with Di today. I was supposed to have brunch with her, but I overslept." I yawned. "So, you sending the package or what? I need it."

"I'll send the three hundred I promised. Then, when I verify this shit, we'll talk," Orlando said.

"Thanks. You can courier it over to The Four Seasons Baltimore."

"Rio, remember what I told you. Be safe. This shit is not a game. Don't trust nobody," Orlando said. "And call Mom. She's worried."

"I will," I told my brother.

As soon as we got off the phone, I blocked my number and called my mother, knowing if I didn't, Orlando would have something to say. I was doing whatever I needed to in order to stay in his good graces.

"Hey, Ma. It's your favorite son," I joked to break the ice. I already knew she was going to be mad.

"Where the hell are you, Rio?" she asked. "I've been calling and texting your phone."

"Oh, I didn't bring it with me. I'm borrowing a friend's phone to call." I hated lying to my mother, but sometimes she left me no choice.

"Well, when are you coming home?" she asked. "And you know you shouldn't be anywhere without a phone. What if something happened and we needed to reach you? Or if something happened to you and someone needed to reach us? How would your father and I find out?"

"Everything is fine, Ma. And nothing is going to happen to me. I'm on vacation and having the time of my life."

"Vacation where, Rio?" she asked.

"Not far. I'm in the United States," I told her vaguely. If I told here where I was, I wouldn't put it past her to send one of the family's bodyguards down to get me. "Listen, I have to go. I love you, and I'll be home soon."

"Love you too, Rio. Do you want to talk to your father before—"

"No, Ma, I'm good." I ended the call. LC Duncan was the last person I wanted to speak to at that moment. He was good at sniffing out lies, and before I even said "hello," he would have already figured out my whole business plan and shut it down.

Oh, well. At least I'd done what Orlando asked and let my mother know I was okay.

My phone vibrated. It was a text from Diana, telling me to meet her at the boutique later. I climbed into the bed and drifted back to sleep with thoughts of Pierre on my mind.

"You are the biggest loser." Diana shook her head at me when I walked into the store later in the afternoon.

"I come bearing gifts, though," I said, holding up two Starbucks cups and a bag of pastries.

She rolled her eyes. "You really think coming in here with some coffee and doughnuts is gonna make up for your standing me up for brunch?"

"First of all, it's not coffee, it's cappuccino; and it's not doughnuts, it's croissants. You know coffee and doughnuts are basic. I don't do basic, and neither do you." I placed the food on the counter then walked over to the rack where she was standing. I reached out my arms for a hug, but she shut me down with her palm in the air like a stop sign.

"Nope. It's not gonna work."

I put on my best fake-sad face. "Diana, come on. You know you're my only friend here in Baltimore. Don't treat me like this."

"You're a damn liar and ain't no truth in you, because you didn't leave Pierre's house until two thirty this morning, which is why you stood me up," she stated, sounding like a cop detailing the evidence against me.

"Damn, does Pierre tell you everything?" I asked, especially curious now that I knew about Pierre's supplier, who also happened to be her boss. Was it a real friendship, or did she just collect information from Pierre to feed it back to Corey?

"Pretty much." She shrugged.

"I'm gonna have to talk to him about that."

"However, there may be a way you can make it up to me," Diana said.

"How's that?" I asked. "You know the prices in here are too damn high for me to buy but so much." There was no reason for her to know that I could afford to buy the whole damn place. Sometimes it's better to play that shit down until you know a person's true intentions.

"Stop being cheap. You know you got it like that. Besides, I'm sure your friend Pierre would buy it for you," she teased.

"You're really sounding a bit jealous, you know that?" I said. "Now, how can I make it up?"

"I need you to come and hang out with my sister and me tonight."

"Where?"

"At the club. She's young, and I need you to kinda help me keep an eye on her."

"You want me to give up my Friday night to help babysit?" I asked.

"No, I'm asking you to come and hang out with me." She touched my arm. "Come on, Rio."

"Well, I—"

The door chime rang out as someone entered the store. We both turned to look, and I damn near fainted when I saw who was walking in. This time, there was no mistaking who he was. He looked exactly the same. I felt lightheaded as he got closer.

"Shit," I said under my breath.

Diana frowned. "Rio, are you okay? You look like you're about to pass out."

I didn't answer her. I couldn't answer her. All I could do was stare at the ghost in the flesh that was headed in my direction.

"Wassup." He nodded toward us.

I searched his face, hoping he would show me some sign of recognition, but he just blinked, then turned his attention to Diana. I swallowed the ball that had formed in my throat.

"Hey, Dre," Diana said dryly. She turned to me and said, "I'll be right back. I have to take care of something right quick."

I said nothing. I just stared at him. Our eyes met briefly, but he just looked at me like he thought I was crazy. I couldn't believe him. He really acted like he didn't know who I was.

"I gotta go. I'll talk to you later, Di," I said, hurrying toward the door.

"Wait!" Diana called after me, but I didn't stop.

"What the fuck is wrong with him?" I heard him say as I pushed the door open and walked out.

I made it my car and sat there, unable to move. A wave of emotions came over me all at once: shock, anger, confusion, and sadness. My chest rose and fell rapidly as I struggled to catch my breath. I needed to calm down so I could think, so I closed my eyes and inhaled, held my breath, then exhaled slowly. When I felt my heart rate finally return to normal, I opened my eyes and looked around. That's when I saw Dre walking out of the store.

I stepped out of my car. He was so busy talking on the phone in front of his car that he didn't even notice me until I was standing right next to his Dodge Charger.

"Hey," I said.

He turned around and saw me. "Yo, I'll see you in a few minutes," he said into his phone, then ended the call.

I stared at him, wondering how long it would take him to acknowledge who I was. I was trying to give him the benefit of the doubt. Maybe he hadn't recognized me because I'd shaved my head and put on a little weight over the past year or so. Or maybe he had recognized me and didn't want to reveal it in front of Diana. But now she wasn't around, so why the fuck was he still acting like a stranger?

He looked at me like I was bothering him. "What's good, man?"

"You're just gonna stand there and act like you don't know who I am?" I snapped.

He frowned and said, "Um, I don't. Have we met somewhere before?"

"You know what, Kennedy? Fuck you. I don't know what kind of game you're trying—"

"What did you call me?" He looked panic-stricken. His eyes widened, and his breath quickened. "What did you just say?"

"I said I didn't know what kind of—"

"No, the name you said."

"I said your fucking name, Kennedy."

"Who the fuck are you?" He stepped closer to me.

I felt a little threatened by the way he was coming at me, but the weird thing was that I was starting to believe he really didn't know me. Maybe he had amnesia or some kind of brain injury from the gunshots.

"It's me. Rio. Don't you know who I am?" I searched his eyes for some sign of recognition, but there was none.

"I . . . I'm—my name isn't Kennedy. I'm not him. I'm Dre. Kennedy is . . . *was* my twin brother." Pain shrouded his face.

All the air left my lungs, and my voice was barely above a whisper. "I'm sorry. I didn't know he had a twin brother."

"How do—how did you know my brother?"

"He worked for my family."

And I was falling in love with him right before he was killed, I thought. I didn't know yet whether that was the kind of thing this guy would want to hear about his brother.

"He was a great guy," I said.

"Yeah, he was." Dre nodded. "Look, I got somewhere to be."

"Oh, my bad. Again, I'm so sorry. I really am."

"It's whatever." Dre shrugged and opened the car door.

I stepped aside and watched him drive away. Then I stood there in the parking lot, unable to move as I tried to wrap my head around what had just happened. *Kennedy had a twin brother.*

My cell phone began vibrating. It was Diana calling.

"Hello."

"Where the hell did you go?" she asked.

"Oh, I had an emergency I had to take care of." I didn't tell her I was in the parking lot because I couldn't handle talking to her in the state I was in.

"Yeah, probably some emergency dick." She laughed.

"Nah, that was probably why you had to go meet with ol' boy in the back room," I said, hoping to get some insight on who Dre was and why he was at the store with her.

"Hell no, never that. That's Corey's business partner. He came to pick up the bank deposit, that's it," she said.

"If you say so." I got back into my car.

Now I was even more intrigued. I was already on a mission to find out about the weight Corey was moving out of the boutique. The fact that Kennedy's brother was also involved just made everything that much deeper.

"So, are you going to hang out with me tonight or what?" Diana asked.

Hanging with Diana at the club would be the perfect opportunity to gather some more information. I was determined to show Orlando that the moves I was making were solid.

"Fine. I'll turn the fuck up with you and your baby sis, I guess."

Corey

19

I had just left the gym when I got a text from Diana: Everything is a go. I'll be bringing Rio to the club tonight.

After Marcus tried the Sprinkles, he couldn't stop raving about how good the shit was. So, I didn't waste any time hitting Diana up so I could see what this dude Rio was about to see if I could get in on the action.

I remembered the night she brought him to VIP. He seemed nice enough, and there was no mistaking his sexuality: he was obviously gay and proud. Because of this, I'd tried my best to ignore him. When it came to openly gay men, I made it a point not to be too friendly. But now, this was about business, so I had to make an exception as I sometimes had to do with Pierre.

The question now was whether I would tell Dre what was going on. Maybe I would just wait. After all, I didn't have enough information yet: cost, quantity, nothing. So, I didn't have anything to tell. Then there was also the fact that Dre hadn't really been forthcoming with information for me lately either. He still hadn't said shit to me about meeting those dudes Marcus told me about.

I thought about it for a few minutes, but ultimately, I decided to at least give him a heads up that Rio would be at the club. Dre's ass could be so disrespectful sometimes, especially with gay dudes, and I didn't want him saying anything that would make Rio uncomfortable. If Rio's drugs were as good as Marcus said, I didn't want Dre insulting him before we could make a business deal.

I checked my watch. It was four o'clock, around the time he usually made the afternoon deposit. I left the gym parking lot and headed to the bank to see if I could catch him.

Dre was just leaving the bank when I pulled up. I parked behind his car, but he looked so into his own thoughts that he didn't even notice my car as he approached. I could tell something was wrong from the frown on his face.

"Shit," I swore under my breath. We'd been so careful over the past few months, always making sure our deposits were below the limit that would set off bells for the Feds. Seeing the tension in his face gave me cause for concern.

"Dre!" I called out. He finally looked up.

"Hey," he said and walked over to my car.

I opened the door and got out. "What's wrong?"

"Huh? Nothing. Why?" He frowned at me.

"I mean, you lookin' stressed, like something's wrong. Did something happen in the bank?" I asked.

"Nah, everything's good. I just got a lot on my mind, I guess." He couldn't make eye contact. Something was up.

"You sure?" I peered at him.

"Positive." He handed me the receipts from the deposit he just made. "See for yourself. Money's looking good."

I glanced at the slips of paper with a sense of relief and then handed them back to him. "A'ight, man."

He raised an eyebrow and asked, "So, you came here to check the deposits? You checking behind me now?"

"Hell nah. I needed to holla at you for a minute."

"Well, you found me. What's up?"

Dre was acting so strange that for a second, I had almost forgotten why I was looking for him in the first place. "I just wanted to give you a head's up about this guy that's coming to meet with me to—"

He interrupted me. "I ain't coming tonight. Whoever it is, you're gonna have to handle it."

"I—oh . . . I don't have a problem handling it. I was just trying to—"

"I'm heading out of town, and I'll be gone a few days. I already told your boy Marcus to hold shit down till I come back," Dre said, confirming what Marcus had already mentioned. But Dre didn't say why or where he was going.

"You told Marcus?" I said, knowing that Dre would read between the lines and understand that I was not happy about this shit.

"He's who you put in charge, ain't he?" I detected a little sarcasm in his tone, and I clenched my jaw to keep from snapping back at him.

"I did," I told him. I needed to remain calm while I tried to figure out what the hell Dre was up to.

"He's gonna keep doing the pickups on the south side and make sure they're good. I won't be gone that long."

Dre seemed to zone out for a second.

"Dre, you sure nothing's wrong?" I asked him again.

"Nah, I just ran into . . . met this . . ." His words drifted off, unfinished, as his eyes wandered over the parking lot.

"Who?" I pressed.

"Nobody. Look, I gotta hit the road. I'll check in with you in a couple of days." He turned and walked toward his car.

I had more questions, but I decided not to pry. I got back into my SUV and moved so he could back out of his parking space. Dre definitely had some shit going on that he wasn't telling me, but I had my own shit going on. All my energy needed to be focused on getting a supply from this guy Rio before Pierre took over the whole damn market.

"Damn." I gave a low whistle as Diana stepped into the VIP section. She took off her white denim jacket, and her form-fitting magenta dress, which barely covered her ass, had everyone staring.

"You like?" Diana winked at me.

"Hell yeah," I said, giving her a hug and grabbing her ass for show since folks were looking at us.

"I'm glad," she said, then turned toward the two people who were with her. "Corey, this is my younger sister, Mona."

"Wow, I can see beauty runs in the family," I said. I could see why Dre had made a move on her.

"Thank you." Mona flashed a pretty smile.

"And you remember Rio, right?" Diana said.

"What's good, Rio?" I extended my hand.

"Good seeing you again." Rio's grip was a little more masculine than I had expected, especially considering the ensemble he was wearing: ankle-length black pants, a tight-ass silk shirt, and a pair of Giuseppe Zanotti studded loafers that I'd been eying at Saks. This was the kind of outfit I might wear sometimes if I could afford to be out and proud.

"What are y'all drinking?" I offered as I led them toward the bar.

"Whatever you're buying," Rio said.

"Don't let Rio fool you, Corey. He has coins and lots of them." Diana laughed.

"Not true," Rio said. "Chic World done took most of the coins that I had."

"That's money well spent. We do appreciate our customers. Right, boss?" Diana nudged me.

I put my arm around her and pulled her to me. "We do. But Rio is my guest, and so is Mona, so drinks are on me all night."

"Wait! You're Diana's boss?" Mona sounded excited.

"He is the boss here," Diana answered before I could. "He owns Wet Dreams."

"Oh, wow." Mona grinned.

"Now, let's get these free drinks." Diana grabbed her sister's hand and pulled her away from me. I would have to ask her later what that was all about.

Two rounds later, we were all talking, laughing, and having a good time. I made sure Diana stayed next to me as I tried to get a feel for Rio by asking general questions.

"So, where are you from, Rio?"

"New York," he said. "Born and raised."

"I see. And what brings you to B'more?"

He glanced around the club, nodding his head to the beat for a few. Was he hesitating, or just feeling the music? I couldn't tell.

"Just a little getaway, so to speak. I had a little time on my hands," he finally said. "I'd never been here before, so I decided to check it out."

Diana must've picked up on what I was trying to do, so she jumped in to help. "Rio, I've been meaning to ask, what the hell is it that you do?"

Rio paused again. I shot Diana a look to see if she was also noticing his hesitation. She sipped her drink and smiled at me, looking unconcerned. Since she knew the guy better than I did, I decided to just sit back and see how this played out.

"I'm an investor, and I own a couple of businesses," he said.

"Sounds a lot like you, Corey." Diana nodded. "Speaking of business, where's Dre?"

"He's out of town," Mona volunteered.

Diana didn't even try to hide the frown on her face. Mona must have picked up on it too, because she changed the subject in a hurry.

"This is my jam! Come on, Diana, let's go dance."

Diana looked over at me, and I told her, "Go ahead and take her down. Come on, Rio. Let's go have a Cuban in my office. You smoke?"

"Sure. I'm up for anything tonight," he said playfully.

My stomach did a flip. Was he flirting with me? Did he pick up on some vibe that told him I'd be cool with that? I hoped like hell this was just the way he was with everyone.

"This is a dope space," Rio said when he entered my office.

"Yeah, it's taking me a minute to get it the way I want it, but it's getting there," I told him.

"Is that an Ervin Johnson?" He stepped closer to the painting that hung behind my desk.

"You know your black art, huh?" Reaching into the humidor on my desk, I took out two fresh cigars and passed one to him.

"Damn right I do," he said. "I've been thinking about commissioning one myself."

Interesting. I was starting to think Diana was right about this guy having money. You don't just go commissioning artwork unless you have a few coins.

"Guillotine or punch?" I asked, giving Rio a choice of cutters.

"I'm a V-cutter man." He took a seat in one of the chairs facing my desk.

"Damn, dude, you a G, huh?" I laughed, passing the V-cutter I kept just in case someone preferred it.

Rio laughed. "Contrary to popular opinion, I ain't no punk."

"I see that," I told him. We lit our stogies, and smoke filled the room.

"So, tell me what kind of business you're in," I said after a few minutes of silence.

Rio took a long puff of his cigar and eyed me like he was trying to read my intentions. All he said was, "Family business."

Diana

20

For it to be Mona's first time at a club, she sure seemed like a pro on the dance floor. The flirtatious diva in the middle of the dance floor, hitting all the latest dance moves was different from the Bible-toting, Sunday-school-teaching introvert whose bedroom was right down the hallway from mine. As she swayed to the music, she caught the attention of quite a few guys.

"Okay, I need another drink," I said, pulling her off the floor.

"OMG, that was so much fun!" Mona laughed.

"Yes, it was." I couldn't help but laugh along with her. Her excitement was contagious, and I was glad that she was having fun.

We found two empty spaces at the bar. "You got some moves, girl. I have to admit, I'm kinda surprised. I wasn't expecting you to be out there like that."

"Believe it or not, the kids teach me a lot—especially the after-school ones. They always say 'Miss Mona, this is the cool dance. Come and do this!' Most of the time I feel like I look crazy, but I guess I learned a little something."

"Oh, you learned a lot."

"What's up, Di? You want Riesling or Moscato tonight?" asked Freddy, one of my favorite bartenders.

"How about two Cosmos?" I asked.

"Coming right up." He winked at me and went to mix our drinks.

Mona smiled at me, obviously impressed. "Wow, sis. The bartender knows you like that, huh? You must be a real VIP."

I waved away her comment. "Please, he's just good at his job."

She gave me a skeptical look. "Nah, it's more than that."

When he returned with our drinks, Mona reached for her wallet.

Freddy looked at her like she was crazy. "You're with her, right?"

"Yeah?" Mona said, sounding confused.

"No charge."

"Take it as a tip, Freddy," I said.

"Nah, Di. You know better than that. Let me know if y'all need anything else."

"Okay, what the hell is going on, Di?" Mona asked when he was gone.

"What?" I took a sip of my drink.

"It's like you have a secret life that I don't know about. First, Ashton, and now tonight, people are treating you like you're a celebrity, and you're all boo'd up with your boss."

"I *am* a celebrity." I laughed.

"I'm serious, Di."

"Well, first of all, Corey and I aren't boo'd up. Let's get that straight," I told her.

She rolled her eyes. "Oh, really? I can't tell. His hands are all over you. Is that your boyfriend? Is that why Ashton was mad?"

"No, he's not my boyfriend, and no one is thinking about Ashton's white ass," I snapped. "But, since we're sitting here playing twenty-one questions, it's your turn. How the hell did you know Dre was out of town?"

Mona's eyes widened, and she took a long swallow of her drink.

"Oh, no, you're not that damn thirsty." I took the martini glass from her hand and put it on the bar. "Answer the question."

"Fine." Mona took a deep breath. "He told me."

"Told you when?" I could feel my anger rising.

"A couple of hours ago when he was getting on the road. He wanted me to know so I wouldn't be looking for him." Mona shrugged like it was no big deal.

"You only met him for a few minutes in the store. How the hell did he get your number?"

"He doesn't have my number."

"Then how the hell did he get in contact with you?"

"Instagram. He slid into my DMs."

I leaned my head back and groaned. "Your DMs."

"Yeah, I took a pic while I was in the boutique yesterday and tagged my location. That's how he found me on IG. Isn't that romantic?" Mona had the nerve to be blushing.

"No, that's stalkerish! Don't you see how creepy that is? And I told you to stay away from him." I shook my head, wanting to add that I'd also told him to stay the fuck away from her too, and neither one of them was listening.

"It's not like I talked to him or anything. He just jumped in my inbox to let me know. If you think about it, it's kinda polite." She finished her drink. "I think he's nice."

"He's not. He has an agenda, trust me."

"What's his agenda?" she asked innocently.

"The fact that you don't know what it is just proves my point. You need to stay away from him."

"Okay. . . ."

"Don't respond to any more of his messages. As a matter of fact, block him," I continued.

"Okay, okay," she whined. "I won't."

A handsome guy walked up to us. "Excuse me, beautiful ladies. I hate to interrupt your conversation, but I'd like to buy you both a drink if you don't mind."

I turned to get a better look at him, but his attention was clearly on Mona, who stared back with big doe eyes. They were smiling at each other, and I could practically feel the electricity between them. I'd seen him before, here in the club, on more than a few occasions. He'd even hit on me a couple of times, but from the way he was gawking at my sister, I could tell I no longer existed in his mind.

"Thanks, we're fine for now," I said, pointing to the glasses in front of us.

"Thanks anyway, though," Mona cooed.

"I'm Troy," he said.

"I know," I told him, even though I wasn't the one he was introducing himself to. "You told me that the last time you tried to buy me a drink."

His shine dimmed a little, until Mona reached out her hand, a dazzling smile still on her face. "I'm Mona. Nice to meet you, Troy."

"The pleasure is mine," he told her, sounding like one of Chick-fil-A's best employees.

"Excuse us, Troy," I said, standing up. "We'll be back."

"Sure thing." He took a couple of steps back. "Hopefully I can find you later, Mo."

"Definitely." Mona nodded at him. If I hadn't pulled her by the arm, forcing her to get up, she'd probably still be sitting there.

As we passed Troy and maneuvered our way through the crowd, she asked, "He was nice—and cute. Why did we leave?"

"Because he's corny. And because I have to pee," I told her.

"Isn't the bathroom that way over there by that sign?" She pointed across the club to the restroom sign near the entrance.

"Ewww, that's the public restroom. I'm not using that." I turned my nose up. "There are private restrooms upstairs for VIP."

"Oh yeah, I forgot you were a celebrity." Mona laughed.

Tay, the security guard who normally worked the door, stood near the bottom of the steps. He moved the velvet rope and let us through. Mona and I were halfway up the steps when, all of a sudden, we heard a commotion, and people started screaming.

"Die, faggot!" a man yelled just as gunshots rang out. Then, all hell broke loose.

I ducked down and scrambled toward the top of the stairs. I reached behind me to grab Mona, but I couldn't feel her. I turned around to look, but she wasn't there. People were panicking, running everywhere.

"Mona! Mona!" I screamed as I scanned the crowd.

"Diana!" I heard Corey's voice. I looked up and saw him reaching for me. Rio was right behind him.

Then, another shot rang out. I turned to see Tay fall to the ground, and I screamed. Corey grabbed me and pulled me up the steps.

"Let me go! I have to find my sister!" I tried to get away, but his grip was too tight. More shots rang out, and I was terrified, sobbing, "Mona! Mona!"

"Get her!" Corey said. Rio grabbed me and held on tight as he pulled me to the floor.

"Get your ass down, Di!" Rio yelled. "You're gonna get yourself killed."

I relented and lay down on the floor, shutting my eyes and covering my ears. *Dear God, please let her be okay,* I prayed silently. There would be no point in me living if anything happened to my sister, especially if it was my fault.

Rio

21

Corey and I were in the middle of discussing business when we heard the first gunshots. He bolted out of his chair and ran out of the office. I was right on his heels as we stepped out into the chaos. Corey pulled his pistol from his waistband, and I took out the one I kept strapped to my ankle. Keeping low, we headed for the stairs, where Corey found Diana, crying and screaming her sister's name.

As he went to grab for her, I looked down the steps just in time to see a guy raising his gun in our direction. My instincts—and years of training as a Duncan—kicked in, and I aimed my firearm at his chest. I pulled the trigger, striking him dead center. He crumpled to the floor.

Huh. Pop would be proud, I thought.

"Get her!" Corey yanked Diana off the staircase and shoved her toward me. She was still screaming her sister's name, struggling to get back to the stairs, so I wrapped her in a bear hug as I pulled her down low for safety.

"Get your ass down, Di! You're gonna get yourself killed!" I tried to control her at the same time I was scanning the area for any more gunmen. When Corey took off down the steps, I moved to stand up for a better view of the dance floor below, but Diana grabbed onto me.

"Rio!" she yelled.

"It's okay. I'm not going anywhere," I assured her, kneeling beside her. She had finally calmed down enough that I wasn't worried she would run.

My heart was racing as fast as hers. I kept my weapon drawn and scanned the VIP area as best as I could from my vantage point on the floor. The screaming had stopped, so I eased over to the balcony to look downstairs. The only people yelling now were Corey and members of his security detail. Everyone else seemed to be gone. Shattered glass sparkled all over the place, and the flipped over table and chairs made it look like we'd been through an earthquake.

"What the fuck! Tay!" Corey screamed. He was standing over the body of the sexy Latino security guard from the door. He was still alive, but he was bleeding and moaning. Two other security guys made their way over. They lifted him up and out the front door. In the distance, sirens wailed, signaling that the police would be there any minute.

"Shit," I said, standing up.

"Get his ass to the hospital!" Corey instructed, rubbing his forehead and pacing back and forth.

"Mona!" Diana moaned. I helped her up, and she pushed past me. "Has anyone seen my sister?" she started yelling as she went downstairs.

"What the fuck!" Corey roared again, looking down at a second body. "Who is this muthafucka?"

"That's the new bar back that started the other night," one of the bartenders answered.

My eyes landed on the motionless guy they were talking about. His gun lay by his side, and there was no doubt that he was dead, courtesy of me. And although I'd blown his ass away in self-defense, I damn sure wasn't going to wait around and give a fucking statement.

"Mona!" Diana screamed again.

This was my cue to leave. I pulled her toward the exit and said, "She's probably outside where everyone else is."

"Get this dead muthafucka outta here too!" I heard Corey yell as we made it out the front door. Maybe sometime I'd tell him about my kill shot, but for now, I just wanted to get the fuck out of there.

Diana was sobbing hysterically as she frantically pushed her way through the parking lot, where people were rushing to their cars and hauling ass away from the club.

"Di, try calling her phone," I suggested.

She ignored me and started yelling for her sister again. "Mona!"

"Di!" I said, grabbing her shoulders to stop her. "Call her fucking phone!"

Snapping out of her hysteria, Diana looked at me with tears in her eyes and mumbled, "My purse is upstairs."

I could see she was about to have a total meltdown, which I didn't want her to do in the parking lot. It would only draw attention to her, and when the cops showed up, she'd be the first one they wanted to talk to. I grabbed her arm and led her to my car. I pulled out of the parking lot just as the first sirens could be heard in the distance.

Diana turned toward me and started flipping out. "Where are you going? I have to find my sister! Turn around! Go back!"

I took out my phone and handed it to her, trying to remain calm. "Diana, call your fucking sister and see where she is. She probably left."

She stared at the phone for a moment. "Shit, I don't know her number."

"I'm telling you she's fine, Di." I tried to comfort her. "You were yelling her name loud enough for the fucking world to hear and she ain't answer. She left. I'm telling you."

"But she's probably looking for me. She's probably scared. Take me back so I can get my purse," Diana snapped. "I have to find her."

"That place is swarming with cops, and they're not gonna let your ass in to get your purse. At this point, it's a crime scene. Call someone and ask for her number. Call your parents."

She whipped her head around and looked at me with genuine fear in her eyes. "I'm not calling my parents. Do you know how late it is? They'll kill me. Shit, they're probably gonna kill me once they find out I took her to a club and there was a fucking shootout."

"Okay," I said. It wasn't worth arguing about that. I had plenty of experience with how much influence parents can have over your life. "Check her social media and see if you can reach her," I suggested, since going to her parents' house to see if Mona went home was out of the question.

"Her Instagram!" Diana gasped, scrolling through the apps on my screen to send her sister a DM.

I drove through the streets, not knowing where I was headed and not having the use of my GPS since Diana had my phone. I stared at the steering wheel and realized for the first time that my hands were shaking. My emotions were all over the place. This wasn't the first shootout I'd been involved in—after all, I was a Duncan and it came with the territory—but it was still unnerving, just the same. One of my reasons for escaping to Baltimore was to get my mind right, and the chaos of the night had taken me back to a mental space I was trying to avoid. Maybe Orlando was right. I wasn't really ready to deal with all of this.

"Hello?" Diana's voice was shaky as she answered my phone. "Huh? Yeah, we're fine. Hold on."

She passed the phone to me, and I saw Pierre's name on the screen. "Hey."

"Oh my God, are you okay? What the hell happened?" Pierre screamed through the phone.

"We're fine. Some dude started shooting at the club. We made it out okay," I told him.

"Where the hell are you now? Do I need to come and get you?"

"No, you don't need to come and get us. We left, but I don't know where we are," I told him.

There was a beep, and I pulled the phone away from my ear to check the caller ID. It was an unfamiliar number, which I didn't usually answer, but I had to this time in case it was Mona.

"Hey, I'll call you right back."

"Okay," Pierre said. "Don't forget."

"I won't." I clicked over to the other call. "Hello."

"H–hello? Rio?" Mona's voice cracked.

"Mona, where—"

Diana snatched my phone. "Mona, where are you? I've been looking all over for you!" she cried. "Who? Oh God, we're on our way."

"What happened?" I asked. "Where is she?"

"She's at Johns Hopkins."

"Siri, give me directions to Johns Hopkins Hospital," I said into my phone.

Fifteen minutes later, we arrived in front of the ER. Diana hopped out as soon as my wheels stopped moving, and she ran inside while I parked.

I sent Pierre a text—We're at the hospital looking for Diana's sister. I'll call you once I know what's going on—before I passed through the double doors of the ER entrance.

Diana rushed up to me breathlessly. "I can't find her. She's not here."

"What do you mean?"

"I mean I can't find her!" Diana snapped at me. "I asked the lady at the desk, and there's no record of her being here."

"Calm down," I said, not caring that it sounded more like a warning than a suggestion. I handed her my phone. "Call her back."

Diana took the phone and redialed the number that Mona had called from. "Mona, we're here at the emergency room. Where the fuck are you? . . . Are you serious? . . . We're in the waiting room now. . . . Well, hurry up!"

"Is she here?" I asked.

"She's in the back," she said.

"And? How bad is it?"

"She's back there with someone else who got hurt," she answered, flopping down into a nearby chair.

"Diana, I know you're upset and your nerves are frazzled, but bitch, you're gonna have to take a few deep breaths and calm down, because I can't take it." I squatted down in front of her and placed my hands on her shoulders, forcing her to look directly at me. "Your sister is safe. You talked to her, and it sounds like she's fine. Now, get your shit together."

Diana closed her eyes and took a few deep breaths, then said, "You're right."

"Okay, you good now?" I asked.

"Yeah, I'm good." She nodded.

I settled into a chair next to her.

She looked at me and asked, "How the hell did you remain so fucking calm?"

What had happened that night was nothing compared to being kidnapped and held at gunpoint, then being right beside my captor when he was killed, but I didn't want to tell her that. I also didn't tell her about standing a few feet away from my potential lover when he was shot, and then hearing his last words whispered in my ear. And although I could never erase the images of those violent encounters from my memory, they provided me with an inner strength that I could draw on in situations like what happened in Wet Dreams. LC and Chippy Duncan made sure that all of their kids had the training and the skills to survive just about anything.

"Let's just say I don't scare easily, bitch. I'm in control at all times," I told her, fighting the memories of Kennedy that now filled my head.

"I don't know how true that is, but I'm grateful." Diana looped her arm through mine.

"Diana!" Mona came through the doors and ran over to us.

"I'm glad you're okay." Diana hugged her tight for a minute, then leaned back and said, "I'm still gonna fuck you up, though. Why the fuck did you leave?"

Mona's words came spilling out. "It was crazy. I was following you up the steps, and then there was all this yelling, and I slipped and fell. I thought I was about to lose my life until I felt someone catch me," she said. "Then they started shooting, and he carried me out of the club."

"Who?" Diana asked.

"Troy!"

"Who the hell is Troy?" I asked.

"The guy that tried to buy us drinks?" Diana looked surprised.

"Yeah, he caught me, but then we fell, and I landed on his arm. Then when the shooting started, he picked me up with his other arm and carried me out the door," Mona said.

"Daaaaaamn!" I was impressed with the heroic actions of whoever this Troy was.

"Right?" Mona nodded toward me. "So, we made it outside, and I was looking for you, and I was gonna go back in, but Troy stopped me. Then I saw that he was hurt, so I offered to drive him to the hospital to get checked out. I mean, it was the least I could do after he saved me, you know? I kept calling and calling you, but you never answered."

"I left my phone in my purse upstairs," Diana told her.

"Where is Troy now? Is he okay?" I asked.

"Yeah, they think it's just a sprain. They're wrapping his arm now. He should be out in a minute," Mona said.

We sat down and waited for him. I wanted to see this super-hero. Twenty minutes later, a fine-ass man with his arm in a sling walked out. Mona ran over and threw her arms around his neck.

"Ouch!" Troy winced and gave her a weak smile.

"Oh, I'm so sorry." Mona stepped back.

"Uh, Troy, I guess I should thank you," Diana told him.

"Man, that was crazy. I can't believe all that went down like that." Troy shook his head. "When I saw ol' boy taking out his gun and heading over to the steps . . . then Mona slipped and fell. And then he started shooting. It all happened so fast."

"I can't believe I fell." Mona looked embarrassed. "It was those heels." She was more concerned with how she looked than the fact that she'd basically just had a near-death experience. She was either incredibly young and silly, or she had nerves of steel.

"I'm glad he was able to catch you," Diana said. Then she looked down and snapped, "Heffa, where the hell are my shoes?"

We all looked at Mona's feet, which were covered by a pair of hospital booties.

"Oh, those. They're in Troy's car."

"Yeah, she broke the heel off one, though, when she tripped," Troy said.

"Those were four-hundred-dollar shoes!" Diana squeaked.

"I almost lost my life. That's priceless," Mona quipped.

Troy got his discharge papers, and we all exited the hospital together. As we walked, I slowed down to walk beside him. "So, did you know the guy with the gun?" I asked.

"Nah, I'd never seen him before, and I've been coming to the club quite often for the past few weeks," Troy said.

"Did you see him before he took out the gun?"

Troy slowed his pace to put a little distance between us and the girls. He lowered his voice. "It was kinda weird. At first, he was working behind the bar. That's when I first saw him. Then, he got a phone call and damn near dropped the bucket of ice he was carrying. He came from behind the bar, and that's when I saw him reaching for his piece and I knew shit was about to go down. He started yelling and shit at the security dude about gay people."

"That's wild," I said.

"Yeah, if I ain't know no better, I would think whoever called him told him to make a move," Troy said.

There was no doubt in my mind that this was a designated hit. The gunman didn't go after anyone else in the club. He was aiming straight for the VIP section. The question was, who was his intended target? Was it me, or someone else?

Corey

22

To say I was stressed would be an understatement. My head was pounding as hard as my heart, and I felt like I could pass out at any moment. But I didn't have time for that. I was too busy giving orders and making sure there wasn't a trace of blood on the floor where the bodies of Tay and the shooter had lain moments earlier. No doubt the police would be doing a thorough investigation of the entire premises, and I needed to be ready. While the downstairs was being handled, I rushed upstairs to my office to make sure any and everything resembling narcotics was put away in the wall safe hidden in the closet where it wouldn't be found.

I heard a loud voice downstairs yelling, "Who's in charge here?" I straightened myself up and went down to speak with the cops who'd just come in.

They spent a couple of hours interviewing the few witnesses they could find, taking statements and going through the mess in the club. As far as all the witnesses were concerned, a lone gunman had attempted to get into VIP, and when Tay wouldn't allow it, he called him a gay slur, shot him, and ran out of the club before anyone could catch him. I was grateful my staff was so well-trained. I didn't know about the part where the guy called Tay a faggot until I heard one of the bartenders telling it to the cops. I couldn't be sure if it was true or just something he made up as part of the cover story for the cops, but I had a pit in my stomach over it. Did this shit have anything to do with my father and what he said last time I saw him? The worst part was I couldn't ask the bartender about it, because the thug I was pretending to be wasn't supposed to give a shit about that.

"It's safe to say we'll be closed for a few days," I said to the officer in charge. "I can't believe this. We've never had any type of incident like this. Just a shoving match every now and then. Our security staff is trained."

"Yeah," he said, taking a final look around. "And we don't have any records of this being a trouble spot, that's for sure. We'll be on the lookout for the gunman and keep you posted, but we really don't have that much to go on. I wouldn't get my hopes up."

I tried to look sincere as I said, "Yeah, I guess I really should have had those security cameras fixed a long time ago." The monitor for the custom system was in my office, and it was designed to be easily disabled for situations just like this. I would turn that shit back on as soon as the cops were gone. Knowing that the corpse of the shooter and the bloody rags from our quick cleanup were in the trunk of a car in the back parking lot, I was more than happy to see them leave. I gave the cop a thank-you that was just as fake as their promise to look for the perpetrator. They wouldn't do shit; he knew it, and I knew it.

When the uniformed officers were finally gone, I took out my phone and checked out all the calls that I'd missed. I called the number that was most important, deciding to go ahead and get the conversation over with.

"What the fuck happened?" Dre yelled.

"Bad news travels fast, huh?" I asked. "Don't worry. I handled everything."

"I can't be away for one fucking night without shit jumping off." Dre sounded frustrated and not the least bit worried. "So, a muthafucka just came through shooting?"

I wanted to say "I'm fine. Thanks for asking, muthafucka," but instead I answered, "Something like that, but like I said, I handled it."

"How did he even get past fucking security? Who was working the door? Was it Tay's big ass? I told you he was soft. Just because a muthafucka is big doesn't mean he's hard."

I walked behind the bar and poured myself a much-needed shot, throwing my head back to gulp it down. "Dre, he didn't even come through the front. He's some new bar back that had just started working. And he's dead."

"He's what? Dead? Shit, now we have to deal with a fucking murder investigation? The cops are gonna be all over the place, Corey."

"The cops have already come and gone, and as far as they know, there was no murder. There wasn't even a body. I told you I handled it." I poured a second shot.

"I can't believe you killed him." Dre seemed like he wasn't comprehending what I was saying.

"Dre, will you fucking listen to me? I didn't kill anyone."

"You said he was dead."

"Yeah, but I ain't kill him. Rio did. And we got rid of the body before the cops got here." I said it slower this time so his stupid ass would understand.

There was a brief silence, and for a second, I thought I'd lost my signal until Dre finally said, "Who?" real quiet-like.

"Rio. He's a friend of Diana and Pierre," I told him. "He was here when everything popped off, and dude was aiming for me. Rio covered me and took him out with one fucking shot."

"You've gotta be kidding me."

"What's wrong?"

"Corey, stay the fuck away from him. Don't talk to him, and don't deal with him, period."

"Dre, what the fuck are you saying? Do you know Rio or something?" I asked, curious as to why he was so adamant about this guy. From what I could tell from our brief conversation, Rio seemed like a decent dude and a smart businessman.

"I don't know him, but I know of him," Dre said.

"What the fuck does that even mean?" I said, leaning down to pick up one of the fallen barstools and sitting on it.

"Rio is a Duncan."

"Okaaaay?" I was losing patience with his mystery bullshit. My head was pounding, my nerves were shot, and I was tired. "Dre, listen. Maybe we need to have this conversation in the morning when I can think straight, because right now, what you're saying ain't making sense."

"Let me make it real clear, Corey." Dre's voice became serious. "The Duncans were who my brother was working for a couple of years ago, and that's why he's dead. Rio Duncan and his family caused Kennedy's death."

I dropped the bottle of whiskey I was getting ready to pour from, sitting there in shock for a minute, remembering the story of Corey's twin brother. He was shot and killed in New York a couple of years ago, but I never really got the facts behind his death. Dre never really spoke about it. That was when Dre and my father became close. My father could relate because his own brother had been murdered. It was one of the things that bonded the two of them.

I was totally confused. Rio's family had something to do with Kennedy's death, and now he was here in Baltimore, hanging around Diana like they were besties. Was that some type of plot to get close to me and Dre? And if it was, then why? Before Dre gave me this news, I was going to call Rio to thank him for having my back that night. Now, I wasn't sure what to do.

Diana

23

*The gunshots were happening all around me, and the scream-
ing was so loud I couldn't think. All of a sudden, I felt myself
being grabbed from behind and pulled down to the ground. Then,
I saw the shooter standing over me, gun pointed at my head. I
was about to die.*

*"Please," I begged. "Please don't do this!" I started sobbing
uncontrollably.*

"Di! Diana!" My mother's voice was panicked. I felt her shaking
me, and I realized I'd been having a nightmare.

I sat up in my bed, gasping for air. My head and neck were
covered in sweat. "Huh?"

"Lord have mercy, girl. Breathe." She sat on the edge of the bed
and began rubbing my back.

"I . . . I had a bad dream."

"I know. You were crying out in your sleep for the past ten
minutes. You done woke your daddy up, and you know he gotta
be to work early," she said. "What's going on with you?"

"I'm sorry, Momma." I leaned against her. "What time is it?"

"Almost five. Almost dawn, but only an hour later than when
you came home."

I closed my eyes and prayed that she was too tired to go into
a full lecture, which was the last thing I needed right now. Last
night had been hell, and now I was reliving it as I tried to sleep.

"I'm sorry, Ma. I didn't mean to come in so late," I told her.

"Not only did you disrespect my house, Diana, but you had
your sister disrespecting it too. It's bad enough she ain't go to
work the last two days. Now, I know you're grown, and I don't
have a problem with you living here as long as you want to, but
I've told you time and time again that if you stay here, you—"

"Momma, I know," I told her, falling back down on my pillow. I'd come home late unnoticed on more than one occasion. Hell, I rarely made it through the side door before three on a regular night that I went out. But because Mona had gone out with me this time, my mother had probably tried to wait up or at least listen out for our return.

"I don't try to be all up in your business, Diana, and I don't know what's got you spooked out of your sleep, but you need to get it together. Now, you wanna tell me what's going on?" Momma stared at me, waiting for an answer. She was beautiful, even in a headscarf, nightshirt, and no makeup, which she hardly wore except to church. But beneath that beauty was a woman who was tough as nails and wouldn't hesitate to beat my ass if she knew where I had taken my sister—and what had happened there.

I looked away, not knowing if she had already talked to Mona while I was sleeping. My sister's relationship with our mother was much closer than mine, and she might have cracked under the pressure of Momma's interrogation. I was more of a Daddy's girl. I wasn't going to put myself in a position to be caught in a lie, so I just said, "I'm fine. Nothing's wrong, Ma."

"There's something going on with you, Diana." My mother's intuition had probably told her something was wrong, and then my nightmare just confirmed it for her. She stood up and looked around my room. Designs that I'd drawn and pictures out of style magazines hung on the walls, along with clothing items I'd created or started on. I knew she was about to fuss about my room being a mess. That was normally next on her list.

I sighed. "Momma, please. I'm going to clean my room this weekend. Thanks for coming to check on me. I'm sorry I woke you and Daddy up."

"Get some sleep, girl." To my great relief, she leaned down and kissed my forehead, turned off the light, and finally left my room.

I pulled the covers over my shoulders. As much as I loved living rent free and being able to stack my money, I really needed to start thinking about moving out.

"Diana?" The light came back on, and Mona entered my room. "You 'sleep?"

"Bitch, you know I ain't 'sleep," I whispered. "I know you heard Momma in here."

Mona came and sat in the same spot where my mother had been. "What did she say? Was she mad?"

"Stop asking me questions you already know the answer to, Mona."

"Yeah, she came in my room last night, fussing and asking questions."

I sat up and looked at her. "Shit. I knew it. And what did you tell her?"

"I didn't tell her anything. She asked where we went and why we came home so late. I told her out with some of your friends and then to get pancakes." Mona shrugged.

"Pancakes?" I laughed.

"It was the only thing I could think of. I figured that's what people normally do after they leave the club. That is when they haven't been in a shootout like the OK Corral, of course." She shook her head. Even though she was joking, I could see the lingering fear in her face.

"That's not what normally happens, Mona. And I'm truly sorry all of that went down while you were there. I wanted you to have a good time and enjoy yourself." I reached out and touched her arm. "Are you okay, really?"

Mona had been fairly quiet on the ride home. At the time, I was glad because I was still trying to process everything that had gone down myself. We'd narrowly escaped death, and I'd seen a dead man lying on the floor. I was so caught up in my own thoughts that it didn't even dawn on me to make sure my younger, more naive, inexperienced-at-partying sister was okay mentally.

"I'm okay. I think I'm still in a little bit of shock, but I'm good. You would think that I'd be a lot more freaked out, but I'm not. That probably has a lot to do with Troy, though." Mona climbed under the covers, and I moved over. "He was so nice and sweet. I feel horrible for breaking his arm. I'm going on a diet starting today."

"You didn't break his arm. It's sprained. But I'm glad he was there to rescue you," I said.

"My very cute rescuer." Mona giggled.

"Oh, Lord." I groaned. "Here we go. Just yesterday you were geeked over Dre. Now it's Troy."

"Dre wasn't there to rescue me. Troy was," Mona said. "Why are you acting like this?"

"Like what?" I frowned.

"Like you don't want me to do anything or go anywhere. You think you're the only one around here who wants a life?"

"No, I don't think that at all."

"I can't tell." Mona stood up.

I was going to stop her but then decided there was no point. The last thing I wanted to do was get into an argument with her. Momma's bionic ears would overhear us and be back in the room in a second. Besides, I was tired.

I got up and turned off the light that Mona had left on, climbed back into bed, and drifted off to sleep. When I woke up hours later, I headed down the hall to Mona's room to talk. I didn't feel right about the way our conversation had ended, and I wanted to make sure we were good.

I knocked on her door, but there was no answer. I turned the knob and eased the door open, peeking my head in and calling her name before stepping inside. I looked around. Unlike my room, Mona's was neat, and everything was in place. Her bed was perfectly made, and she was nowhere to be found.

I stepped back into the hallway and listened for her voice, thinking she may have been somewhere else in the house with my mom, but I didn't hear her. I went back into my room and glanced out the window, looking for her car, but it was gone.

Just as I picked up my phone to call her, Corey texted me: Don't open the boutique today. Meet me at the club. And don't talk to Rio until I talk to you.

I didn't know what was up with that, but I figured it had something to do with the shooting last night. I texted back and told him I'd be there as soon as I could.

I dialed Mona's number.

"Hello," she answered.

"Hey, where are you? I went looking for you, but you were already gone."

"Oh, yeah. I had a couple of errands I needed to run this morning, that's all. What's wrong?"

"Nothing's wrong. I just wanted to finish the conversation we started earlier."

"I thought we were finished. I said all I had to say, really."

For a moment, I was taken aback by Mona's tone and her overall dismissive attitude, but I decided to look past it. After all, we both had barely escaped death the night before, and she was probably still dealing with it.

"Hey, that's fine. I just want to make sure you understand that I'm not trying to control you or tell you what to do. I'm just looking out for you, that's all. That's what big sisters are supposed to do, right?"

"Uh, yeah, you're right. And I get it. But, Di, I'm kinda in the middle of something right now. Can I come by the store later and maybe we can talk then?" Mona asked.

"The store isn't opening today," I told her.

"It's not?" She sounded surprised. "Oh, does Corey know you're not opening?"

"He's the one who told me not to open it. I'm heading over to the club to meet with him in a little while."

"Oh, cool. I'll call you later," Mona said, then hung up before I could say anything else.

I sat on the side of my bed, hoping she and I would be able to hash everything out later. My phone rang again. This time it was Rio. Following Corey's instructions, I ignored the call. I looked around my junky room as I got up to find something to wear, making a mental note to straighten up the mess later. Even though I decided I would be moving out soon, I wanted my remaining time there to be as peaceful as possible.

Rio

24

I was too wired to sleep when I finally made it back to my hotel room. I tried calling Corey to make sure he was good, but he didn't answer. I sent him a text that said, Just checking on you. Give me a call.

Pierre was probably asleep, so I didn't try to call him. I sent him a quick text, letting him know I'd made it home. Then, I helped myself to the mini bar and drank while watching HGTV in an effort to get rid of the thought that I'd taken a man's life. The fact that it was in self-defense really didn't matter. As different as I felt from most of my siblings, there was one thing I had in common with all of them: I was a killer. Even when I wasn't involved in family drama and I was miles away from family members, death still had a way of finding me. There didn't seem to be any escaping it. Murder was an undeniable part of the Duncan family dynamic. The darkness in my head that I'd felt lifting a few days ago started creeping back in.

Knock. Knock. Knock.

I'd fallen asleep with my dark thoughts, and now a knock at the door jolted me awake. I jumped up and rubbed my eyes, checking the time. I'd been asleep for hours. Looking through the peephole, I saw a bellhop at my door.

"Yeah?" I said when I opened the door.

"Sorry to disturb you, Mr. Duncan, but this package just arrived by messenger with specific instructions to bring it directly to your room."

I looked down at the small box he was holding and immediately recognized the return label for Duncan Laboratories, along with the word **FRAGILE** in bold lettering on the top.

"Oh, thank you so much. I've been expecting this." I took the box from him.

"No problem, sir."

I reached into my pocket and handed him a twenty-dollar bill and then closed the door. I placed the box on the coffee table and sat on the sofa, staring at it. The excitement of doing my own thing with what was inside was now overshadowed by what had happened at the club the night before. Now, I wasn't sure what I wanted to do.

I picked up my phone. I had two missed calls from Orlando and Pierre, but before reaching out to either one of them, I wanted to call Diana, then Corey. Neither one picked up or responded to the text messages I sent.

I took a quick shower to clear my head, then called my brother.

"I got the package," I told him.

"Good. I saw where it was delivered. My suggestion is to not sell all of them to this guy. Just let him get a few at a time until we get a better feel for who he is and what he's about. And after we find out more about his other supplier," Orlando said.

"I met Corey last night."

"Damn, that was fast."

"I told you it wouldn't take long."

"Well, what did you find out?"

"Corey owns a club called Wet Dreams. I met him, and he seems decent." I purposely left out the part about saving Corey's life and killing some guy. No need to get Orlando all worked up about something that probably had nothing to do with me—or at least I hoped it didn't.

"But I'm not going to rush into anything just yet. Don't worry," I told him.

"Rio, is everything okay? You sound weird."

"Nah, I just got up, that's all. I'm still kinda out of it. You know I'm out here enjoying the party scene, and I'm not an early riser like the rest of you." I pretended to laugh.

"Well, a'ight, if you say so. I did get some info about this guy Pierre."

I held the phone closer to my ear. "What did you find out? Anything we need to be concerned about?"

"Everything you told me checked out, other than his name."

"His name?"

"Yeah, his legal name is Peter, not Pierre. Seems like he inherited the bar and a whole lot of money and other property from his lover who died about a year ago. He's pretty loaded, that's for sure."

"A'ight, that's good." I was relieved to hear that Pierre had told me the truth, even if he had changed his name a little. I mean, Pierre was a more intriguing name than just plain old Peter. Who doesn't want to be more intriguing?

"I'm gonna see what else I can find out about this dude Corey he was dealing with, and I'll get back to you in a couple of days," Orlando said, then hung up.

I picked up the box and placed it into the hotel safe, next to the gun I'd used the night before. I went to get dressed, because I needed to go find something to eat, and then I would go by the boutique to check on Diana.

My phone rang again before I finished choosing my outfit. This time it was my sister.

"What the fuck is going on?" Paris yelled in my ear.

"Nothing, I'm chilling. Why?" Had she somehow heard about what happened at Wet Dreams? Paris kept her ear to the streets, and even though I hadn't told her I was in Baltimore, there was a slight possibility that she'd found out. I wouldn't put it past my sister to have some kind of connection down here that I didn't know about. That bitch had dudes in every city willing to anything for her. For all I knew, she had one of them keeping an eye on me.

To my relief, that wasn't the case.

"Because Orlando just asked me if I'd talked to you. He's been asking that a lot lately, which we both know he never does. So, that means either you've talked to him, or someone has said something to him about you. Either way, what the fuck is going on?"

I sighed. "Nothing's going on."

"Liar."

"I'm not lying, Paris," I lied. "What's going on with you?"

"Don't even try it, Rio. Something's going on. Where are you, anyway?"

"I told you, I just needed to get away. I should be home in a little while."

"Little while like a couple of hours, days, weeks?"

"No, not hours or days, that's for sure." I laughed. "But I'll be home soon."

"Are you boo'd up? You must be. That's what it is, isn't it?" Paris squealed. "You met a boo jank!"

I sighed. "Fine, it's something like that."

"I knew it! So, tell me. Who is it? Are you in love?"

"His name is Pi—Peter, and he's really nice. He treats me like I'm god damn royalty, Paris. And you should see his penthouse. It's amazing." I lay back on the bed and began telling her about the past few dates I'd had with Pierre, in an effort to both satisfy her curiosity and distract me from visions of the night before. Talking about him also made me realize how much I did like him.

"Rio, he sounds incredible. Is the sex amazing? Did he rock your world?" She laughed.

"No sex yet," I admitted.

"What? Oh, shit! This must be love."

"I ain't saying all that, but I am really feeling him."

"So, when do I get to meet this Peter? Wait, is he white?"

"No, he isn't white. Why would you think that?"

"I don't know that many black men with the name Peter. Hell, the only Peters I know are Peter Griffin and Peter Brady from television," she joked.

"You're a damn fool, Paris."

"You act like you don't already know that. Besides, we act just alike. So, when do I get to meet Peter? Are you bringing him home when you come?"

"Hell no! Why would I do that? Are you crazy? Have you lost your damn mind?" I sat up and said in a voice nearly two octaves higher than normal.

"No, I'm just saying if he's special, you should bring him home and let the family meet him," Paris said innocently.

"Fuck you, Paris."

"Why it's gotta be all that?" she snapped.

"Have you ever met anyone special and brought his ass home? You're trying to be funny."

"I'm not. I was trying to be supportive and helpful. But what the fuck ever, Rio. You go and have fun doing whatever the fuck it is you're doing with whoever the fuck you're doing it with." She hung up.

The conversation went left so fast that I almost felt bad. But I knew my sister too well. The last thing she was trying to be was helpful or supportive. She was trying to be messy. It would never be simple for me to just bring a guy home like that, and she knew it. Even if my parents loved me, my sexuality would always make certain parts of our relationship difficult. No matter how much I enjoyed getting to know Pierre, if we ended up falling in love, being together would have its limitations. And was love even worth it if it couldn't be limitless?

Speaking of Pierre, my phone rang, and his name showed up on the screen. In the mood Paris had left me, I was tempted to just ignore his call. But I knew he was calling to make sure I was okay after last night. My family issues were not his problem. So, I answered the call.

"Hello."

"Hey, you. I was starting to get worried," Pierre said. "Are you okay?"

"Yeah, I'm good. Just getting up and getting out of the shower," I told him.

"Sounds tempting. Is that an invitation?" He laughed.

"I wish, but not this time."

"I can't believe there was a shooting at the club. I heard Tay got hit."

"Yeah, he did. I need to call Diana and see if she's heard anything. I tried reaching Corey, but he didn't answer. I'm going to try and call him a little later. I'm sure he's pretty busy, but I just wanna make sure he's good," I told him. "That shit went down so fast, and then afterward he was giving orders, but I could see he was a little shaken. I was trying to get Diana under control to help out."

"Wait, so you were with Corey when the shooting happened?" Pierre asked.

"Yeah, we were all upstairs in VIP."

"Rio, were you the guy who came out of the office with him?"

I paused for a moment before answering, then said, "Yeah, we went into his office just a few minutes before to smoke a cigar. We'd just lit up when we heard the commotion."

"Oh, shit! I heard there was a guy that came out the office, but I didn't realize it was you," Pierre said.

"Yeah, it was me."

"I wonder why he didn't mention that," Pierre said.

"What do you mean?" I asked.

"He called me a little while ago."

"Really?" Hearing that Corey had called Pierre but hadn't responded to my calls or texts raised a red flag—a big one. Something was off. Everything had been fine, and I'd saved his life, but now he was suddenly ghosting me.

"Yeah, he said we needed to talk later and he'd come by the club. He's not opening tonight, so he probably wants to see if he can do business here. I don't think I want that to happen." Pierre sighed.

When I didn't say anything, he said, "Hello, Rio, you still here?"

"I'm here."

"My bad. I thought I lost a signal or something."

"Nah. My mind was just somewhere else."

"Well, what are you doing for the rest of the day? Do you wanna do lunch or something?"

"I have some running around to do, but I'll call you later. What time are you meeting with Corey?" I asked.

"I don't know exactly. I just hope he's not on some bullshit like Dre usually is. I can't be bothered."

Dre. As soon as Pierre said the name, I realized what, or rather who, was most likely behind Corey's sudden "unavailability." Dre must have said something about me, especially if Corey had mentioned I'd been at the club with him. That had to be it.

"Well, listen. I gotta get ready to get out of here," I told Pierre.

"Okay, I got a lot to get done too. Wet Dreams might be closed for a couple of days, which means more business for Oz. We're gonna be packed tonight, so I gotta make sure we're ready," Pierre said. "Speaking of which, you have any more goodies for me, by chance?"

I thought about the box that the bellboy had just delivered. With the crowd that Pierre was expecting the next couple of days, I had no doubt we would be able to sell what I had and then some. But I was still uneasy.

"I'll get back with you on that," I said.

"Okay, well, either way, I want to see you, so let's plan to meet up tonight at the bar. Then you can come over to my place for a late-night snack."

"That sounds like an offer I can't refuse," I said. "Call me after your meeting with Corey."

"Will do."

When the call ended, I quickly got dressed. I thought about grabbing my pistol out of the safe, then decided I wasn't going to need it. While waiting for the valet, I tried calling Diana again, but she didn't answer. Luckily, I remembered she'd used my phone to reach her sister. I hit redial on the last unfamiliar number in my phone.

"Hello?" Mona answered.

"Hey, Mona, it's Rio. I'm trying to reach Diana, but she's not answering. Is she home?" I asked.

"Nope, she's not."

"Okay, I'll go over to the boutique and see her there," I told her.

"She's not opening today. Corey called and told her not to open up. They're actually over at the club, I believe. She went to meet him there like ten minutes ago." Mona gave me all the information I needed without even realizing it.

"Thanks, Mona."

I damn near pushed the Asian valet out of the way as soon as he got out of my car.

"Excuse you, Mr. Duncan!" He rolled his eyes at me.

"Sorry," I said as I climbed in. "I'm late for a meeting."

"I see." He nodded curtly without giving me the flirtatious smile he normally did. I'd give him an extra tip next time I saw him, and a better apology. Right now, I had somewhere to be.

Corey

25

"I'm heading back later tonight."

"I thought you were gonna be gone a couple of days," I said to Dre. "You don't have to rush back if you're somewhere handling business. I got everything under control here."

"Have you heard from that muthafucka Rio?"

"No, I haven't." After what Dre had told me last night about Rio's family connection to Kennedy's murder, I'd been avoiding him. He called and sent a couple of text messages, but I didn't respond to any of them. "But, Dre, the man saved my life, though. I at least owe him a conversation."

"You don't owe him shit. And real talk, I wouldn't be surprised if that whole situation last night was set up by him. You don't think it's kinda strange that he pops up and all of a sudden there's a fucking shooting at the club?" Dre asked.

"I don't know," I said. "I mean, he was probably just trying to get to the safe. It was a dude who worked for us. He was hired before Rio even came around."

"That don't mean nothing. Rio was probably hanging around the boutique, trying to get on Diana's good side at the same time his man was being hired at the bar. If it woulda been a fucking robbery, don't you think he woulda had somebody with him?" Dre said skeptically. "Nah, Corey, this was a hit, and it was probably set up by that muthafucka Duncan."

"Then why did Rio take the guy out?" I asked.

"He was probably gonna take his ass out anyway. Come on, think about it. The timing is just too perfect to be a coincidence. I'm telling you, he had something to do with it."

I tried to make Dre's theory add up. He was right about some things, but if Rio wanted to take me out, he could've easily done that himself when we were alone in my office. Then again, there was also the fact that Rio was now supplying Pierre's club drugs. Pierre stood to gain a lot of business since I would be shut down for a couple of days. Were they working together?

"Look, you don't have to cut your trip short. Handle your business. We'll deal with Rio when you get back," I told him.

"Damn right we will. I'll holla back in a little while," Dre said.

I leaned back in my office chair. If life was different, I would be hopping on a plane and heading somewhere tropical for some much-needed rest and relaxation. I had more than enough money to do so, and with the club being closed, I should've been able to. Hell, Dre had no problem going wherever he wanted, whenever, to do God knows whatever, so I should too. Instead, I had to worry about whether the shooting at Wet Dreams was set up by Rio, or maybe even worse, something set in motion by my gay-hating father.

I needed to go back downstairs and help Marcus and Freddy with the cleanup. Just as my hand touched the door knob, there was a knock at the door.

Thinking it was Diana, I snatched it open. "About damn time you got here."

"Um, I didn't know I had a specific time to be here."

Surprised at the sound of the baritone voice, I took a step back. "What's good, Rio?" I cleared my throat. "I thought you were—"

"Diana, I know. But, nah, she's downstairs. I told her I needed to speak to you in private if that's okay." Rio looked over my shoulder like he wanted to get into the office.

"Uh, yeah, that's cool. Come on in." I opened the door so he could step inside.

My eyes widened as he walked past me. Looking at him now, no one would ever suspect that Rio wasn't straight. He had on a pair of designer jeans, a white T-shirt, and a pair of crisp Jordans. To top it off, he wore a black NY Yankees fitted ball cap and his eyes, which were gray the night before, were now dark brown. All that flashy, flamboyant fashion was gone. I damn near had to do a double take to recognize him.

"You, uh, look . . . different."

Rio did a little turn-around. "Yeah, I decided to change it up today. I like to do that from time to time."

I realized I'd been staring, so I turned away from him. "I hear ya," I said with a little extra bass in my voice. "I got your texts, man. It's been crazy around here."

"Understandable, but you'd think you might have a free moment to call the guy who had your back last night. What's up with that?" Rio sat in the same seat as the night before.

I chose not to sit behind my desk. I wanted to maintain some leverage over him because I still wasn't entirely sure whether I could trust him. Leaning on the front of my desk, I said, "Nothin'. Just been making calls, trying to get the place cleaned up."

"You clean up the mess I made last night?" Rio asked.

Obviously, he'd come up the stairs, so he knew the blood was all gone. He was referring to the body and whether we'd gotten rid of it.

"I did. Mess is all clean," I answered, trying to read his body language. There was nothing about his demeanor that suggested he was traumatized from last night, or even slightly shook. This was a guy who'd been around dead bodies before, and that had me wondering, *Who the fuck is this guy?*

"A'ight. Just making sure. I wanted to let you know that I could clean up my own mess if you needed me to. I've made a mess before," he said, confirming what I'd already guessed.

Was Dre's brother one of those messes? I squinted a bit and tilted my head, studying his expression, which gave me no clues.

I looked Rio in the eye and said, "I heard."

Rio sat back, nodding slowly. "So, I guess you had a conversation with Dre."

"Yeah, he told me all about you and his brother and what happened," I lied. Maybe if he thought I already knew, he'd spill some details.

"Kennedy," Rio said, and a pained look came across his face. It definitely wasn't the expression I'd expect if he was the one who killed Kennedy. I was even more confused.

"He says you're the reason Kennedy's dead—that you're the one who killed his brother."

Rio jumped up out of the chair, agitated. "What? That's a lie! I didn't kill Kennedy. He was working security for my fam—

me . . . when he was shot." He stopped pacing and turned to look at me. I swear his eyes were glistening like he was about to cry. "I didn't kill him. But I was there when he died. He took a bullet for me . . ." His voice dropped to almost a whisper as he finished with, "And I loved him."

"You loved him?" I wanted to make sure I'd heard him correctly.

"Well, I could have loved him. But he died before it happened." He collapsed back into the chair.

"Dre's brother was gay? He never told me," I said, shaking my head.

Rio shrugged. "It wasn't anything too many people knew, I guess. But I'm sure you know how that goes."

I felt like I'd been punched in the gut. "What the fuck do you mean by that?"

"I mean what I said. His sexuality wasn't something people knew about, the same way they don't know about yours." Rio stared at me.

"There aint' shit for people to know about mine. I don't know what the fuck your bitch ass is insinuating, but—" I puffed out my chest a little and took a step toward him with my fists clenched.

He dismissed my aggression with a wave of his hand. "Calm down, Corey. All that rah-rah shit ain't needed right now. You don't have to do that shit for me. I get it. That's why when I knew I was coming over here to chop it up with you, I switched it up. I wanted to make sure you were comfortable," Rio said. He was so calm and reserved that it damn near put me at ease. "I know what the deal is. You wanna stay in the closet, that's on you."

"Ain't nobody in the damn closet. You're wrong," I told him.

"Nah, I'm right and you know it. But, like I said, that's on you. I just find it insane that you feel the need to. It's fucking 2018!"

"Shut the fuck up. You don't know shit about me." My anger was boiling to the surface. After all the time I'd spent trying to keep it concealed, how did this muthafucka come in here and figure me out in, like, a day? Was it that obvious? And if he knew, then who else knew and wasn't saying it? I suddenly felt like I was in a lot more danger than I'd realized.

"Do you know who the fuck my father is? You out here talking reckless will get you fucked up, Duncan or not!" I threatened.

Rio stood up suddenly. I squared up, prepared to defend myself if he decided to take a swing. But, to my surprise, he started laughing. I looked at him like he was crazy, but that just made him laugh harder.

"Yo, you're funny as fuck, you know that? Did you really just say I don't know who your father is? Boy, please—and I'm not using that as a term of endearment. I came to talk business with you man to man because your bitch ass was ducking and dodging my calls. But that's fine." He turned and walked toward the door.

When he opened it, I saw Diana standing in the doorway.

"What's up, Di?" Rio said casually, as if he hadn't just blown up my whole world.

"Uh, Rio . . . what . . . why . . .?" She looked past him to me, and our eyes met. I knew she was wondering what the hell was going on, because I'd sent her a text earlier telling her not to talk to Rio if he called, and now, here he was.

"I was just leaving. I'm sure Corey will fill you in, and I'm pretty sure he's gonna tell you not to fuck with me anymore. So, it's cool," Rio said. "I don't want you to get in any trouble, especially with you being his beard and all." The door closed loudly behind him.

Diana stomped over to me and asked, "What the hell was that all about?"

"Nothing," was the only answer I could give her. There was no way I could tell her that Rio had just tried to drag me out the closet. The topic of my sexuality was taboo between me and Diana—we basically never discussed it. I'd been with women before, so I knew enough about fat asses or big titties to comment on them from time to time like they turned me on, but she'd never asked if I was seeing anyone. My cover story in the beginning was that I just didn't trust gold-digging hoes, and that's why I paid her to be by my side at the club, kind of like an insurance policy against them. But I'd never tried to push up on her, either, and now I was wondering if that had been a mistake. Rio and Diana were friends, so he might say something to her now, and if she started thinking too much about our "arrangement," she might realize Rio was right.

I damn sure didn't need him talking to her or anyone else. I had to figure something out before he opened his mouth.

"It was something," she said suspiciously. "First you call me in a panic, tell me to rush down here and not to talk to Rio, and then when I get here, not only is he here, but y'all are arguing."

"We weren't arguing!" I yelled.

She raised her eyebrows and cocked her head back. "*Oh, please.* I heard you yelling before I made it to the top of the steps—the same way you are now."

I took a deep breath. I hadn't even realized I raised my voice. "Damn."

She sat down, leaning forward with a kind look on her face. "So, you wanna explain what's going on?"

"What all do you know about Rio?" I asked, sitting in the seat Rio had just gotten up from. I could still smell his cologne and instantly recognized it as one of my favorites.

"Not much. Shit, we just started hanging out a couple of days ago. I know he has great taste in clothes."

"I'm serious, Di." I knew she was trying to ease the tension, but now wasn't the time for jokes.

Diana's slight smile faded. "Fine. I know he's from New York, and I know he's paid. And I'm thinking because he's supplying Pierre with party favors, that means he's connected to the game. But I don't think he's a dealer. Oh, and he ain't no punk. He proved that last night."

"Well, I know a little more about him than you do," I told her.

"And what's that?" Diana peered at me.

"Rio is the son of LC Duncan. So, being connected to the Duncan family is an understatement. He's a *member* of the family."

"Who's the Duncan family?" she asked. Even though she sold some shit out of the boutique for me, I forgot sometimes that Diana was pretty innocent when it came to the true workings of that world.

"The Duncans are one of the most powerful families in New York. His father, LC Duncan, owns Duncan Motors."

"So, his family sells cars. What's the big deal?" Diana leaned back and relaxed in her chair.

I shook my head. "They sell more than fucking cars. They sell dope—and plenty of it. Rio's family runs one of the biggest narcotics rings in the country."

"Shut the fuck up. Are you serious?" Diana stared at me, wide-eyed with surprise. "The same Rio who just left out of here?"

"The same Rio."

"Wow. I should've sold him more shit. He clearly could afford it."

"He's also a murderer," I told her.

She shook her head adamantly. "What? He killed that dude in self-defense. Hell, if he hadn't, we'd both probably be dead."

"That's not what I'm talking about. According to Dre, Rio's family killed his twin brother, Kennedy."

"Wait. Dre had a twin brother?"

"Yeah."

"I never knew that. And Rio had something to do with his death?" She frowned.

"Yeah, he just sat here and told me he was right there when Kennedy died," I told her, purposely leaving out the fact that Kennedy was protecting Rio when he was shot. It was better for me if she believed Rio was a killer.

"Rio is here to cause trouble, Diana. Taking Pierre's business is just the tip of the iceberg. He's here to take us out. That's why he befriended you."

"Uh-uh. I don't believe that, Corey. Rio didn't even know what I was involved in." Diana shook her head. "There's no way."

"I just told you his family has money, power, and control of the drug game. Don't you think they know what we're doing here in the city? You're talking about the Duncans, the family that took out Sal and Vinnie Dash. Shit, they're probably the reason my father is sitting in prison." I knew the part about my father was a lie. He'd been busted by the FBI, DEA, and ATF, who were after another dealer in the city. Dad had become sloppier in his old age, and his arrest was his own fault.

"Shit, Corey. I'm sorry." Diana sighed. "What are we gonna do?"

"Right now, just stay the fuck away from him. Don't talk to him, period," I told her. "We're just gonna sit tight until Dre gets back. Don't worry, we'll handle it."

"This is so damn crazy. He seemed so cool. What's crazy is I hardly recognized him when he opened that door. He looked so different."

"That's what I'm talking about. He came in here all thugged-out and shit. Maybe that's the real Rio, and all that other flaming shit was the act."

Diana jumped up. "I gotta get to Pierre and tell him."

"I already called and set up a meeting to talk to Pierre later today."

"Nah, I need to talk to him now." She rushed out of the office, and I followed right behind her.

We made it down the steps and were headed toward the front door when my phone rang. It was Dre.

"Yeah," I answered.

"What the fuck is going on? What the fuck happened to Marcus?" he yelled.

"What are you talking about? Marcus is here at the club." I turned around, looking for him, but I didn't see him. "Freddy, where the hell did Marcus go?"

"He got a phone call and ran out for a second. He said he'd be right back," Freddy answered.

My heart started racing. "Dre, what's going on?"

"I just got a call. Somebody just shot up Marcus's car. He's dead," Dre said. "Not only that, but they also got Curtis and Serge, too. They're all fucking dead, Corey."

I gripped the phone, too shocked to say anything. Not only was one of my most loyal foot soldiers dead, but two of my most loyal workers. Dre was right—we were being targeted. Someone was trying to take us down, and it had to be Rio Duncan.

Diana

26

"Get home and stay there."

"What's going on?" I asked Corey. I could tell from his commanding tone that something was very wrong, and I was afraid.

"Just do what I said. Don't leave your house, and stay the fuck away from the store!"

"What? Why? Corey, please tell me what's going on."

"Just do what I said, Di. Go home!" he said then yelled out, "Freddy! We gotta get the fuck out of here!"

Panicked, I got into my car and drove straight home. The house was fairly quiet when I walked in. I suspected my sister and mother were out shopping together like they normally did on Saturdays, and my father was somewhere drinking a beer and watching some sporting event.

I went into my room and shut the door, then sat on the bed, going over everything Corey had said as I tried to make sense of it all. I couldn't believe what Corey had told me. Rio seemed like he was genuine. I'd had a really good time hanging out with him and playing matchmaker to him and Pierre, and it hurt to think that maybe I was being used.

"Pierre!" I had to call him and warn him. I grabbed my phone from my purse.

"Hey, gorgeous!"

My words spilled out in a rush. "Pierre, I need to talk to you."

"You and everyone else in B'more today. I swear my phone has been ringing off the hook all damn day, and I'm standing here now talking to my wine distributor, who thought I wasn't gonna see that he fucked my order up. I'll call you back in twenty. Jerome, now you know—" Pierre's voice disappeared as he ended the call.

My nerves were on edge, and I needed to smoke a blunt ASAP. It was something I only did when I was super stressed. I'd say that being shot at, then finding out Rio might be dirty, not to mention the drama with Ashton earlier in the week, qualified as some serious stress. A smoke was most definitely warranted.

I reached up to the top shelf of my closet where I kept my extra blanket, and I felt around until I found the small velvet bag. Inside was everything I needed. I'd just locked my bedroom door and was preparing to lay everything out on my desk when I heard something. I paused and listened a little closer. Sure enough, someone had come into the house. I gathered everything and tossed it back into the bag and shoved it into one of the drawers. My much-needed smoke break would have to wait.

I sat back down on my bed and turned on my laptop, deciding to do a little research. I typed *Duncan Motors* in the search engine, and all kinds of results popped up. I looked at the homepage for their business, which featured all kinds of luxury vehicles. Then I clicked back through the search results to find images. It brought me to pages full of photos of the Duncans, a handsome black family that put me in the mind of the Huxtables plus a couple of extra kids. I clicked on one of the family photos from an old feature in *Ebony*, and sure enough, there was a much younger Rio beside what I assumed were his brothers and sisters. The article highlighted the accomplishments of his father, who came from a small town called Waycross, Georgia. He opened a small car lot, eventually moved to Atlanta, and climbed the ladder of success, which eventually led him to settle his family in New York. It was the classic tale of a self-made man, African-American style, and it made no mention of anything illegal. The Duncans seemed like a nice, normal—albeit super wealthy—family.

I continued to look through articles and photos, trying to find as much information about Rio and his family as I could. Before I knew it, an hour had gone by, and I realized the house was still very quiet. Wondering who I'd heard coming in earlier, I walked down the hallway into the den. My mother was sitting on the sofa, watching TV alone.

"Where's Mona?"

"I don't know." She shrugged and reached for the green fleece hooded jacket that matched the pants she was wearing.

"Momma, did you really wear a whole sweatsuit to the store?" I groaned.

"What's wrong with it? It's cute, and it matches. The lady at the store liked it so much that she asked me where I got it from," she said proudly, extending her legs so I could see the green sneakers on her feet.

My mother was the ripe age of fifty-three, but she dressed as if she were ninety-three. He wardrobe consisted of sweat-suits, sequins, leopard print, and graphic tees with Bible verses. And she had a thing about matching. If she had on a red shirt, then she also had to have on red everything else: shoes, accessories, purse, hat. I may have been a talented styl-ist and designer, but I damn sure didn't get my talent from her. I tried and tried to spruce her up, but it never worked.

"Did this woman happen to be wearing a velvet sweatsuit of her own?" I asked.

"No, but she was wearing this cute polka dot shirt and pants that I was loving. She even had the polka dot shoes to go with it," she said with no trace of irony in her voice.

"I give up," I said, walking back into my room and dialing Mona's number.

"Where the hell are you?" I asked when she answered.

"I told you I had some running around to do. I got another call. Let me call you back." She hung up.

"What the hell?" I said aloud to no one. Everyone around me was acting crazy. I prayed Mona's strange behavior wasn't because she was somewhere with Troy. I mean, he'd been her personal superhero and all, but she still didn't really know him. She had just met him the night before. Seeing him today was too soon, and the last thing I wanted was for my little sister to look thirsty.

Not knowing what else to do to calm my racing thoughts, I decided to take a nap. It felt good to lie down, but as soon as I closed my eyes, my phone rang. I saw that it was Ashton and ignored the call. He'd been trying to reach me since the incident in the parking lot, and I'd hoped he'd get the picture after I ignored him long enough. So far, he hadn't.

I sent him a text that said, Leave me alone or you'll end up blocked. It was probably what I should've done in the first place.

I turned over, closed my eyes again, and this time, I fell into a deep slumber—until my phone started ringing over and over again until I couldn't ignore it.

"Damn it, Ashton," I whispered, reaching for the phone to turn it off. Then I saw that it wasn't Ashton, but Dre.

"Hello," I answered with a scratchy voice.

"Are you 'sleep? Why the fuck aren't you at work?"

"First of all, who the fuck are you talking to like that?" I almost raised my voice, then realized my mother was right down the hall.

"Look, I don't have time to go round and round with you. I need you to get your ass over to the boutique," he demanded.

"I'm not getting my ass anywhere. The boutique is closed for the day," I told him. "Leave me alone."

"Diana, listen to me—"

"No, I'm not listening to you. I keep explaining to you that you're not my boss, and you damn sure don't tell me what to do. I work for Corey, not you. He knows I'm not at work. Now, goodbye." I hit the END button.

I couldn't believe Dre had the nerve to talk to me the way he did. His mouth was truly getting out of control. I knew it was because I'd turned his ass down time and time again. He might have been sexy as hell, but his attitude was fucked up and a total turn-off at this point. Even if I was no longer with Ashton, I wouldn't sleep with Dre.

I got up and walked back over to my computer. Rio's picture was still in the middle of the screen where I'd been doing my research. I couldn't believe he'd orchestrated all the drama that was going on and had put our lives in jeopardy. I thought we were friends, and I had genuinely enjoyed getting to know him. Now, I was just as disappointed and disliked him as much as Dre. The only difference was that one of them was just an asshole, and the other one had tried to kill me.

Rio

27

I parked my car beside Pierre's Maserati, which was in front of the entrance to Oz. It was a couple of hours before Happy Hour, but a handful of people were already inside. I nodded to the security guard and headed straight to the back, where I knew Pierre would be. I'd learned that he didn't make his appearance until what he considered prime time.

He didn't notice me until I arrived at the small table where he was sitting, wrapping silverware in napkins. One thing I liked about him was that he didn't mind getting his hands dirty and doing whatever needed to be done in the place.

"What's up?" I said.

He looked up from his work. "Well, damn, Rio." He looked me up and down. "This is what we're doing today?"

"What are you talking about?" I frowned.

"This." He gestured to my outfit, then pointed to my face. It was the first time he'd seen me without colored contacts. "And those. If you're going for the dark and dramatic look, you've succeeded. It's working for you. And here I thought I'd gotten to know the real you. I see some things aren't as real as I thought they were."

"Come on now, Peter. Let's not try to be funny." I smirked.

A look of surprise came across his face; his mouth opened, but nothing came out. I knew I'd caught him off guard.

I winked at him and said, "Now, get up and give me a hug."

Pierre stood up. "Well, I guess. I'm not used to this aggressive Rio. I think I like him."

We embraced, and he kissed me softly on the neck. A warm feeling filled my chest, and I smiled.

"So, what happened with Corey?" I asked after we separated.

"Nothing. He didn't show. But with all the shit that happened a little while ago—"

"What happened?" I asked, thinking Corey must have said something about our interaction at the club earlier. He was pretty pissed off when I left, but I had no doubt he was just mad because I'd figured out his little secret. The question was, how far would he got to protect that secret now?

"I heard three more of his guys got ambushed. Somebody has it out for him," Pierre said then sat back down and started wrapping again.

"What? When? Where?"

"I don't know all that. I just heard they took some of his people out. I do know one of them was shot near the club at about noon," Pierre told me.

"I left the club just before noon." I told him. My mind began racing. Twice within a twenty-four-hour period, I'd been in the vicinity where someone was killed, and both times involved someone connected to Corey. Our conversation earlier had gone completely left without warning. I went there meaning to help and show my support, and none of that had happened. Without question, we wouldn't be talking business anytime soon. It was too risky, and the last thing I needed was to be involved with someone who seemed to have a target on his back.

"Then I guess you missed all the action," Pierre said. "I'm glad you left. That could've been you instead of the dude who got killed."

"Man, I can't believe this." I shook my head.

Pierre's phone rang, and he took it out. "It's Di. You know she'll tell me all the tea."

"Put her on speaker and don't tell her I'm here."

Pierre hit the speakerphone button and said, "Hey, ho!"

"Man, I need a drink. Are you at the bar?" she asked.

"Yeah, I am. Why? What's wrong?" Pierre asked in a voice that even I could tell was fake.

"Don't act like you haven't heard what happened, Pierre. You know what's going on," Diana said.

"No, I don't. Girl, I've been here working. I'm sitting here now trying to get stuff together. You know how I am. Everything gotta be right."

"Listen, have you talked to Rio?" she asked, her voice serious.

Pierre glanced up at me, then said, "Not since earlier this morning. Why? What's up?"

"You're not going to believe this, Pierre, but your new boo is in the drug game," she said.

"Shit. So are you. And anyway, I already knew that," Pierre replied, giving a slight shrug as if she could see him. "Why do you care? You do know who your boss is, right?"

"No, Pierre, he's not a street dealer. He's beyond that."

Pierre looked up at me. "What do you mean beyond that?"

"He's a fucking drug kingpin from New York. His name is Rio Duncan, and his family is—"

Pierre took the phone off speaker and held it close to his ear. I couldn't hear what Diana was saying anymore, but based on the look on his face, she was giving him an earful. I closed my eyes and took a deep breath. I had been planning on telling Pierre about my family's business when the time was right. It wasn't as if I was hiding who I was from him, but I was sure it seemed that way now that Pierre had heard it from Diana and not me.

He stared at me, his face void of emotion as he continued listening to whatever she was saying.

"But that makes no sense, Diana. What would make Corey think that?" Pierre frowned. "Shit. I don't believe that's what's going on at all."

"What?" I whispered.

Pierre held up one finger toward me. "Mm-hmm, but if that was the case, why would Rio shoot the guy last night?"

As I tried to eavesdrop, my own phone began ringing, and I quickly snatched it from my back pocket, easing out of the room. "Hey, O. What's up?"

"Rio, you've gotta get the hell outta Baltimore. It's not safe. Get home," Orlando said in a rush.

I figured he'd gotten wind of the shootings at Corey's club. "O, I'm fine. It's just a misunderstanding, and I've got it under control," I explained.

"No, Rio. I mean it. Get home now. This is serious, and you don't need to have your ass down there. The last thing either one of us needs is for Dad to somehow get wind of—"

"What?" Pierre yelled, startling me. "That's ridiculous!"

"O, I gotta call you back," I said and hung up. I walked back into the small room and found a now very flustered Pierre holding his phone. "What's wrong?"

"Where do I begin?" He shook his head.

"Listen, Pierre, I wasn't trying to hide who I was or anything. It's just that I was waiting—"

Pierre shook his head. "You can apologize for that shit later—and believe me, you will. But, Rio, this shit with Corey is crazy."

"What do you mean?" I frowned. "What did Di say?"

"Di says Corey told her that you came to town to take over his business. That's why you're here in Baltimore."

"What? That's not true," I protested. "I came here to—"

Pierre held his hand out to stop me. "Wait, I'm not done. The incident last night was all a setup, and he told her you had something to do with the shootings today."

I exhaled loudly. "What the fuck? Are you serious? This is ridiculous."

"Did you have something to do with Corey's brother being killed?" Pierre stared at me.

My eyes fell to the floor for a second, then I looked back at him. "I was there, but I didn't kill him. I swear."

He paused for a while, studying my face. I kept my eyes on his, hoping he'd see the sincerity in them. Finally, I guess he decided I was telling the truth. "Okay," he said.

"I explained all of that to Corey this morning. He knows that already."

"Maybe so, but at this point, it is what it is," Pierre told me. "Corey and Dre are hell bent on finding you. You've gotta get away from here. You know this is the first place he's going to look."

"Not if I find his ass first."

"What? You're sounding just as crazy as they do. The last thing Corey is gonna want to do is talk. Someone has declared war on his turf, and right now, he thinks that person is you."

"I'll be back." I walked over and gave Pierre a brief embrace.

"Rio, where are you going?"

I didn't answer as I walked away. I could hear Pierre calling after me, but I kept going, jumping into my car and speeding out of the parking lot.

I couldn't believe the tailspin that my life was now in. A few days ago, I was enjoying life, being held in Pierre's arms as we stood on his balcony. Now, bodies were falling all around the city, and according to the streets, I was the cause. Somebody was setting me up. My brother was right; Baltimore was no longer safe for me, but I wasn't going anywhere until I cleared things up.

I had enough sense to know that with everything going on, the last thing I needed was to be out without some kind of protection. I drove back to my hotel to get it. As soon as I walked into my suite, I felt like something was off. I looked around, and everything looked the same, but it still didn't feel right.

Then, I heard movement coming from down the hallway. I didn't have time to go into the safe and take out my gun, so I would have to use whatever I could as a weapon. I went to slip out of my shoes, then realized they were sneakers. Those soft-ass rubber soles wouldn't hurt anyone. So, I grabbed the first thing I saw on the coffee table and walked as quietly as I could toward the noise. It was coming from the second bedroom. The door was slightly ajar, and I could tell that someone was standing near. My heart was pounding so loud that I was sure whoever was on the other side could hear it.

Taking a breath, I closed my eyes and then kicked the door wide open.

"Arrrrrgh!" I roared.

"Damn it, Rio!"

"What the fuck?" I opened my eyes and blinked a few times, shocked to see the person now in front of me. "Paris?"

She gave me a big smile. "Surprise!"

Corey

28

"Damn, what we gon' do, C?" Tay asked. Even with everything going on, I knew I had to come by the hospital and check on him. I had made calls to the rest of my street soldiers and told them to lay low until further notice, and operations were halted until Dre got back and we called a meeting. No doubt this would hurt us financially, but it was also damaging to our reputation. I had to make sure I took care of it before word got back to my father, because God knows if he found out, he would have my head on a platter, even from jail.

"Right now we're on stand down. The Duncans are a force to be reckoned with, and we need to be smart. But don't worry, we gonna handle it," I assured him. "You just rest up and get better."

"Yo, I'm fine. I'll be back at work by the weekend. The bullet went straight through my shoulder—no major damage." Tay winced as he tried to sit up.

I smiled and put my hand on his arm. "Whoa, chill, Tay. No need to rush. We need you, but we need you to be healed first."

"Thanks, man, but if you're at war, then I'm at war. We in this together. I got your back, whatever you need." He looked up at me sadly. "And man, I'm sorry to hear about Marcus. He was a good dude." There was something about the way he said it that made me nervous, like he was implying that he thought Marcus's loss was more personal to me.

"Uh, yeah, we need all the soldiers we can get right now," I said.

"Hey, like I said, whatever you need."

I stuffed my hands in my pockets and stepped away from him. "I gotta get outta here. You gonna be a'ight? You need anything?"

"Nah, I'm good. But you know I'm a big dude. You could've brought a brotha a crab cake from Koco's, a chicken box and half and half from Northeast Market . . . somethin'!" Tay laughed, breaking up the awkwardness between us.

"My bad. Hell, you know I got a lotta shit going on right now. I got you next time. I promise."

"It's a date?" Tay raised an eyebrow at me.

I clenched my jaw and said, "We'll see. But I'll holla at you tomorrow for sure."

As I was headed toward the door, Tay called out to me. "Hey, Corey."

"Yeah?" I turned around.

"Be careful. Like you said, this Duncan dude is a force to be reckoned with."

"I know, and I will," I said.

As I walked out of the hospital and headed toward my car, I replayed our exchange in my head. *Does he know? Was he flirting?* He'd worked for me since I opened the club, and he'd never spoken to me in that manner. Then again, we'd never really been alone without anyone nearby. I'd heard it mentioned that he might be gay, but because of my own hidden lifestyle, I stood clear of any discussion about him or any other suspected male. I didn't have time to contemplate it now, though. I was in the middle of a war and had to keep my mind focused.

Making sure my supply was secure was a priority, so I headed over to the boutique. I didn't want to take the chance of anyone seeing my car in the lot, so I parked a few stores down and went through the back door.

I unlocked a storage area that only Dre and I had a key for. Inside were locked cabinets that held shoeboxes full of narcotics. In the back of the storage room was a large safe where we kept a stash of money, guns, and larger quantities of marijuana. I grabbed a stack and tucked it in my jacket, and then reached back in the safe and took out a 9 mm pistol. I had just locked the safe and stepped out of the storage area when the front door chimed.

Damn it, I told Diana not to come here today. Just as I was heading to the showroom of the boutique to cuss her out, I heard a voice that wasn't hers. I froze.

"This should only take a second. I just gotta put this shit away. You know I appreciate you doing this for me, right? You really came through for me. It means a lot. You know what I'm saying?"

"It was no biggie. I could tell you were in a jam, and I'm glad I could help out. Besides, I need the money anyway," a female answered.

"Oh, so that's the only reason you did it? For the money? You sure you weren't trying to get in good with me?" He laughed.

"Nah, it was the money, trust me."

I walked out of the back room and entered the darkened store. "Dre? What the fuck? I thought you weren't getting back till late tonight."

"Shit, Corey! You scared the hell outta me. What are you doing here?" His eyes went everywhere except on me.

Why does he look nervous right now? I wondered.

"I came to make sure everything was good over here. Wait, Mona? What the hell are you doing here? What the fuck is going on?" I asked.

"Nothing's going on," Dre said, but his voice cracked a little. It sure didn't sound like nothing was going on. "Mona made the runs for me and picked up cash, that's all. I met her here so I could pick it up."

I looked at Diana's sister, and even though I already knew the answer, I asked, "Does your sister know about this?"

She looked down at the floor. "No, but I didn't think it was a big deal."

"It's not a big deal," Dre told her.

"He gave me a gun. It was no big deal." Mona reached into her purse and took out a small .22 to show me.

"It is a big deal, and your sister's gonna be pissed when she finds out. I can't believe you, Dre." I snatched the gun from her. "You can go ahead and leave."

She glanced over at Dre. "What about my, uh, payment?"

Dre reached into his pocket, took out a set of folded bills, and handed it to her. She stuffed it into her purse without counting it.

"I'll call you later, sweetheart," he said.

Mona smiled innocently at him. "Okay."

I waited until she was gone before I said anything. "Yo, what the fuck was that? Why would you have her do the fucking pickups? She could've gotten robbed, or raped, or worse. Are you fucking crazy?"

"Calm down, Corey. It was only three spots she had to hit, and they knew she was coming. I told them I was going to be wit' her, so they ain't even know she was alone. And like she already told you, she was packing." Dre said it like he'd sent her to the corner store to pick up a bag of Hot Cheetos instead of to the hood to pick up drug money. "Besides, who else was gonna do it? We're down three people, and we still got shit to do. You're making a big deal out of nothing." The strength was back in his voice now. He sounded more like his usual self.

"No, you're jeopardizing the life of a young girl for no reason. And again, when the fuck did you get back?" I asked.

Without answering my question, Dre walked past me and went to the back. I followed him and watched as he unlocked the storage room. He opened the safe and put the thick envelopes of cash inside.

Finally, he said, "I just got back, and I came straight here to meet Mona. I was gonna call you after we were done. You over here bitchin' about me when you should be worrying about Rio Duncan and handling that shit."

"There's no way he's working alone," I told him. "Marcus, Serge, and Curtis were all killed around the same time. He had help."

"You're right. He probably has guys here working with him. Who has he been around?" Dre asked. "He has to have someone with him."

"He isn't around anybody. I've only seen him with Diana and . . ." My words drifted off.

"And who?" Dre asked.

I shook my head. "Nah, other than Diana, I've never seen him with anyone."

Dre wasn't buying it. "Who were you gonna say?"

I hesitated for a minute, wondering why I was trying to avoid telling him. Truth was, I didn't really have a good reason. I said, "Diana said he's been hanging with Pierre," then quickly added, "but I think that's more personal than business."

"You sure about that?" Dre raised an eyebrow at me.

Rio was supplying drugs for Pierre's club, so they did have some sort of business relationship, but I still couldn't believe Pierre was connected to this in any way.

"It's Pierre, man," I said. "You know he's the farthest thing from a gangster of anybody we know."

Dre disagreed with me. "Pierre may be harder than you think. I ain't underestimating nobody. Hell, real talk, your girl may even be involved in this shit some kinda way."

"What girl? I know you've lost your damn mind for real, Dre."

"Isn't it ironic that Rio Duncan arrived into town and suddenly befriended the woman who has total access to our shit—and the one guy who has the most to gain? You think that's a fucking coincidence?"

Next to Dre, Diana was the only other person on this earth that I trusted with my life. I couldn't conceive of her ever doing what Dre was suggesting. Besides, she'd made a lot of money working for me—money she was using to pay for her college classes. Putting me in harm's way would jeopardize everything she'd been working toward as well.

"Diana wouldn't do that to me. She's got way too much invested," I told him.

Dre looked like he was getting frustrated with me. "He's a fucking Duncan!" he yelled. "He can afford to buy whatever the fuck she's invested and way more. And if I find out she has anything to do with this shit, I'm taking her ass out the same way I'm taking out anyone else." Dre's voice was cold and his stare menacing. "Ain't nobody around here safe."

Diana

29

I was in my room getting ready to go over to Oz when I heard the kitchen door open. The only time anyone came through that door was when they didn't want to be seen by my mother, who was always posted up in the den near the front door. I listened to the sound of light footsteps coming down the hallway, then the bedroom door across from mine softly closing.

I walked into Mona's bedroom without knocking, and I couldn't believe what I saw. She was sitting on the side of her bed, smiling and fanning herself with a fan made of fifty-dollar bills. When she saw me, she quickly tried to hide the money behind her back.

"Where have you been? And where did that money come from?" I asked.

"I told you I had some errands to run." She shrugged, trying to look casual, even though guilt was written all over her face.

"And the money?"

She let out a big, dramatic sigh. "Fine. I went to the casino and I won. Don't tell Momma. You know she'd be mad I went without her. But it wasn't planned at all, I swear."

I exhaled the breath that I'd been holding and sat on the bed beside her. "Girl, I was worried."

"Worried about what?" Mona smirked.

"About you and where you were. I thought you had snuck off to be with—"

"With who?" Mona had a worried look on her face.

"With Troy," I told her.

She relaxed and said, "No, I wasn't with him. And even if I was, I don't have to sneak off. What's wrong with Troy?"

"There's nothing wrong with him. He's a nice guy, and he did save your life and all."

"Exactly. And I like him, so I'm going to go out with him, just so you know," Mona told me.

"I didn't say you couldn't go out with him. I just didn't know where you were, that's all. What's wrong with you? Why are you so agitated? Is this about what happened last night? Listen, I'm sorry you had to go through that, I really am. I know it was kinda traumatic. I wanted to talk to you about that earlier, but then you left without saying anything." I rubbed her back. "I know you're probably upset, but this is why I tried to warn you. Being out at the club isn't always glitz and glamour. Shit pops off."

"I'm agitated because you treat me like I'm a fifth-grade kid instead of a woman. I'm stronger than you think I am, Diana. I don't need you to protect me. You don't like Dre, you don't like Troy . . ."

"Hold up. Is that what this is about? Dre? You're right. I don't like him for you," I told her. "Dre is way too . . . experienced, for lack of a better term. He has a lot of shit with him, and you don't need that in your life, Mona. Trust me."

"Stop trying to tell me what I need and don't need. I'm twenty-one years old, which means I'm legal. You're right, shit popped off last night, but I handled it, didn't I? You were the one freaking out and forgetting your phone, not me. My shit was in my bra, where I keep it when I'm in a crowd so I don't lose it," she said matter-of-factly.

I pulled back and cocked my head to the side. "Oh, it's like that?"

Mona's door opened, and my mother stuck her head in. "Mona, I ain't hear you come in. When did you get home?"

"Oh, hey, Momma. I got in a few minutes ago. I came through the side door because I had to pee," Mona lied without missing a beat.

"I was waiting on you. Cato's was having a clearance sale, and I wanted you to come with me to pick out some stuff," Momma said.

I cringed at the mention of Cato, one of my mother's favorite stores. It wasn't even close to our house, but I swear she lived on their website, and she would drive hours to get there whenever they were having a clearance sale. I'd given up on trying to get her to wear a few of the more conservative pieces I'd brought home from Chic World.

She looked at me and said, "Your phone in there ringing."

I hopped up and excused myself. Grabbing my phone off my bed, I saw that I had a missed call from Ashton. He was definitely getting blocked. As I was about to do it, a text came through from him. There were two simple words: Come outside.

I rushed over to my window and looked outside. He was parked directly across the street from my house. *What the fuck?*

I didn't hesitate to rush out the front door. When he saw me coming, he got out of the car, smiling. He had the nerve to be holding his arms out like he was going to get a hug.

"What is wrong with you? What are you doing here?" I tried my best not to yell, not wanting my mother or sister to hear me, but I needed him to leave immediately. Even though I didn't know what time my father would be returning home from wherever he was watching the game, I knew it would be soon. The last thing I wanted was to have to explain the presence of this random white guy.

"Damn, you're beautiful." He dropped his arms to his side, but then reached out a hand toward me.

"No." I stepped back.

"I came to talk to you in person since you won't talk to me on the phone," he said. "Diana, I miss you. I gave you some space, and I tried to be patient, but I love you."

"*This* is space? How the hell did you even find out where I live?" I hissed.

"I went to the boutique—" he started, but I cut him off.

"The boutique is closed today, Ashton."

"I know. I saw that when I got there, but then I saw your sister coming out, and well, I followed her here," he said sheepishly. "I know you're pissed. And I'm sorry. But I had to find you somehow."

I was still stuck on the first part of what he'd said. He had to be mistaken. There was no way he'd seen Mona coming out of the boutique. "You're lying."

"Lying about what?" He gave me a confused look.

"My sister coming out of the boutique."

"I'm not lying. How else would I have followed her? She walked right out and got into that car right there." He pointed to the older model Honda that used to belong to my mother until she gave it to Mona.

"Go home, Ashton." I turned and jogged back toward my house, trying not to stumble on the grass in my high-heeled boots. I slammed the door and stalked back to Mona's room, but she wasn't there. Stepping back into the hallway, I saw her coming out of the bathroom. I grabbed her by the collar and damn near dragged her into her room.

"Let me go! What's the matter with you?" she whined.

I shoved her on the bed, and then through clenched teeth, I asked, "Were you at the boutique a little while ago?"

She tilted her head, and in the same voice she'd used earlier while lying to our mother, she said, "What? No."

I got up in her face. "Don't fucking lie to me. Were you there?"

She dropped her head and said quietly, "Yeah, I was."

"What the fuck for? Who were you with? And again, don't lie to me," I warned.

"I . . . uh . . . it . . ." she began, stuttering.

"*Who?*" I asked, this time louder.

She couldn't make eye contact with me as she admitted, "I was with Dre."

I grabbed her arm roughly. "Mona, I'm not playing with you. Tell me what's going on—and your ass better tell me now. What were you and Dre doing at the boutique?"

"The errands I ran earlier . . . they were for him. I met him up there to drop something off to him," she said, her voice barely above a whisper.

My original thought had been that they were fucking in the back of the boutique. The fact that that wasn't what they were doing brought some relief, but also raised a whole new set of questions I was afraid I already knew the answers to.

I glared at her. "What kind of errands, Mona?"

"I just went a couple of places, dropped off some shoes, and picked up some money. That's all," she said.

"You what?" I gasped.

"It was really quick and easy, Diana. Nothing serious."

"Nothing serious? Have you lost your immature-ass mind? Do you realize what the hell you just did, Mona? Those weren't shoes; those were drugs. Dre was using you as a mule! There's no telling what could've happened to you!" I snapped.

There was no trace of surprise on her face, which told me one thing: she knew damn well there were no shoes in those boxes. I felt sick to my stomach.

"Nothing was gonna happen, Di. Dre made sure I was safe. It was only three or four stops, and he stayed on the phone with me each time. I also had a gun—"

"A what? Where the hell did you get a gun from, Mona?"

"From Dre. He gave it to me." She shrugged.

"Oh my God! What the hell is wrong with you?" I stood up and began pacing back and forth. "You do know the reason he had you run these so-called 'errands' was because the guys who usually do them were shot and killed this morning, right?"

She finally looked shocked. "What? No, I didn't know that."

"Yeah, that's what happens when you deal drugs. You get shot and die," I said. "I guess you were lying about the damn casino, huh? What else have you lied about?"

"Nothing, I swear. He just called right after you left this morning and asked if I wanted to make some quick money, and I said yes. He paid me three hundred dollars. I never thought I was in any kind of danger. I mean, you work for him, so I thought it was okay." Mona began tearing up.

"No, I don't work for him. I work for Corey, and I damn sure don't run errands. I get paid to run the boutique and look cute at the club. That's it. Corey would never put me in a situation where my life was in danger—believe that," I said.

"I'm sorry, Diana. I really am." Tears were rolling down her cheeks.

"Where the hell is the gun at?"

"I gave it back."

"I'm going to kill Dre." I got up and stormed out of Mona's room. She was right behind me.

"Diana, wait!" She grabbed my arm. "You can't go after him."

"Don't tell me what I can't do." I snatched away from her.

"You've gotta listen to me. Dre is planning something big. Really big. I overheard him talking to somebody," she said.

"Big like what?" I peered at her.

"I think a robbery."

"Mona, what are you talking about? What did you hear?"

"He was talking on the phone, and he said they were snatching up all the sprinkle muthafuckas at Oz." Mona sighed. "I don't know what that means, but he said it was a message to Rio Duncan that they aren't to be fucked with."

"Shit!" I grabbed my keys and purse and rushed out the front door. As luck would have it, Ashton's ass was still parked across the street, leaning on his car. He perked up when he saw me come out.

"Didn't I tell your ass to leave?" I yelled.

"I was hoping you would come back out and talk to me. Where are you going? What's wrong? Diana, talk to me."

"Leave me alone, Ashton! Leave me the fuck alone!"

Rio

30

"What the hell were you planning to do, Rio? Turn my damn volume up?" Paris laughed.

I stared at the TV remote that I was holding like a gun. "Fuck you, Paris."

"I missed you too, boo." She ran over and gave me a hug. I had to admit, she was a sight for sore eyes, and after everything I'd been through over the last twenty-four hours, I was glad she was there.

"I need a drink," she said." I know you got some liquor in this posh-ass suite."

"Damn right I do!"

We walked back into the living room, and I poured us a drink.

"What the hell are you doing here?" I asked. "I told O that I had everything under control. He didn't have to send you."

"Orlando didn't send me."

"How the fuck did you find me then?"

Paris took a long swallow of Jack Daniel's. "I overheard Orlando talking to Junior. He was asking about Baltimore and telling him to send a lookout down here. I put two and two together." She downed the rest of her drink. "I jumped on a flight, and voila!"

"Sneaky ass. But how did you find exactly where I was? Here?" I gestured to the hotel room we were sitting in.

"Come on, Rio. I looked for the swankiest five-star hotel, then I found the valet who looked like the easiest mark. "I told him you were my brother. You know it didn't take me but a few minutes to get him to confirm you were staying here." She looked down at her outfit, a skin-tight dress with her cleavage spilling over the top. "With these assets and a little cash, I got him to let me into your room." She adjusted her breasts and winked.

Then, she peppered me with questions. "Now, what the hell is going on with you—and why are you dressed like an extra in a bootleg rap video? Who are you trying to be thugged-out for? And what do you and Orlando have going on? Since when are y'all buddy-buddy?"

"Nothing's going on," I lied.

"Then what do you have under control? And why does he need Junior to send a lookout?" She gave me a knowing look.

It was no use trying to lie to her again. She would find out everything eventually, especially now that she was here. So, I downed my shot and then told her everything that had transpired since I arrived in the city: the boutique, meeting Diane, Corey, convincing Orlando to partner with me and supply Sprinkles to Pierre, and the shootings.

"That's it," I said when I was finished.

"Damn, Rio. You caused this much trouble in a week?" She was laughing. No matter how much drama or danger was going on around us, she always found a way to laugh.

"I ain't cause nothing," I said. "When I first got here, everything was so damn perfect. Diana was cool, and she introduced me to Pierre, and I was starting to be . . . happy. And now . . ."

"Now what?" Paris slid closer to me on the sofa and put her arm around me.

"Now I got people out here accusing me of shit I ain't do, and I'm in a street battle by myself over something I don't even want." I leaned back and said, "I'm back to being a Duncan."

"Rio, you ain't by yourself. Don't ever think that," she said. "You always got me. And that's better than any army out here in these streets."

I stared at her. She looked so much like our mother, and it made my heart full. I gave her a tight hug. "You're right. And I'm glad you're here."

"Good."

I got up and walked over to the safe in the closet, taking out my gun and grabbing another .45. I tucked them both in my pants and said, "Come on, let's go."

"Go where?" she asked, jumping up.

"We're taking a ride."

"A ride where? Do I need to change? You damn sure do."

I rolled my eyes. "Whatever. Bring your ass on. And make sure you got backup."

She ran back into the second bedroom and came out carrying a large Balmain bag and a pistol. How she managed to get on a flight with a weapon was beyond me, but my sister was a trained assassin, so she had her ways. "I stay having backup. Let's go!"

"A bar? I guess I can find a cute guy to enjoy tonight," Paris commented when I parked at Oz. She took a mirror out of her bag and checked her appearance, refreshing her lipstick, and then turned to ask, "How amazing do I look?"

I smiled. "You look fine, but you ain't gotta do all of that."

"How do my girls look? Are they sitting up?" She tugged on her shirt to expose a little more cleavage. "I see some cute guys in line." The crowd was a little thicker than when I'd been there earlier, and a line had started to form outside the door.

"You're doing too much," I said.

She took out her gun and was about to put it under the seat of my car when I stopped her. "Nah, bring it."

"They're checking," she said, pointing at the security working the door.

"This is Pierre's bar," I told her. "Security won't check us. We're good."

"Oh, so it's a gay bar?" She sounded slightly disappointed as she adjusted her shirt again to put the girls away.

"I tried to tell you." I laughed.

We were walking toward the entrance when I saw Diana come from around the corner. She rushed inside. From a short distance away, I could tell she was anxious about something.

I increased my speed and told Paris, "Come on."

"What's up, Rio?" The security guy nodded when we got to the door. "Who is this beauty you got with you?"

"This is my sister, Paris."

"Welcome to Oz." He looked Paris up and down and gave her a smile that said he liked what he saw. Men always did.

"Well, damn." Paris stopped and smiled back at him. "Seems like there might be someplace better than home."

"Not now, Paris," I said, grabbing her hand and pulling her inside.

"Okay! I was just being friendly," she protested as she tugged her arm away from me.

I led her over to Pierre's section, expecting to find him there with Diana, but it was empty. The bar was only so big, and they couldn't have gone far. I was about to walk toward the kitchen area when I saw Pierre beckoning me from the other side of the dance floor.

I nudged Paris. "There he is."

"We have a problem. A big one," Pierre said when we approached him. He led us back into his office, where Diana was already standing. She didn't look too pleased to see me.

"Hey, Di, what's wrong?" I asked.

She glanced over at Paris with a look of distrust on her face.

"This is my sister—"

"Paris," Diana said before I could. "I know."

"How do you know me? Have we met?" Paris frowned.

"No, I saw her in your family photos while I was looking you up on the internet," Diana said. "After Corey told me who you were and why you're here."

"Corey's wrong," I told her. "I'm not here to cause trouble."

"Are you sure? Because it seems to be a lot of it these days. And now you've got backup." Diana cut her eyes at Paris.

Never one to back down, Paris stepped up next to me and narrowed her eyes at Diana like she wanted to punch her in the throat. "Look, heffa. He's my brother, and I came to check on him. And you're right, I'll back him up whenever he needs me."

The tension in the room was rising, so Pierre came and stood in the middle of us. "Listen, this isn't helping the current situation. Di, Tell Rio what you told me."

Diana looked at Pierre, then to me, and said. "Dre told someone he's planning to send you a message."

"What kind of message?" I asked.

"He's gonna do something here at Oz. He thinks you and Pierre are working together to move in on his and Corey's territory," Diana said.

"Which is preposterous, because I damn sure don't wanna do that," Pierre snapped.

"Shit." I turned to Pierre and said, "We've gotta get these people out of here—now. You've gotta shut the place down."

Pierre didn't like that idea. "But she didn't actually hear him say it. What if it's just a rumor?" he said. "I got a line of folks wrapped around the building."

"What if it's not?" Paris offered. "Then you may end up with a line of dead bodies instead. Which would you rather do—take that chance tonight, or live to do business another day?"

Pierre swallowed hard. "You're right. I don't have a choice."

We followed him back out to the bar. He walked over to the deejay booth and had him turn the music down. At first, people didn't notice, until he tapped the microphone and said, "Attention! May I have your attention? Listen the fuck up!"

Finally, all eyes were on him. The crowd quieted down, and he continued. "We're gonna have to clear out of here. We have a . . ."

"Sewer emergency!" I yelled. He turned around and gave me a thankful look.

"A sewer emergency, and we have to shut the water off. Oz is closing for the night. We're sorry," Pierre said as people on the dance floor started filing out, moaning and groaning all the way.

Pierre came back over to us. "I'm gonna go tell the kitchen staff to clear out too."

"We'll wait right here," I said.

We stood and watched everyone slowly leave, and once the place was empty, the rest of us followed suit.

"Everybody good?" the security guy asked as Pierre put the lock on the door.

"Yes, we are," Paris volunteered. "So, what do you have planned for the rest of the night?"

"Nothing."

"I'm sure we can find some—"

Pow! Pow! Pow!

Paris's words were interrupted by gunshots, and we all ducked for cover. Glass from the bar's windows and door shattered all around us. I spotted a black SUV where the shots were coming from, and I returned fire. Diana and Pierre were screaming.

"Stay down!" Paris yelled at them as she fired her weapon.

The large security guard tried to grab her to protect her, because he had no idea that he was dealing with a seasoned professional. She eluded his grasp, remaining right by my side. We took out the windows of the SUV as it sped out of the parking lot. Then, another set of shots rang out, this time from a car in the back of the parking lot, and we ducked down. I glanced over and realized they weren't aiming at us, but at the SUV. We remained still until the SUV was out of sight and the gunshots finally stopped.

"Fuck!" I yelled as I got up.

"Everybody okay?" Paris called out.

I ran over and helped Pierre and Diana off the ground. "Y'all good?"

"Yes." Diana nodded with tears in her eyes.

"I'm fine," Pierre said, looking at the damage to the front of the bar. "I'm glad nobody was in there."

"I guess it wasn't a rumor after all," Diana said breathlessly.

"Who the fuck is that?" I pointed to the car where the other shots had come from. It was still parked in the same spot.

Diana gasped. "You gotta be kidding!"

"What? Who is it?" I asked.

"It's Ashton," she said.

"The fucking white boy?" Pierre frowned. "Oh, shit."

The car door opened, and sure enough, a sexy-ass white guy jumped out and came running over to where we were. "Is everybody okay?"

"We're fine, Ashton," Diana told him with more attitude than you would expect toward a man who was trying to protect her. "I can't believe your stalking ass did that."

"Shit, I'm glad you did," Paris told him. "Good looking out."

"You've gotta get out of here. You know the police are on the way." Pierre looked over at me. "And the muthafuckas who did this might be coming back, too."

"He's right, Rio," Paris agreed.

I shook my head and told Pierre, "I'm not leaving you here alone."

"It's fine. I got him." He nodded toward the security guard.

"Shit, you need to be asking her to stay." The guard pointed to Paris. "You're a bad bitch."

"Thank you." Paris winked.

"Diana, you and Ashton can go with them," Pierre said.

"No, stay here. I need you two to do something for me," I told them.

"What?" they asked simultaneously.

"I need you to start a rumor."

Corey

31

"Yeah, I got the call a little while ago. We'll link up tomorrow so you can get your bonus." Dre was on the phone when he walked into the den. When he ended the call, he looked at me and said, "I told you that shit would be handled."

I sat up on the sofa. There was a basketball game playing on the television, but I was too distracted to watch. Shit was already crazy enough, and of course, my father was trying to reach me. I'd been avoiding his calls all evening, knowing he would have an earful for me. I was sure word had somehow gotten back to him about Rio Duncan and the chaos he'd caused. No doubt he had plenty to say about it—none of which I wanted to hear, especially when my only response would be: "Dre says it will be handled." That wasn't good enough.

Dre and I had two different ways of handling things, and whether he liked it or not, I was the one in charge. To me, the best thing was for us to lay low and come up with a well thought out plan before we made a move. Dre didn't agree, and now, hearing part of his phone call, I realized he'd totally disregarded my orders.

"What do you mean, it's handled? Who the fuck are you now, Olivia Pope?" I asked.

"Who the fuck is that?" Dre frowned. His hard ass was too busy running the streets and chasing pussy to watch *Scandal*, I guess.

My phone rang. It was Diana calling. I ignored it, but she immediately called back.

I answered. "Yeah?"

"Dre, Rio's dead!"

"What? What are you talking about?" I struggled to keep my voice from rising an octave or two.

"There . . . there was a . . . a shooting," she sobbed. "He . . . he was at Oz and he caught two in the chest."

I was in complete shock. My eyes went to Dre, who was standing in front of me with a look of contentment on his face.

"Diana, slow down. Tell me exactly what happened."

"Rio was with Pierre, and they were leaving Oz an hour ago. It was a drive-by."

"Fuck," I whispered. "Where is Pierre?"

"I think he's with the police," she said.

"Listen, everything is gonna be okay. I'm gonna call you back," I told her. "Where are you?"

"I'm at home."

"Good. You're safe. Stay there, and don't go anywhere until I call you."

"Okay," she said, still sniffling back tears.

When she hung up, I got up off the couch and stepped to Dre. "What the fuck did you do?"

Dre smirked. "I guess you heard, huh? I told you I handled that shit."

"Rio was shot in a drive-by at Oz. You did that?" I clenched my jaw to try to suppress the anger I felt bubbling to the surface.

"Hell yeah. I see good news travels fast." He was obviously pleased with this news.

"This shit ain't good news. What the fuck is wrong with you? When did you even make that call? I told you we needed to lay low and think this shit out before doing anything. You done stirred up a hornet's nest now, muthafucka. You put a hit out on a Duncan."

"And that would've been the dumbest shit ever. Why the hell would you even want us to punk out like that, Corey?" Dre asked. "If we wouldn't have reacted to this shit, everybody in Baltimore and beyond would think they could carry us any kind of way. I wasn't 'bout to let that shit happen."

"But that wasn't your call to make, Dre. It was mine," I said coldly.

"Oh, for real? That's how it is, Corey? I thought we were a team. Now you saying you call the shots around here?"

"I'm saying your way of handling it just put all of our lives in jeopardy, and you ain't think that shit all the way through. You said it yourself that family is vicious and powerful. Don't you think when LC Duncan finds out we had something to do with this, he's gonna come after us? We ain't got that much power, money, or enough respect in these streets like he does. We're fucked." I threw my hands up in frustration.

"Corey, it was because of Rio Duncan that my fucking twin brother is dead. Or did you forget about that shit?" Dre's voice was filled with emotion, and he had a wild look in his eyes. "How do you think I felt knowing the man responsible for taking my brother's life was also around here trying to take out our livelihood? You really wanted me to sit around and not do shit? Do you know how much of a slap in the face that was for me when I heard he killed Marcus?"

"Dre." I walked closer to him. "I'm sorry all this shit happened. I really am. But—"

"But what?" Dre stared at me. "What was I supposed to do, Corey? Let him kill you next? I couldn't let that happen."

We were now standing so close that I could feel his breath on my face. I saw the hurt and pain in his expression and instinctively wanted to comfort him. I pressed my forehead against his and put my arms around his neck.

"Dre."

He remained silent as he wrapped his arms around me and pulled me closer, then pressed his lips against mine. His kiss was soft at first; then our mouths opened, and it became passionate. My mind was reeling with confusion, but my body went into auto-pilot as desire took over.

I closed my eyes and tugged to remove his shirt as his lips moved to my neck. It had been so long since we'd been together. Each time, we'd sworn it would be the last, but there were moments, like the one we were in now, that our attraction was inescapable.

We undressed one another and made our way down the hallway to the spare bedroom that we used for moments like this. I refused to allow him to have sex with me in my bedroom, because it was where I laid my head every night. I couldn't bear having to sleep in the same bed night after night, thinking about him, wanting him, missing him, longing for him, and knowing I could never truly have him. By the time we made it into what was now known as "our room," we were both naked.

Normally, when Dre and I were together, it was hot, fast, and passionate. Tonight, to my satisfaction, we took our time pleasuring one another and enjoying it. Even after our love-making was over, Dre held me in his arms and we talked. As I began drifting off to sleep to the sound of his voice, I reminded myself that we could never be together. As much as I enjoyed lying beside him, and knowing that I was in love with him, the business we were in wouldn't allow us to be out with our love.

When I woke up, Dre was gone. I sat up in the bed and ran my hands along the spot where he'd been. I got up to go into my own bed, and that's when I heard Dre's voice coming down the hallway.

"I will. I promise. Don't worry," he said.

I looked at my watch and checked the time. It was four in the morning, so I assumed he was talking to one of his many women. Diana was right about Dre being a whore, in more ways than one. It was another one of the many reasons we couldn't be together.

I heard him say, "He'll be dead before sunrise."

I slipped into my room, wondering who the hell he was talking about. Rio Duncan was dead, and there wasn't anyone else we had to be worried about. Pierre definitely wasn't a threat to us or anyone else, especially with Rio being gone. I climbed back into bed and waited for him to return. It was a little while before I heard his footsteps enter the room. I rolled over, expecting him to get back into bed, but he just stood in the doorway.

"Dre? What's wrong?" I asked, sitting up on my elbows and squinting in the darkness.

"I'm sorry, Corey," he whispered.

"Sorry for what? What are you talking about? Who were you on the phone with?"

He took a step closer to me and raised his arm. That's when I spotted the Glock in his hand.

"Dre, what the fuck?"

"I . . . I don't wanna do this, I swear." His voice was shaking.

Reality hit me like a sledgehammer. "It's me, isn't it? You told someone I'll be dead before sunrise?"

"Corey, I love you," Dre said.

"Don't do this, Dre. You don't wanna do this. You know my father is going to kill you if you do this."

"He's the one who I was talking to on the phone," Dre said sadly, taking a step closer with his gun pointed at my face.

I closed my eyes and prepared for a death that would be all the more painful because it was inflicted by someone I loved. A single shot rang out, and I roared out, "Nooooooo!" waiting to feel the hot metal rip through my body.

Rio

32

"Are you okay?" I asked Corey. He was trembling, and his eyes were unfocused. He was clearly in a state of shock.

Paris, who was standing behind me, put her gun away. She reached down and picked up a shirt that was laying on the floor near the bed and tossed it over to him.

"Wha—How . . . I . . ." Corey stammered.

"No, I'm not dead," I told him. I tapped Dre's body with my foot, making sure it didn't move. The bullet had caught him right at the base of his neck, leaving a small hole that was now spewing blood.

"But he is." Paris giggled and looked at me. "Good shot, bro."

"Who are you?" Corey asked her as he pulled the shirt over his head.

"Oh, I'm Paris," she said. Then, looking down at Corey's naked crotch, she added, "And you are?"

"We'll let you get dressed in private." I pulled her out of the room.

"What the hell is wrong with you?" I asked when we were in the living room.

"What? I just asked his name, that's all." She shrugged with an innocent look on her face.

"You know his name, heffa! I can't believe you. Trying to make a move on a man—a gay man at that—who just witnessed his lover being murdered."

"I gotta give it to you," she said. "Starting that rumor was genius. You were right. As soon as Dre heard it, he let his guard down and came straight here."

"But what are we gonna do now?" she asked, suddenly becoming serious. "I mean, we came here to kill both of them. I wasn't expecting this shit."

"Neither was I." I flopped down on the couch. "Well, I guess the good thing is we only have to clean up one body instead of two."

"Make that three."

We turned around to see Corey aiming a gun straight at us. He had tears in his eyes.

I tried to reason with him. "Corey, listen, put that gun away. You're about to make the biggest mistake of your life."

"He's right, Corey, you are. You can't kill both of us at the same time, and whichever one you don't kill first is going to be the one who kills you," Paris explained. She was deadly calm, and it seemed to throw him off. His eyes went from mine to hers.

"Listen to her. Put the gun down, man. We can talk about this," I told him.

"Talk about what? How you showed up here trying to take over my business? How you just killed my business partner and best friend?" Corey said.

"No, we just saved your life."

"He wasn't going to kill me. He loved me," Corey insisted. "And I loved him."

This muthafucka is totally irrational right now, I thought. I wanted to smack some sense into him, but I knew I had to defuse the situation, since he currently had the upper hand.

"Corey, listen to me. I know everything is confusing right now, but you need to just put the gun down and chill." I went to take a step toward him. He tensed up and raised the gun a little higher on my chest.

I stopped moving. "You really don't want to do this."

"You really don't." Paris shook her head.

"Both of you shut the fuck up!" Corey yelled. Beads of sweat formed on his forehead.

"Fine, I'll go first," I said. "Shoot me!"

"Oh, hell no! You're not going to be the one he kills, and then I have to explain this shit to Momma. Shoot me, Corey." Paris jumped in front of me, and the gun was now pointed at her.

"No!" I yelled and pulled her back. "Don't fucking shoot her. She has a kid for God's sake Her son already doesn't have a father. You can't take away his mother, too!"

Paris turned around and yelled at me, "Fuck you, Rio! My son has a father!"

"Yeah, which one is it? Do he know? Hell, do you even know?" I shouted back at her. "What kind of mother are you anyway? Where is your son while you're here?"

"You're just mad because I get more dick than you do!" Paris responded.

In the midst of our argument, we had slowly eased closer to Corey, who was so confused by our exchange that he didn't realize it. His gun was now in arm's reach, so I made a move to grab it from him. He lifted his arm in an effort to get it away from me, leaving his midsection open for Paris to kick him. She caught him right in the stomach.

As he fell forward, his finger pulled the trigger. The gun fell to the floor, and Paris grabbed it. Then, the sound of someone kicking in the front door took all three of us by surprise.

"Rio! Paris!"

We all turned to see Orlando running into the living room with his gun drawn. Behind him was our older brother, Junior.

"O?" I was so confused.

"More like 'Oh, shit!'" Paris whispered.

"What the hell is going on?" Junior asked, looking at me like this was all my fault.

"Who the fuck are you?" Corey scrambled to get up.

"Stay down," I said to him, knowing that my brothers wouldn't hesitate to shoot him if they felt that he was a threat to any of us.

"Paris what the hell are you doing here?" Orlando asked her.

"I came to check on Rio. What the hell are you two doing here?" she asked.

"We got word that Rio was dead, so we came to kill the mutha-fucka who put the hit out on him." Orlando looked at Corey.

"It wasn't me. I swear." Corey held his hands up. "It was Dre."

"Where the fuck is Dre?" Junior demanded to know.

"He's dead. Rio already took care of him," Paris said with pride. "One shot to the base of the head. Clean, too."

Orlando and Junior turned their attention toward me. Orlando spoke. "I told you it was dangerous and to get the hell back home."

"And I told you I could handle it," I replied. "I know how to handle my business, Orlando, even if y'all don't think so."

"Did you know that someone was sending orders from jail and putting hits out because he heard there were gay men working for Corey?"

Corey sat up and admitted, "That's my dad."

Orlando looked at him for a minute, and I worried he was about to put a bullet in his head. Finally, he asked Corey, "Did you know Dre was the one he was sending orders to?"

A look of horror came across Corey's face. "No, I ain't know that," he said quietly. "I had no fucking idea—until tonight." Corey finally got off the floor and was now sitting on the edge of the sofa, looking discombobulated and terrified.

"What do you mean, until tonight?" I asked.

"He told Dre to kill me too," he whispered.

We all stood quietly, staring at Corey. I knew this was overwhelming for him, and despite our conversation the day before in his office, when he looked like he wanted to kill me for bringing up his sexuality, I still felt the need to help him.

"Hey, Junior, O, there's a mess in the other bedroom I need help cleaning up. Paris can show y'all where it is," I said. My brothers and sister took the hint. Junior disarmed Corey, and then they left him and me alone to talk.

I went and sat beside him. "Hey, it's gonna be okay."

"My father tried to have me killed by my best friend, and Dre was going to do it." He was staring at the floor, looking like he might cry at any moment.

"But he didn't," I said. "Neither one of them was successful. Dre is dead, and you're still here."

"Diana told me ol' boy heard them on the phone before it popped off." He seemed to be talking to himself. "He told me he was out of town. He probably wasn't even out of town."

Suddenly, he jumped up and rushed over to a small table near the hallway entrance. Laying on it was a cell phone, which he began fumbling with. The screen lit up, and he started scrolling.

"Son of a bitch," he whispered.

"What?" I asked him.

"He's been talking to my father for weeks now. They've been plotting this for weeks," he said. "This had nothing to do with you or your family. My father wanted me dead. My own fucking father wanted me dead, and my best friend tried to kill me."

"Corey, come on." I reached for the phone and glanced down at the messages he had been looking at. There were several text exchanges between Dre and someone named Pop. He was right.

"My father wanted me dead. My father wanted me dead." He kept repeating it over and over. "They both wanted me dead. My father and my best friend."

I put my hand on Corey's shoulder and tried to comfort him. I knew exactly how he felt, because my own father had offered up my life at one point. I wouldn't wish that kind of pain and confusion on anyone—to feel like your life is worth nothing in your father's eyes.

"Uh, Rio." Paris's voice caused us both to look up.

"Yeah?" I said.

She walked over and handed me her phone. I looked at it for a moment, confused, until she motioned for me to speak into it.

"Hello?"

"Rio." The sound of my father's voice caused the hair on my arms to stand up and my heart to race. He was the last person in the world I wanted to talk to, especially right now.

"Yes." I sighed, preparing myself for the verbal lashing that I knew he was about to unleash. He would make sure to list every misstep I'd made along the way while I was here in Baltimore.

"You're alive," Pop said quietly.

I closed my eyes and said, "I'm sorry." I didn't know why I felt the need to apologize.

"Come home, son," he said.

"Huh?" I was confused. "But, I—"

"You heard what I said. Come home. It's time."

"Yes, sir." I knew there was no point in arguing. Besides, it was time for me to leave. I'd had enough Baltimore excitement to last for a while.

"Good. Oh, and Rio." Pop inhaled deeply and paused for a moment before he said, "I'm glad you're alive."

***

Two days later, I was packing up my bags to leave Baltimore. Orlando and Junior had already left, and Paris was scheduled to fly back in a few hours.

"You got everything?" she asked.

"Yep, I do," I told her. "I'm glad I bought that extra suitcase, or everything wouldn't fit."

"Damn, Rio. You bought that much stuff?" She shook her head.

"Jealous?" I teased. "What time does your flight leave?"

"At five, so I need to be there by four-thirty."

"Don't you mean four o'clock? You have to be at the airport at least an hour before the flight leaves, Paris."

She smirked. "Yeah, right. You really think I'm gonna sit around an airport for an hour? You act like you don't know who I am sometimes. I get there right before take-off—and I never miss a flight."

I double-checked the bedroom and bathroom to make sure I hadn't left anything behind, then went to the safe and removed all of my items, including the box containing the Sprinkles Orlando had sent to me. I'd never given them to Pierre. I hadn't even spoken with him since the night of the shooting. He hadn't called me, and I hadn't called him. Even though it had been established that everything that happened at Oz had nothing to do with me, I still felt responsible. He probably thought I had too much shit with me that he didn't want to deal with. And he would've been right, which was why I became distant.

As I tossed the box into my duffel bag, there was a knock at the door.

"That's probably the bellhop for our shit. You ready?" I asked Paris.

"Ready when you are," she said.

I opened the door, and while our belongings we being loaded onto the cart, I took one final look around, and then we headed downstairs.

"You leaving us, Mr. Duncan?" the Asian valet asked.

I gave him a smile. "Yeah. I been here long enough, don't you think?"

"Well, I hope you enjoyed your stay here in Baltimore. I'm sorry to see you go," he said.

I reached in my pocket and handed him two hundred-dollar bills. "Hey, thanks. I was kinda rude to you the last time you got my car, and you've been nothing but nice to me. Plus, you told me all about Chic World, and for that, I'm grateful." My association with Diana had had some pretty dangerous unintended consequences, but at least I was going home with some fly-ass outfits that no one else in the New York clubs would have.

"Wow, thanks, Mr. Duncan," he said. "I'll be right back with your car."

"Uh, isn't that the name of the boutique where all of your trouble started, Rio?" Paris asked.

"True, but it's not about how you start. It's about how you finish." I winked at her. Little did she know that the boutique was where we'd be headed once we left the hotel.

"Wait, *this* is Chic World?" Paris turned her nose up after I parked in front of the store.

"Don't judge a book by its cover," I said, opening my door.

"Okay, you and these damn philosophical adages, or whatever you wanna call them, are annoying."

We walked inside, and Diana walked over and gave me a big hug.

"Aw, you're leaving?" she said. "I don't want you to leave."

"I'll be back," I told her, though it sure as hell wouldn't be any time soon.

"Ohhhhhh, this jacket is fly! Does it come in some more colors?" Paris yelled from the other side of the store, where she was going through the racks.

Diana glanced over and said, "Yeah, it does. Red, yellow, and silver, plus the black that you're holding."

"I'll take them," Paris said.

"Which one?" Diana asked.

Paris raised an eyebrow. "All of them."

"All-righty then." Diana looked back at me. "I see great taste and long coins run in the family."

"Whatever." I laughed.

"Have you talked to Pierre?" she asked.

"Nah, I haven't." I sighed. "How is he?"

"Why don't you ask him yourself?" Diana said, nodding toward the front door.

I turned to see Pierre walking in. My heart began racing, and I became so nervous that I could feel sweat pooling under my arms.

"Hey, Pierre!" Paris sang his name loud enough for everyone in the store to hear. I knew she was trying to be funny.

"Hey, diva." He walked over and gave her an air kiss on each side of her face.

I took a deep breath and held it as I watched him approach me.

"I'll get those other jackets for you, Paris. Oh, and I have some more stuff over there I think you'd probably like." Diana quickly excused herself.

"How are you?" I asked Pierre.

"I was wondering the same thing about you." He gave me a weak smile.

"I'm good now that I'm standing here with you."

"So, you were gonna leave without saying goodbye?"

"I, uh, didn't want to, but . . ."

"But you were." He smirked.

"Yeah, I was," I confessed. "I guess I thought you would be glad to hear that I was gone."

"And I guess I thought you would've at least asked me to go with you," he said, locking his eyes on mine.

"You did?"

He nodded. "But it's okay. I . . . understand."

As we stood there staring at each other, I thought about how happy I'd been the first few days with Pierre. The time we spent just getting to know one another felt really special. When I was with him, I could be myself. I wanted that feeling to continue, but now it was too late. It was time for me to leave.

"I'm glad I did get the chance to see you before I left though," I told him.

"Me too, Rio. And I hope I get to see you again soon." He leaned in and kissed me on the cheek, and we embraced for a few moments.

"I'll call you," I promised.

He didn't say anything else to me before he turned and headed back toward the door, stopping to hug Paris and telling Diana he would meet up with her later.

Paris rushed over to me. "What the hell did you do? You're just going to let him leave like that?"

I shrugged my shoulders. "What do you mean? What was I supposed to do?"

"Bitch, tell him how you feel," Paris snapped.

"Offer to stay longer," Diana added.

"Invite him to come with you!" Paris followed up.

I shook my head. "Yeah, right. And what do you think our parents would do if I showed up at the house with Pierre? How do you think our brothers and sister would treat him? The same way they treat me? I don't think so."

Paris sighed. "You're wrong, Rio. True, Daddy and Vegas would probably feel some type of way, but they would eventually get used to it. No matter what you think, Rio, I know Daddy loves you. He just sucks at showing it."

I gave her a skeptical look.

"I think everyone else would be fine with it," she continued.

"I don't."

She folded her arms and frowned at me. "How would you know? You haven't ever given them the chance to see."

"You're tripping," I told her.

"Rio, Orlando, and Junior were just here. If they didn't give a shit about you, do you think they would've come to Baltimore to avenge your fucking death?" Paris asked.

"I don't know." I sighed.

"Well, I know. And you're making a mistake by letting Pierre leave here without some kind of declaration," she told me.

"You'd better catch him, Rio. You know Pierre is fine, and he's a great guy. Don't let him get away out of fear." Diana touched my arm. "Trust me, I know."

I looked at both of them, then I damn near ran out the front door.

"Wait! Pierre, wait!"

He was backing his Porsche Panamera out of the space when I yelled his name. He stopped and looked at me like I was crazy.

He rolled down the window and asked, "What's wrong?"

I stepped up to his car. "This is wrong. My leaving like this is wrong."

"What do you mean?"

"Me leaving without you is wrong," I said. As the words escaped my mouth, I felt happier than I'd been in a long time. "Come with me."

"What?" Pierre looked surprised, but pleased.

"Come with me to New York. I want to be with you. I want us to be together." I opened the door to his car.

Pierre put the gear in park and turned his body toward me. "Are you serious?"

"Dead-ass serious." I laughed.

"Well, considering you were dead two days ago, that's pretty serious," he said, stepping out.

I pulled him into my arms and kissed him—enjoying the moment until I heard someone beeping behind us.

"Get a room!" a voice called out.

We both looked over to see Corey pulling into the parking lot.

I turned to Pierre and said, "Go pack. I'll pick you up from your place after I drop Paris off at the airport."

"You're sure about this?" Pierre asked.

"I'm sure." I kissed him again, and he waved at Corey as he drove off.

Corey pulled into the spot that Pierre had just left and parked his car. He climbed out, and I noticed a large figure in the passenger's seat.

"What's up, Corey? And . . . Tay. That's your name, right?" I asked.

"Yeah, man." Tay smiled.

"I thought you were leaving," Corey said, giving me a pound.

"Headed out now," I told him. "You good?"

"Yeah, I'm good. I'm glad I caught you before you left."

"Really? What's up?" I leaned against his car, my arms folded.

"I just wanted to say thanks . . . for everything. I appreciate it," he said with sincerity.

"Hey, no thanks needed. Anytime."

"Oh, and tell Orlando I'm gonna take him up on his offer," he added.

"His offer?" I had no idea what he was referring to.

"Yeah, we talked for a long time last night, and he's gonna help me transition from this line of work. It's time for me to retire." Corey looked a little sad, but I had a feeling he was going to be okay.

Hearing that my brother had offered to help Corey was surprising, especially knowing that he was gay. Maybe Paris was right.

"Well, you know if you need me, I'm a phone call away," I told him.

"Uh, yeah . . ."

I laughed. "Corey, you do know you can be gay and have platonic friends who are gay, right?"

He blushed. "Yeah, this is all kinda new to me. My bad."

"It's fine. You sure you're gonna be okay, though?"

"Yeah, I am." He nodded toward Tay.

"Don't worry, I got him!" Tay gave me a thumbs up. The look that passed between them let me know that he wasn't just talking about his security job.

"Rio! We gotta go!" Paris walked out of the boutique, both arms full of shopping bags. "I can't miss this flight."

"I thought you weren't worried," I said.

"Just unlock the damn door. Bye, Corey, we gotta go!" she yelled as she passed by us.

"Thanks again, Rio," he said.

We shook hands.

"Hey, maybe you can come hang out in New York one of these days," I offered as I opened my car door.

"Maybe I will. I'm sure we can find some trouble to get into."

I shook my head. "Ugh! From your lips to God's ears, let's pray that doesn't happen. I think I've had enough trouble in one week to last me a lifetime."

Enjoy this sample of Carl Weber's

New York Times bestseller,

The Family Business

now a television series on BET.

Paris

1

"Okay, Paris, let's go over this one more time. What exactly did the man who shot Councilman Sims's son look like?"

It was late, almost three in the morning, and standing in front of me was an obnoxious New York City homicide detective with bad breath and a Brooklyn accent. He and his partner, a homely brown-skinned woman who needed to do something with her ugly-ass weave, had me sitting in a small, dimly lit room somewhere in a police station in Brooklyn. This was the fifth time he'd asked me the same damn question, and there was no doubt in my mind that he was going to ask it again, because I wasn't saying shit.

You see, less than two hours before, I'd witnessed the shooting of my date, Trevor Sims, son of New York City councilman and congressional candidate Ronald Sims. Regrettably, Trevor didn't make it. He died five minutes after he was shot, right in my arms, which was why I was covered in his blood from head to toe. To say I was having a bad night was an understatement. I was having a terrible fucking night.

"Trevor, dammit! His name is Trevor! Stop calling him the councilman's son. He has a name," I corrected him as tears welled up in my eyes. I would have paid a million dollars to be anywhere but where I was right then.

"Correction, Paris. Had. He had a name," the bad-weave bitch stressed. "Trevor's no longer with us, because he's dead, and we're trying to figure out who did it. Now, I hate to break this to you, but you're the only witness we got to his shooting, so we're going to go over what you saw again. And, Paris, this time I want some fucking answers."

"Look, I told you I ain't got nothing to say. I just wanna go home. Look at me." I spread my arms apart so that they could see my blood-soaked DKNY dress.

The dog-breath detective laughed. "You're not going anywhere until we get some answers, Paris. We've got a congressional candidate's son in the morgue. Do you have any idea what that means?" He paused only for a second and then answered his own question. "That means the newspapers and media are going to be crawling all over this. Which means the chief of detectives is gonna be crawling up my lieutenant's ass, wanting some answers. Which means my lieutenant's gonna be crawling up my ass, looking for those answers. So, until I get them, I'm gonna be crawling up your ass."

"You can crawl wherever the hell you want to," I said flatly, folding my arms in defiance. "I ain't got shit to say."

I stared at the cop and wondered, if Trevor's dad were a garbageman or the janitor at Jamaica High School instead of a councilman running for Congress, would we even be going over this so thoroughly? My fellow clubgoers were being questioned all over the precinct about other victims of tonight's shootings, but Trevor's death was drawing the most attention because of his father's political connections and the fact that it was the only shooting outside the club, not inside. I was sure the mayor would have something to say about it in the morning. I just hoped they left me and my family out of it. God, my dad was gonna kill me just for being there.

"Why don't you have shit to say? Because of some stupid 'no snitching' code of the streets?" the female cop snapped. "Is that it? You got some stupid moral code?"

I stared at her briefly, then exploded in anger. "Are you for real? Do I look like I'm worried about some moral code of the streets? Bitch, I'm wearing a ladies' Rolex that's worth more than both your damn salaries combined." I flashed my wrist in front of her face. "Look, I'm a party girl, not a gangbanger. I've got Kim Kardashian on speed dial, not Lil' Kim. But maybe you don't know who I am, so let me introduce myself. My name is Paris Duncan, daughter of LC Duncan, the owner of Duncan Motors, the largest African American–owned car dealership chain in the tristate area. He donated almost a million dollars to the PBA last year, so why y'all hassling me? Maybe you need to make a few calls and find out just who the fuck I am and where I come from."

"We already know who you are," she replied irately, "and personally, I'm not impressed with you or your nigger-rich daddy. I just—"

I sprang to my feet, pointing my finger up in her face. "Don't be talking about my father, bitch. You don't know him!"

"I don't need to know him! And I'll talk about whoever I damn well please. Now, get your finger out my face and sit your ass down before I break it and you."

"I'd like to see you try." I was about to step around the desk and show her just who she was fucking with. Good thing for her that her partner cut me off.

"Paris, please sit down. Don't pay attention to her. She's not going to do anything to you. Just have a seat so we can talk, please. This is about Trevor, not you and her. Let's focus." He guided me to my seat, then turned to his partner. "Anderson, sit your ass down!"

Would you believe that hooker with a badge did exactly as she was told? I turned my attention to her partner, who pulled his chair up next to me, gently encouraging me to sit down, like he was on my side. I gave that heifer a smirk that said I knew who had the real power in that partnership.

"Okay," he said. "So, if it's not some code, then why won't you cooperate? We're not the enemy here. We're just trying to find out who killed your boyfriend, so why won't you help us?"

"He's not my boyfriend. He was just a good friend. We just started dating." What I really meant was that he was a friend I never should have gone out with. "And the reason I ain't talking is because my lawyer's not here . . . yet," I replied. "I know my rights."

"You ain't got no rights," his partner barked.

"Anderson, will you please shut the hell up?" he snapped so I didn't have to. He turned to me, speaking so nonchalantly I almost felt like he meant it. "Paris, you're not under arrest, so what do you need a lawyer for?"

They were playing one hell of a game of good cop/bad cop, and I bet all those fools they interrogated fell for it—but not me.

"Yeah, famous last words. I'm not trying to cause any trouble. I'm just protecting my rights. Y'all ain't gonna get me caught up in no shit. My father told me about how cops play games and set people up, and he also told me to never say a word until I had a lawyer present." I sat back cozily, as if I were on a piece of designer furniture at home instead of this rickety old piece of shit in a police station.

"Look, we're not trying to play games or entrap you. You're a party girl . . . a celebutante," he said, making air quotes with his fingers. "I get that. But the longer we're playing around here, the longer your boyfriend's killer goes free. Don't you want justice?"

"He's not my boyfriend. How many times do I have to tell you that? And of course I want justice, but I also want to be alive to see it. Those dudes that killed Trevor are still on the street. I'm not getting involved with you so that they can come knocking on my door." I mumbled, "I'm not stupid. I watch *Criminal Minds* and *Law and Order.*"

"Look, Paris, we can protect you. And we've got a pretty good idea who these guys are, but we just need a witness—someone who can identify at least one of them—and I know you saw who did this, didn't you?"

I didn't answer him, but couldn't restrain a nod in the affirmative.

He smiled, then said, "He was a big, dark-skinned black guy with a bald head, wasn't he? He was the one who shot Trevor, wasn't he?" I gave him a half nod, and he turned toward his partner with a nod of his own. "Look, Paris, all I need you to do is write down what you saw and look at a few pictures, and then you can get on out of here."

"That's it?" The thought of escaping that place had me lifting my head, but I wasn't convinced by a long shot. "That's all you want from me?"

"Yep, that's it," he said. "So, are you ready to go on the record with that? Write this down for us? Please." He picked up a legal pad and a pen. "You write this statement and I can have you out of here in a half hour, tops."

"I can have her out of here right now, and she doesn't have to write down a thing."

I cut a smile as my brother-in-law, Harris, stepped into the room, followed by a balding white man in a bad suit. Harris was the husband of my older sister, London. He was one of the best attorneys in New York and worked exclusively for our family business, Duncan Motors.

"What he said," I added, suddenly perking up.

"Who the hell are you?" Anderson asked.

"I'm her lawyer, and unless she's being arrested for something, I'm taking her home." He held out a hand to help me up out of the cheap-ass chair. "Come on, Paris."

"Lieutenant, she knows who the killer is," Officer Unbe-weave-able whined to the white guy who'd come in with Harris.

He just shrugged. "Cut her loose."

"Bye, guys," I said as I snatched my purse from the table. Walking to the door, I turned to Brooklyn's ugly-ass partner and smiled. "You impressed now, bitch?"

I almost skipped past Harris and the lieutenant, grinning from ear to ear, until I saw the imposing figure standing in the corridor outside the door.

"Uh-oh." I nearly let go of my bladder and peed on myself. Just the sight of my father, LC Duncan, standing there with his trademark fedora, tailor-fitted overcoat, and gray scarf draped over each shoulder scared the crap out of me. A huge part of me would rather have gone back in the room and faced the cops than dealt with the scowl on my father's face.

"Daddy, I didn't do anything. I swear."

LC

2

Eight hours earlier . . .

I walked into the large conference room of Duncan Motors for
our annual year-end board of directors meeting, followed by my
wife, Charlotte, who I called Chippy. Already seated at the table
was Orlando, our tall, slim, brown-skinned third son. He had a
phone to his ear as he worked an iPad like it was a piece of him.
He didn't say much, other than to acknowledge his mother with
a wave as we took our seats. Orlando wasn't being rude or anything; he was engaged in a phone conversation with one of our
distributors about a shipment of pre-owned Bentleys for one of
our six high-end pre-owned car dealerships.

Like myself, Orlando was a workaholic. He ran a tight ship, for
which the devil was in the details. He was the company's chief
operating officer, in charge of running the day-to-day operations
of our dealerships. Only thirty-three years old, he was turning
into one hell of a man, if I did say so myself. Of course, like everyone, he had his flaws of a sort. He had no idea I knew anything
about it, but we were going to have to address it in the very near
future.

"We're good, Pop. They turned the cars over to our guys in
Maryland, and the shipment will be delivered sometime tomorrow," Orlando called out to me with a thumbs-up before con-
tinuing his conversation. In addition to our pre-owned car dealerships, we also owned three Toyota dealerships, which made us
one of the largest African American dealers of cars in America,
as per *Black Enterprise* magazine.

Chippy shook her head. "Will that boy ever learn to slow down?"

"Somebody has to pull the load around here," I replied, wishing the rest of my children had what Orlando possessed. They all contributed to the family business, but none of them had his work ethic. He was the first one in the office every morning and the last one out every night.

"I heard that," my youngest and more defiant son, Rio, chimed in as he walked into the conference room and took his seat. Rio was wearing a bright yellow paisley shirt that could be seen halfway across Queens.

He glanced over at Orlando, who had just finished up his conversation. "No offense, bro, but I bust my ass around here just as much as you. You're not the only one who makes a lot of money for this family. I don't hear anybody complaining when the money from the clubs gets deposited on Monday morning, or about the two BMW 650 convertibles DJ Two-Tone bought on my recommendation last week."

Rio spearheaded the marketing and promotions aspects of Duncan Motors, a creative endeavor he came up with himself. He paired the two things celebrities loved most: exotic cars and parties. Where there were celebrities, there were fans willing to buy everything their idols purchased. I wouldn't admit it to him, but his brainchild was a brilliant, unquestionable success that had only served to expand the family's reach in ways I didn't think possible.

Orlando nodded, acknowledging his brother's work, but I took a different path, rolling my eyes in my youngest son's direction. "Do you call going out to a club all night and sleeping until three and four in the afternoon busting your ass?"

"Nope," Rio huffed, meeting my gaze with one of his own. "I call it the night shift. When you're sleeping, I'm working. Why can't you understand that? Is this because I'm gay?" Rio pulled his sunglasses down, peering over them as he struck a very feminine pose.

"Don't mess with your father, Rio. Not tonight, all right?" Chippy warned, with a look that said she meant business.

Rio shrugged his shoulders and gave her an angelic smile. Of all our children, he was the closest to Chippy. She loved and accepted him as is—no exceptions. I, on the other hand, loved my son but just couldn't accept his lifestyle. I just couldn't wrap my head around the fact that my son was a homosexual. I didn't think I ever would. His sexual preference disgusted me.

"I'm not messing with him, Momma. I'm just trying to make a point. I bring business into this company too." Rio sat back in his chair and folded his arms. "I just think a little recognition would be nice."

"Are you finished?" I asked. The look on my face said everything that didn't come across my lips.

With a final glance from his mother, Rio softened his demeanor and nodded. "Yeah, Pop, I'm finished."

I turned my attention away from Rio just as a cute little bundle of energy came into the room, scurrying around the conference table and chairs as if they were her own personal playground. That little bundle of joy was my granddaughter, Mariah, and with her mother on her heels, she bolted just out of reach behind me and her grandmother.

"Mariah! What did I tell you about running in here?" her mother shouted.

Mariah's mother, my eldest daughter and fourth child, London Duncan Grant, was a tall, classy, butter almond–colored woman, the spitting image of her mother when she was the same age.

"It's okay, London," I said, handing my only granddaughter one of the lollipops I carried in my suit pocket just for such occasions. She was the apple of my eye. I loved my children, but my granddaughter stole my heart from the moment I set eyes on her. As far as I was concerned, I would lay the world at her feet. "Let her be. She has just as much right to be here as the rest of us. One day this will all belong to her, anyway."

Mariah took the lollipop out of my hand and gave me an affectionate kiss on the cheek before taking off again. When she passed my eldest son, Junior, he caught her with one arm and deposited her in his lap as he took his seat. She giggled at her uncle's sudden display of strength. If she were older, she wouldn't have questioned it at all, because Junior was six feet five inches tall and a solid 270 pounds of pure muscle.

As big as he was, Junior could be as gentle as a lamb—unless provoked. He was in charge of our car carrier and transportation fleet of trucks, along with overseeing our service mechanics. He wasn't involved much with the financial end of our company, but he could drive and fix anything with an engine, which in our business made him very valuable indeed.

"Humph. Daddy, you'd let that girl get away with murder if you could. I don't recall you ever saying anything like that to us when we were growing up," London said with a slight attitude as she took a seat beside her husband, Harris Grant. He and my daughter had met while she attended George Washington University in Washington, D.C., and Harris was attending Georgetown University Law School.

Harris was always thinking, and that keen mind of his had allowed him to graduate magna cum laude from Georgetown. In the years since he and London got married, Harris had become an integral part of all our business affairs and was now the company's in-house legal counsel. This allowed London to happily relinquish her duties as sales manager and focus on being a loving mother and devoted wife, something she took very seriously and sometimes to extremes.

"Y'all were my kids. It was my job to raise you right. Mariah's my granddaughter, and it's our job to spoil her." I smiled at my daughter, then lifted my hand to my wife, who gave me a high five.

"Well, that ain't making my job any easier. That girl is just as spoiled as can be."

"Ha! That's what the fuck I'm talkin' about, Mariah," Paris, Rio's twin and perhaps the most attractive of our children, blurted out inappropriately as she walked in with some man I didn't know behind her. "Let them spoil you, girl. You gonna be just like your aunt Paris, aren't you? Kiss the boys and make them motherfuckers cry!" Paris laughed, but no one in the room— other than Rio—joined in.

London glanced at her younger sister and rolled her eyes. "Could you please stop cursing in front of my daughter? What is wrong with you?"

"Stop tripping, London. She hears much worse than that just sitting out in the service area with Junior and them."

"Well, I haven't heard that, but I heard you—"

Harris gently took his wife's arm and mumbled, "London, it's not worth it."

London glanced at me and my wife and then at her husband before she sat back in her chair obediently. "This is some bull. They'd never let me get away with this."

"Daddy," Paris said in this gushing voice that customarily rose in pitch when she was seeking my approval. It usually worked, too, except when it had to do with men. Yes, she was a daddy's girl; there was no question about that. I didn't know why, but I had a weakness for my youngest daughter, despite the fact that she always seemed to be getting herself in some kind of trouble I had to bail her out of. "Daddy, I'd like you to meet Trevor. Trevor, this is my father, Lavernius Duncan Sr."

"Pleased to meet you, sir. Ma'am," he said, greeting Chippy as well. "You have a wonderful daughter."

"Uh-huh," I said. Still holding the young man's hand in mine, I turned to Paris, who was smiling like she'd won the lottery. "So, in what hole did you find this one, Paris? Please tell me you didn't buy the suit he's wearing, like you did the last one." I spoke loudly to be sure the young man understood I didn't care if he heard my insult.

"Daddy!" Paris shrieked. Her pretty, high yellow face turned beet red from embarrassment. I loved Paris dearly, but I never was one to mask my disappointment in her, especially in her choice of men.

"We met at Antun's catering hall in Queens Village, sir, and it's not like that at all. The suit's mine," Paris's date asserted, to my surprise. The rest of the family was taken aback, too, from the looks on their faces. Most of Paris's little male friends were, unfortunately, bad boys, thugs, or sheep, and were intimidated by me. Surprisingly, this one wasn't.

"Oh, really? Tell me how it is, son," I urged, my curiosity piqued by the nature of the stranger in our midst.

"We were having a fund-raiser for my father's election campaign when I met Paris, sir. Nothing improper. I believe your wife was there also."

I glanced over at Chippy, who nodded.

"His dad is Councilman Sims," Paris added, trying to take back control of the conversation.

"Ronald Sims? He's running for Congress, isn't he?" I was keenly aware of New York's political landscape and the players in all five boroughs, especially Queens. Ronald Sims was definitely a player who was on the rise.

"Yes, he is." Trevor smiled.

I was sure he was hoping for a quick thaw between us, but he'd forgotten one thing: Paris was my daughter, and I knew his only objective was to get her into bed. He was going to have to show his face around here a hell of a lot more, and preferably on days I wasn't conducting a board of directors meeting, if he expected me to thaw.

"So, no, I don't need anyone to buy me a suit—but my father could really use your support in his reelection campaign," he added.

I let out a hearty chuckle that filled the room, and then glanced over at Orlando and Harris, who both nodded their heads and discreetly began to type into their iPads. "You know what, young man? I admire your moxie—or rather your swagger, as it's called these days. I've always been one to preach involvement in family endeavors to my children. Good to see your father is of a like mind. We'll have to see what we can do for our future congressman."

I nodded at Paris, who seemed pleased as she placed her arm in Trevor's and led him toward the door. While not quite up to the level of her sister, perhaps there was some hope, after all, when it came to Paris's choice in men.

Chippy leaned over and whispered in my ear, "Dear Lord, LC, has Paris lost her mind and invited that man to sit in on one of our board meetings?" I glanced back over toward the door and, to my dismay, watched Paris and her new friend take two empty seats by the entrance. Why the hell she would have that man sit in at one of our board meetings was beyond my comprehension. Perhaps Chippy was right; she'd lost her damn mind.

"Uh-huh, that's exactly what she's doing." I took a deep breath, trying to calm my nerves, because I was known to have a very explosive temper. Why couldn't that girl be more like her brothers and sister and just use common sense? Ain't no way London or any of the others would be stupid enough to invite a stranger to one of our private business meetings. I was about to storm over there when Chippy took hold of my wrist.

"She's only doing this to impress you. You know she usually doesn't date guys like him. She wants you to see she can pick a smart man like London," Chippy mouthed softly. "We might not be able to speak as candidly as we'd like with him in the room, but let's see how it goes. The kids all know better than to discuss anything beyond the basics in front of a stranger, so it won't matter. We can always ask him to step out of the room if we get on a topic that's not for his ears. The rest we can discuss tomorrow in private."

I glanced over at Paris, who was leaning up against the boy, with her head on his shoulder. She really didn't have a clue, and that scared me.

"Besides, Trevor . . . and his father could be useful to us one day."

I looked over at my wife, a little shocked by her response. "You sure about this?"

"Yes, I'm sure you can handle it. You always do. Now, let's go get us a plate so we can get started." Chippy smiled that prideful smile she sometimes gave me, admiring my ability to always think on my feet and adapt. It was one of the many qualities she said attracted her to me those many years past. Back then, she knew I was a man with drive and a certain "moxie" myself—moxie that rescued her from the cursed path upon which she once strode.

Once everyone was seated, I stood and cleared my throat to get everyone's attention. They turned to me, looking eager for whatever I had to say, probably because they knew the year-end meeting was when I thanked everyone for their individual contributions and handed out rather substantial bonus checks. The only one who seemed to sense something awry in my demeanor was Orlando. He exchanged looks with his mother but came away with nothing.

"First of all, I want to tell you all that your mother and I are blessed to have everybody together tonight, including our new guest," I said, with a nod to Paris's friend Trevor.

I couldn't help but notice how the acknowledgment chafed Harris, the last outsider to become something more within the family and the business. I could see he had already begun assessing whether the young man was a potential threat.

I continued, "As I do at the end of every year, I have called all of us together for a brief slowdown from the crazy pace we set for ourselves. This moment is to reflect and to thank you for your hard work. You're all very special to me and your mother, and not just for your value as part of what we've built here, but as a family. It's not my normal demeanor to be so emotional, but I do love all of you, despite some of our differences. I'm proud of you all." I purposely glanced in Rio's direction. Chippy patted my leg approvingly under the table.

"Damn, Pops!" Rio exclaimed, a mischievous grin forming on his lips. "You tryin' to break a brother down or what? You acting like you got cancer or somethin'." He wiped fake tears.

"Rio!" Chippy scolded.

"Oops. Sorry, Momma."

Rather than burning Rio with my gaze, I said, "Let him be, Chippy." This unusual action got everyone's attention. London shushed Mariah, who was now seated on her lap. Paris stopped fidgeting with her hair for Trevor's benefit. Junior sat with his mouth agape. "Right now, each one of you owns three percent of the company, for a total of eighteen percent. Your mother and I are giving each one of you five percent more."

"Dad, what's up? You and Momma okay?" Orlando asked.

With a glance at Chippy, I spoke, my deep growl diminishing with each successive word, to where it was almost a whisper at the end. "Yes, son. We're okay, but your mother and I will be ending our hand in the day-to-day business operations."

The room was silent, until Paris stood, ready to take on the world to protect me.

"Why, Daddy? Did something happen? 'Cause don't nobody mess with the Duncans. 'Cause—" Paris cut herself off, glancing down at her date. I was sure she would have loved to say more, but Trevor's presence kind of hindered that.

"No, princess. Nothing happened other than old age. All of you are grown now, and your mother and I aren't getting any younger. We'll be retiring to the house on Fisher Island soon, so we wanted to give you all time to adjust to the changes ahead."

"Retiring," Harris blurted out. I guess my right-hand man was caught more off guard than anyone. He looked hurt, too, probably because Chippy and I had kept this announcement very close to the vest, and he was used to being in the know. I was sorry for that, but he'd have to get over it, because it was already done.

"So if you're retiring, who's going to be in charge? Who's going to be you while you're in Florida?" I was sure Junior was simply seeking clarity. Although he was the oldest and possessed unquestionable loyalty to the family, nothing in his makeup said leader.

The room fell silent again as they all waited for my answer.

"I'm glad you asked, Junior. Your mother and I thought long and hard about this," I replied, sure to make eye contact with each of them. "First of all, technically nothing changes. Your mother and I are still the majority shareholders, but someone has to make decisions in our absence, and ultimately . . . we decided the person best suited for the job is Orlando."

All eyes turned to Orlando, and as they studied him, I studied them. They had no idea what the future would bring, and neither did I, but I knew something wasn't right, and that was why I was stepping down so that I could prepare.

Orlando

3

Every eye in the room was upon me the second my name slipped out of my father's mouth. I scanned the room, looking each of my siblings in the eye as I tried my damnedest to hold back a smile. Yes, my father had chosen me to lead them, and I was sure there was going to be some resistance, but he had to choose me. It was the most obvious choice. Who else would he have chosen to lead us—Harris, Junior, or Rio? I don't think so. I mean, Rio didn't have a chance, and although Harris was smart and close to the old man, he still wasn't blood, and everyone knew Junior didn't want the responsibility. Besides, I'd worked my ass off for this business, for this family, so why wouldn't they appoint me its new leader? I just wished Pop had told me ahead of time so that I could have come up with something inspirational to say.

No matter. I'd think of something when the time was right.

I hadn't even gotten a chance to let things sink in before my pain-in-the-ass little sister Paris stood up, pointing her finger at me and shouting with her usual lack of tact, killing the moment. "Daddy, why him? Why would you choose Orlando to be in charge?"

My father's head swiveled in her direction. "You wanna know why? Because I said so, that's why."

Paris's spoiled nature, along with the fact that she was my father's unquestionable favorite, allowed her leeway in most situations, but the look in the old man's eyes was all that was needed to remind her to sit down and not question him any further.

It was obvious to us all that he wanted to say more to my sister but held his tongue due to her guest, the politician's kid. Why the hell would she bring someone she barely knew to a business function like this, anyway? All she was really doing was trying to seek brownie points with the old man. Maybe if she were more focused on business, like the rest of us, instead of partying and men, she'd have his attention the way she wanted it.

Foolishly, she mumbled something to my brother Rio, and my father looked even more pissed.

"What was that?" he snapped, his eyes shifting back and forth between Paris and Rio. "You two got something to say?"

Rio slumped back in his chair, but Paris boldly stood up again and said, "I'm sorry, Daddy, but I gotta say this. What about Vegas? How you gonna put Orlando in charge and pass by Vegas?"

Once again the room fell silent, and this time all eyes, including mine, were on LC. Heck, now that she'd mentioned it, I wished I had asked that question myself. Vegas was my older brother, between Junior and me. He'd been away for almost three years, but everyone in the family, including me, knew he'd been groomed to be the heir apparent since we were little. He was the only one in my family, other than the old man, I'd have no problem taking a backseat to.

Pop glanced knowingly at my mother, as if this had been the subject of many conversations between them. He sighed, then glanced at each one of us. "Your mother already spoke to Vegas about this, and he's one hundred percent behind our decision to have Orlando run the business. As you all know, he's got other things he's taking care of right now."

Yeah, but what's going to happen when he comes back? I thought as I watched Paris take her seat. My little sister and I were going to have a long talk in the near future, because there were going to be some changes around here now that I would be in charge. Her spoiled behind wouldn't like the changes one bit, but she was going to have to deal with it.

"Are you sure about this?" I asked before adding, "Um . . . about the retirement?" Couldn't let them think I was unprepared for the announcement—even if I was.

"Mm-hmm. We're sure about our retirement, son, just as we are about you leading this family." The look he gave me almost dared me to refuse. Of course, he knew I wouldn't, even though it was not going to be easy to deal with my siblings—and Harris.

But life isn't about knowing everything, especially in our business. It's about how you handle the unknown; how you stare it in the eye, laugh in its face, and conquer it.

"Is this something immediate, LC?" Harris asked. I knew he hoped it wouldn't be, because that would give him time to manipulate things to his benefit. Despite the fact that my brother-in-law and I worked well together, it didn't mean I trusted him completely. Maybe it was our matching ambition and intensity that put us naturally at odds.

Harris had made us all a lot of money over the years, but I still questioned my father's reliance on this dude. He hadn't done anything to betray the family, and I didn't have any clear-cut reason to distrust him, so it probably just rubbed off on me from Vegas. He had never trusted Harris, and wasn't shy about his feelings, despite Harris's hard work and apparent loyalty to our family. Vegas never told me what his beef with Harris was, but I was pretty sure it had something to do with our sister London.

"No, Harris. We'll have time before Chippy and I wash our hands entirely of the business, but I felt it was time to let you all know. That way those who may need to step up and pull their weight will have the opportunity to do so. You don't have anything to worry about, Harris. Orlando may be sitting in my chair, but yours will remain next to it. He's going to need your advice and counsel."

"I see. That's good to know," Harris replied, adjusting his suit jacket. It had been established that there was still a need for him, and I was sure he'd do all he could to exploit that. Still, my father had made his decision, and the decision was me. I didn't think it could have been any clearer.

"Congrats, bro," Junior succinctly uttered. He'd have my back in this. He was too easygoing to want to deal with this leadership shit. As good-natured and gentle as he was, that was what Junior did so well—the not-so-gentle stuff.

"You okay with this, bro?" I whispered. I really didn't want him to feel as if I were taking him for granted.

"Yeah, you know me," he said, as expected. "Can't say the same about the rest of them, though. With them you're going to have to prove yourself. Maybe even knock a few heads, if you know what I mean." He let out a chuckle and looked around the room at my other siblings and my brother-in-law.

I already knew where Paris stood in all this. She'd made her position clear, but the rest were riddles, sure not to talk about or reveal their true feelings in front of Momma, Pop, or the outsider at the table. All I had were my assumptions, as Rio, Harris, and London took turns sizing me up the rest of the night.

While they did that, I tried digesting what it was going to mean to head an organization created by the great LC Duncan. What would I do differently once given complete free rein? What I did know was that I had to continue to build the empire my father had worked so hard to establish.

Finally, Harris walked over, extending his hand. "Congratulations, O. How about we sit down at the house with a cocktail and go over your vision for the future? I've got some great ideas for expanding in the South and Midwest."

I wasn't sure what he was up to, but if he was extending an olive branch, I was going to take it. "Sure, Harris, I'd like that. We're going to take this family to the next level. You wait and see."

"We sure are." He gave me a smile that almost looked like a smirk as he walked back over to my sister. "See you back at the house in, say, an hour?"

"I'll be there." I slipped my BlackBerry from my pocket when I felt it vibrate. I'd received a text.

Just got some new shit in right off the boat. You were the first one that came to mind. You interested?

I lifted my head from the phone, then glanced left and right to make sure no one was within eyesight of my BlackBerry screen.

I glanced over at Harris, who was guiding my sister and niece toward the door, then replied to the text.

Damn right I'm interested. I was just given a big promotion at work and have a lot to celebrate. Give me about an hour to slip away.

The return text read, Congratulations. I'll have my sister set everything up for the exchange.

I glanced over at Harris again. Sorry, Harris, but our little meeting may have to wait until morning.